Condition Evolution

Book Three

By

Kevin Sinclair

COPYRIGHT © 2020
KEVIN SINCLAIR

KEVIN SINCLAIR

First edition 2020

THANKS

Thanks first and foremost goes to my wife, who without her support, none of this would be possible. From being alpha reader and editor, to help with all aspects of this crazy journey we have embarked on.

As always, I'd like to thank my children, Ewan, Lydia, William and Alexander, for providing constant interruptions and generally making a nuisance of themselves, but mainly for making me smile.

To the Guildmasters, for all your help, support and friendship. Just a thoroughly fantastic group of people.

To my beta readers, Steve Kenny, Jeff Walsh, Joe Jelliffe, Denny Johnson, Liam Johnson and James Auwaerter, for your time and amazing feedback.

To my Editors, Lewis Packwood and Victoria Sinclair for your excellent work. Gaiusprimus for some amazing proofreading.

And Eko for yet another amazing cover!

CONTENTS

C1

To Torax

As amazing and potentially lifesaving as the ship's new folding drive was, it sure was disorientating.

We re-materialized what felt like an instant later, but there was no way to be sure. We were all wiped out, laying slumped on the floor or in chairs.

"Ember, what the fuck? That was the Thoth!" I shouted.

"I heard, dumbass."

"Why the hell were they coming after us like that?"

Elyek interjected. "If I had to guess, they had no idea you were here. They named me specifically. I am really sorry guys. I don't know what to do. I've been nothing but trouble to you."

"Yeah, you're right. They would have mentioned us if they knew we were here," Ember said.

I shrugged. "I suppose they'd have no way of knowing we're on the ship. You know, after they left you for dead and me stranded on a hostile planet. They wouldn't exactly expect to find us halfway across the galaxy in a shit-hot spaceship, carrying a fugitive. But, more importantly," I said, emphasizing the point with a shake of my index finger, "Fuck those guys. They didn't bloody well check either. If we do see them again, and they start shit, I'm gonna finish shit."

"Shaun, are you ok? You do remember they're our

people, yeah? You know, the ones you really want to save?" she said, then smirked, "Plus, saying *'finish shit'* doesn't sound nearly as cool as you think it does."

"I'll tell you what, I'll leave Gus and Mick alive. Fuck it. I'll even lay off Astrid. But the rest of them...," I paused in anger, "not one of them made any effort with me on that ship, even after everything that happened, and how I was brought into all of this. It's the arseholes on Earth I want to save, not these tits."

Ember laughed hard. "Shaun, you really are just too fucking much. You know why no one approached you, right?"

"Ignorant dicks?"

"No. They were fucking terrified of you. I overheard loads of talk behind your back, and some people even asked about you to my face."

"Terrified of me? I hadn't even massacred an entire space town at that point."

"You hit level 40 in nine months in Anatoli. You transcended on your first day of proper consciousness and took me along for the ride. You were stranded on a supply station for two weeks, after only a week of leaving the game, then killed three Fystr. Ogun was like a child around you. Then you went, half dead, and took Havok from four very well respected, improved human warriors. Followed later by giving a good hiding to the self-styled Thor when he retaliated. All without a mark on you. Thor, or rather Rodger, was a genuinely feared member of both the Thoth and the Seshat," she half shouted at me.

"Really? I never realized any of that was a thing on the ship."

"That's not even the half of it, you absolute moron. I

can't even remember some of the shit I heard whispered about you. Like, how you turned into a pro-bodybuilder in two weeks, or that you carried on your back a massive sentient axe that levitates by itself."

"You're pretty fucking cool, Shaun," Havok said into my mind.

"I know dude, but now's not the time for a fist pump," I thought back, pushing a laugh through our link, then focused on Ember, who was waiting for a response.

"Oh. I never really thought about it like that. But you helped with the Fystr on the supply station. You should be just as feared."

"Shaun, I'm your fucking sidekick. I'm like goddamn Robin over here. Oh, yeah, and you weren't exactly chatty to the people on the ship either."

"I was the new kid. People should have been welcoming *me*," I said petulantly, but I'd already lost this argument and I knew it.

"Stop pouting, Shaun. It doesn't suit you."

"You really think I'm being too hard on them?"

"Of course I do. If we see them again, we need to talk to them." She turned quickly to Calegg and Elyek, "I'm never leaving you guys. It hasn't been long, but we're family now. It's just, we at least need to get them off your trail, Elyek. They might even become allies."

Elyek nodded back solemnly. Calegg grinned his bastard head off at the affirmation of our strong bond.

"Whatever," I angrily waved away the conversation. "Let's focus on Torax. We need bodies, and if these guys are anything like Calegg, then they're the bodies I want backing me up."

Calegg puffed his chest up at the compliment.

Ember wasn't happy with my conversation deflection.

"I thought we'd have more time before our next death-defying adventure," she replied, disappointed.

"Don't whine, Ember. It doesn't suit you," I snapped, still a little angry at the arrival of the Thoth, and that she seemed to defend them and berate me.

In a truly impressive bit of telekinesis, she shot the boot off her foot straight at my face. Even more impressively, Havok deflected it.

Calegg and Elyek looked on in amusement.

I just smirked, which unfortunately sent Ember up a level of irritation. She quickly shot her other boot towards me with a lot more speed and intent.

Havok sorted that shit out, this time cutting the boot in two.

"Havok. Those were the only boots I have!" Ember shouted unhappily. She sulked a little more before talking to Havok again, "Sorry Havok, but he can be a dick at times."

Elyek and Calegg looked to each other, confused.

"Have you never even spoken to Havok yet?" I asked, feeling like Havok was already part of the family after our chat a few planets ago. But they both shook their heads.

"Havok, dude. These guys are family now. Can you see if you can introduce yourself?"

"Anything for you, Shaun," he said back almost lovingly. I felt like it should have creeped me out a little – how devoted he was to me – but it didn't. I fucking loved my axe and second-best friend.

I looked up to see expressions of mild surprise on Calegg's and Elyek's faces. Havok must already be talking to them.

"It's nice to finally talk to you, Havok," Elyek said

calmly.

"How are you alive?" Calegg asked, alarm clearly written on his face.

I hoped Havok wouldn't tell him everything, but moments later Calegg exclaimed, "Over two million!" and my heart sank. Calegg now knew the true nature of Havok, and it was bloody and brutal. He looked over at me, and I just shrugged and smiled. He shrugged back, then said, "It's great to meet you Havok. I hear you have had a lot to do with our success."

Havok obviously spoke back, but their conversation must have ended as Calegg turned back to one of his monitors and checked something.

Elyek had already been busy with their monitor and turned to me and Ember, "It seems we have completely escaped our hunters, for now."

"Well, that's a relief," Ember said, looking up forlornly from her severed boot.

"It is. How far away from Torax are we?" I asked.

"Twenty-six hours, as planned. We are relatively dark to any scanners here, so we can remain stationary for a time if you need to take a moment to reflect," Elyek said.

"Might be nice," Ember replied. "I did pretty much die. *Again.*"

"Yes, I have to say, that was, without doubt, the most intense experience of my life, and I have spent that life acquiring difficult experiences. Your faith in Shaun is not misplaced and being part of this crew fills me with hope for the future," Elyek said.

"We feel the same having you with us, Elyek," I replied, and I meant it. Having an invisible thief, assassin-type looking out for you was pretty cool.

"I think we make a good team, too," Ember said, casting the boot halves into a corner with an aggrieved look, "but can we discuss this over some quality bait from the canteen? I need to replenish my blood supplies."

"I couldn't agree more. Let's bounce," I said, happy at the thought of food.

As we walked, I reflected on how unbelievably amazing my life had become, despite being a desperate fight for survival most days. I mean, we had a top-class spaceship, plenty of spondoolies, the beginnings of a top-class crew, and I was the bloody captain.

We all sat around a canteen table and dined on an eclectic range of dishes. Ember had a tiger prawn salad. I'd chosen a T-bone steak with half a chicken on a massive bed of spinach, covered in a creamy peppercorn sauce. Absolutely rocking low carbs and loving it. Calegg had some kind of meat with what looked like pasta. Alien, but pretty normal. I literally had no damn clue what Elyek was eating. It looked like it was still alive. A bowl of gloopy liquid with chunks of something in it, which I swear moved. If I ever got fat again, it wouldn't be from eating Veiletian food.

We were all tucking in when Calegg blindsided us. "I know I was optimistic about my people earlier, but now we're close, I'm actually shitting an irregularly shaped ore deposit here. I may have overplayed my hand. Part of me never thought we'd actually ever make it this far."

"What exactly do you mean, Calegg?" Ember asked with a little edge to her voice.

Calegg put his hands up in a kind of submissive gesture. "There are people who would love to leave, don't get me wrong. The problem is that some on my planet work for the betterment of themselves, rather than of our people. Our world is filled with mining settlements, but the whole planet is ran from a central government. Not everyone in that government has our peoples' best interests at heart," Calegg said.

Everyone started asking questions at the same time, so I captained the shit out of the situation. "Calegg, you're talking bollocks, mate. There's something you need to tell us, so just tell us straight. Now come on man, what's the score?"

Everyone seemed to agree with my assessment of Calegg's avoidance tactic, and let me have my moment. Calegg looked like a deer in the headlights, then finally spoke, "My father is the head of trading on Torax. He's in charge of all shipments on and off the planet."

"That's brilliant," I exclaimed. "He can help us get people away then."

"I had a huge falling out with him, and that's why I left Torax. He is, how do you describe it… a complete prick. We do not get on, yet unfortunately, anything we do on the planet will have to go through him."

"Right. That's not great. Can you make it up with him?" Ember asked.

"I'll try, I promise," Calegg said, although we could all clearly see the tension in him as he made that promise. He didn't believe he could deliver on it.

"You'll do fine, I know it," Ember said, while Elyek patted him on the back.

"Let's get down there. I don't think hanging on will help Calegg's confidence any. How soon 'til we can land?" I asked.

Calegg sighed, "We can be there in an hour. We've jumped close. And seriously, this ship." He smiled a little with pride, patting the table.

"Well, the Thoth turning up as bounty hunters changes

things, too. I want to... sorry *we* need to get some support. Uprising Inc. needs a crew, yesterday."

"Okay, Shaun. We're going," Calegg said, getting up from the table, "but I'm making no promises."

"I will take us to Torax and watch over the bridge. You should all get tidied up and prepared," Elyek said. "Plus, you won't need me on this trip. I can rest when you all go down to Torax."

"Yeah, we could do with cleaning up. Hopefully, this excursion will be less intense," I laughed.

"I'll stay with you, Elyek. I'm still fresh and I can help talk us past the barrier force," Calegg added.

"Thank you, Calegg. That would be appreciated," Elyek replied.

Ember and I slunk off to our room to get cleaned up for whatever awaited us on Torax.

After we showered and jumped into bed, Ember started chatting, "Hey, Shaun. Have you checked your stats lately? We must have got some gains for that last week. We might even be up for the hundred party."

"Okay. Together?"

"Definitely, mine first."

I nodded happily, "Sure, Ember. Let's do it." I went to her Interface Room. She was waiting already.

Name: Ember Davison

Age: 25 GY

Transcendence Level: 100

Strength: 81/1000

Agility: 110/1000

Speed: 100/1000

Intelligence: 40/1000

Constitution: 116/1000

Wisdom: 51/1000

Mental Resilience: 205/1000
Mental Clarity: 45%
Potential: 83%

"Woo-hoo! I did it! Now let's have a peek at yours."

"Yeah, sure. How has your Clarity gone up? I'm sure it was only like, 38 or something last time we looked."

"Unlike you, Shaun, I occasionally visit my Mindscape and do a bit of work on it. A practice you should start adopting quickly. Now come on, let's go see how you're doing," she said, and we both scooted over to my Mindscape.

Name: Shaun Sutherland
Age: 29 GY
Transcendence Level: 99
Strength: 203/1000
Agility: 74/1000
Speed: 108/1000
Intelligence: 46/1000
Constitution: 200/1000
Wisdom: 7/1000
Mental Resilience: 60/1000
Mental Clarity: 20%
Potential: 99%

"You've got to be fucking kidding me. How's that even possible?" she said, totally astonished.

"Hell, if I know. I did do quite a bit. Maybe it was the bare-knuckle beating I took, or maybe Havok helped me level."

"I'm glad you've had a good jump, Shaun. It means we're that little bit safer doesn't it?" she said, curling into my armpit. It seemed like she was about to go off to sleep when she suddenly jumped up like a mad-woman.

"What! What's wrong?" I shouted, panicking.

"My boot! I need to put it together, and hopefully it will self-repair, or I'm fucked. I'll have to hop everywhere."

I laughed, then rolled over. "Night, Ember."

C2

Slow-Baked Potato

Torax met with my expectations. Because of Calegg's fire-based abilities, I figured red and orange colors, and very rugged. Anywhere a race of fire-wielding, horned people came from was bound to look mildly hellscapey.

We watched the planet through the front screen of the landing craft. Ember stood next to me, leaning against my side. Arriving at new planet wasn't likely to get old anytime soon for us two intergalactic noobs, and luckily Ember's boot had repaired itself, so she was my friend for the approach.

We left the Uprising in orbit because we were unanimous in our agreement that being caught on the ground with her would be the pinnacle of stupidity, considering how many people we'd pissed off. We left Elyek near the space station, which contained a number of Galactic Empire soldiers. Their purpose was to act as a kind of police force, checking incoming and outgoing traffic. Generally, the Torax were not permitted to leave their planet. They could only leave under specific circumstances, although I wasn't sure what all of those were.

Ships arriving at Torax were 99% trade vessels, here to purchase the precious Suldr: fire gems, as Calegg informed me. The Torax people mined, prepared and sold these Suldr. They were apparently an invaluable energy source on spaceships and Torax's only export. It was for the Suldr that we claimed to be here to buy, and we were in fact going to buy some while we were here.

Elyek had explained that most of the ship's functions were powered by the same fuel the ship used to go places. But the energy from the fuel had to be converted, however Suldr could charge many of these functions far more efficiently, thus allowing our fuel to last exponentially longer. It seemed like a bloody good idea to me.

Elyek and Calegg had come up with the plan together, and it was a fucking brilliant feeling, to trust in them to make these plans and decisions. The responsibility was an unwelcome weight, and I was happy to delegate at any time. They had informed the Empire guard that we would be landing the shuttle down on the surface to negotiate the purchase of Suldr. Once complete and our order made ready, we would take the Uprising down to pick up the cargo, which would indeed consist of Suldr. But more hopefully, it would also include a strong group of Torax fighters, hidden of course.

To Calegg's credit, he transported us down in the small craft like an absolute pro, which was impressive considering how nervous he was looking. Facing his father was clearly an extremely uncomfortable prospect for him. We landed our shuttle in a docking bay. It would have been easy enough to find even without coordinates. The entire planet looked almost empty apart from one large city. And when I say large, I don't mean massive, it was just a bang-average-sized city, and was the only place permitted to receive incoming space-faring vehicles.

Calegg told us it was the capital, unimaginatively named Torax Prime. He regaled us on how only the commercial and ruling Torax lived and worked here. The vast majority of the population were spread out across the planet in small mining villages.

This city was where control was exerted, where all money changed hands and where the Suldr was brought to be sold to races far and wide across the galaxy.

When we finally docked, I patted Calegg on the back. "Good job, mate. That was some good flying… I know this is difficult for you, but don't worry about it. We've got your back. We trust you and think you're the man. Okay?"

"The man?" he replied, looking at me, confused.

"You're cool. You know what you're doing, eh. We respect you. Yeah?"

"Yes, Captain. I'm the man. I can do this."

"Sure you can, Calegg," Ember said, smiling.

Not wanting to give him any more time to dwell, I clapped my hands together loudly. "Let's get to it, gang. We've got Suldr to buy, and Torax to smuggle. "I didn't wait for a response and headed to the craft's exit ramp, sending a quick thought to Havok, who flew over to my back with a whoop.

After our successes so far, I was feeling supremely confident about our chances here. That was until the ramp lowered and we were blasted with heat, like the opening of an oven door. It was unreal. I turned away toward Ember, who looked easily as uncomfortable as me.

"Dude, how damn hot is it here?" I asked him.

"I don't know. It feels mild. The hot season can be unbearable at times," Calegg said, nonchalantly.

"Calegg, you mad bastard. This temperature is right at the top end of what Ember and I can handle. Why didn't you tell us?"

"How would I know to tell you? This is fine for me. I know you two like it cold on the ship, but that doesn't really bother me either. Temperature is not a concern for Torax." He turned, giving us both a deprecating smile.

"That's not the point, mate. We're not Torax!"

"Then maybe you should check the surface temperatures of the planets you land on now and again," he said sarcastically. At least our discomfort had taken his mind from his stressful responsibility, although the worried look returned to his face a moment later as he stared intently at an approaching Torax garbed in robes.

All that the Torax knew of our arrival was that we were here to trade for Suldr. Even though there were plenty of people around, only this one old Torax approached us. He did a double-take when he saw Calegg, and his neutral expression turned to a frown. "So, someone gave you a job, Calegg. What do they have you doing? Cleaning their toilets?" he said as he came within a few feet of us.

Calegg stood up straighter. "No, father. I'm their pilot."

The old man turned to look at Ember and me. "You let my son fly your ship?" he asked, genuinely curious.

"Your son is a fine man. We're privileged to have him fly our ship," I answered neutrally, but I already hated the shithead.

"Who are you that allows a Torax such an honored position? I do not recognize your race?"

"We're humans," Ember answered, voice dripping with distaste at Calegg's father's rude opening statements.

"Again, I do not know that race. Where are you from? Are you not aware of our reputation among the galaxy's inhabitants?"

"We're from the Fystr Empire. We know of your reputation. We're not gonna judge you by it," Ember replied in clipped tones.

"The Fystr, you say. Now, I have heard of them. They annexed much of the galaxy. They are immensely powerful, are they not?"

"Sure are, although they're our enemies. Most of the planets in their Empire are filled with humans like us, who are subjugated and oppressed," she continued.

"Interesting. So, why are you here with my son? Something tells me it is more than Suldr that brings you."

Calegg chirped up this time, which I was relieved about. "We need more crew members, father. I intend to smuggle those who would leave on to our ship. We've many enemies, enemies of the Torax people also. My friends here killed Mazltor, ten Tri-bor and an Ang-bor on Necrus. They have much honor."

"Whether they are honorable or not, I will not risk our people, Calegg. We have peace, and we are left alone by the Empire for the most part. We are happy on Torax!" he shouted the last bit to leave us in no doubt about his stance.

I was surprised to hear Calegg reply so vehemently, "You're slaves, nothing more! Mining our planet's precious resources for money-grabbing bastards, who despise us and underpay us for the pleasure. What'll you do when the Suldr runs out?" Calegg started ranting.

"I see you have not matured in your time away," his father said with an expression that conveyed both smugness and disappointment.

"I've matured. You just seem to bring out the worst in me. I'm sorry for my outburst. Please, don't judge my friends by it."

"I will not. Now, are you here for trade, too, or was that a ruse? If it was, then you may leave now."

"We'll still trade," I said.

"Good," he said shortly, "follow me. I will take you to the trade hall, where we can do business in comfort."

We followed along, amid stares and whispers, although most seemed to be directed at Calegg. I was beginning to really struggle in the heat, and that took most of my attention. Our Fystr outfits were incredibly good at cooling us down and wicking away the sweat, but unfortunately they didn't cover my head, which felt like a slow-baked potato.

We approached a large building that looked like it was carved from the rock itself. I wanted to ask Calegg about the building techniques on Torax, but I found I didn't have the energy for it.

"Hey, Havok. Is there anything you can do for the heat? I feel like I'm gonna pop."

"I can stop you dying, but not much else. You're already becoming dehydrated. Ember, too. I'll look after you both as best I can, just drink plenty and don't stay too long," he replied in my head.

I prayed that the trade building would be cooler than outdoors until that became my sole reason for putting one foot in front of another. We were approaching the entrance, and my hope swelled.

But to my unbridled horror, the building was just as hot inside as out. I conjured just enough energy to look at Ember, who was trudging alongside me, head down and looking very much worse for wear, her sweat-drenched hair hanging down. That was enough.

"We're too hot, Calegg. I feel like I'm gonna melt here."

He barely acknowledged me, busy as he was speaking to his father.

"One of you needs to sort out a cooler area for us.

Now!" I said, loudly.

"Father, can we get Ember and Shaun to the diplomat's room? Quickly, they're unused to such heat."

Calegg's dad gave us a look of derision, then beckoned us in a different direction. We finally reached a room that had some kind of air-conditioning; it was pure bliss.

"Thank you," I said to him, "and sorry, what was your name? We haven't been properly introduced."

"I am Chancellor Dolegg," he replied, full of his own self-importance. I was about to reply, when he continued talking, "I am surprised you are so delicate; I had heard the Fystr to be a highly resilient race."

He was a dick, no doubt about it.

"Yeah, the Fystr are. We're not Fystr. We're the bottom rung of their Empire. Try to keep up, Dolegg." Ember answered, full of snark. Whether he picked up on it or not, I couldn't tell. He sat down behind a desk, we three followed his lead and also sat, Havok adjusted himself seamlessly to allow me to sit.

"So, what value of Suldr do you wish to purchase?" he asked.

"How much are they each?" I replied.

"Four senlars, each."

"Four senlars!" Calegg cried out.

"Is he trying to rip us off?" Ember asked Calegg.

"No, not at all. Before I left here, the agreed price was nine senlars, which was still insulting. They're worth at least 15. More, really. But 15 is the minimum."

"The Galactic Council has reduced the price to four, so it is four," Dolegg answered, emotionless.

"We'll take a hundred," I said.

"Very good, human."

"My name is Shaun, Dolegg."

"As you wish, Shaun. I will take the payment now."

"I've a banking chip for a Juntos account. Do you have means to take payment from there?"

"Of course we do. We are a trading hub," he said, feigning offense. He pulled out a small device from the terminal at his desk before continuing. "The amount is 400 senlar. Please place your chip over the scanner."

"No. We'll pay what they're worth. I won't be part of the system that keeps your people down. One that underpays you for your hard work and resources. I'll pay 1,500 senlar, if you feel that's fair."

"It is not about what is fair. It is about what we are allowed to take for our produce. Four hundred, if you please."

"Dude, seriously. You're being shat on from a great height. I could understand you wanting to stay here and mine if you were left alone, but you're not. You're little better than slaves, like Calegg said. This planet is a prison."

"You speak of things you don't understand, human," he replied.

That prompted Calegg to respond angrily, "But I understand, father. There are others here who are not so happy with the arrangements made through you, as I remember. We're being driven into poverty, and when the Suldr have run out, we'll be left with nothing. A shell of a planet with no resources and no future. If you won't stand up against that, then you should give our people the chance to at least leave, if they want."

Dolegg began to laugh, "Of course most of the miners would leave on a wild Chugubi chase. Following adventure, rather than toiling relentlessly for little pay. But they often forget that it is their hard work that keeps our people safe. If they left, they would be leaving our people to certain doom when we cannot meet our quotas. Not to mention they will be killed in the great void."

I was about to ask what the fuck a Chugubi was and assure Dolegg we would take care of the people we took. But Calegg got in long before I could articulate the thought, "All my fucking gods. You're in the Galactic Empire's pocket, aren't you? It all makes sense now!"

His father started blustering speechlessly, "I... how... how dare you! I am a well-respected, trusted member of our governing council. The people understand that the negotiations I carry out are the only thing that keeps food in their mouths. The hard work I do is for the good of us all, I do not just run away because things are hard!"

Turns out his bluster was a ruse; he must have somehow signaled for guards while he waffled on about how important he was.

Seven large, armed and uniformed Torax men came pouring in the room. I jumped up, Havok almost instantly in my hand, as I moved to stand in front of Calegg and Ember. The guards carried rifles, but they weren't lasers, they were more like our Earth assault rifles.

"Guards! Arrest these people," Dolegg shouted, with outrage in his voice. The guards moved forward, but Calegg commanded them to stop.

"Calegg?" One of the guards said, clearly recognizing our friend.

"Koparr, my friend. It's been too long a time," Calegg said with a sad smile.

"Stop talking and arrest them," Dolegg shouted again. The man looked over to Dolegg, confused.

"What for, sir? This is your son, and they were all sitting peacefully when we entered," said the hulking Torax named Koparr.

"They are dissenters trying to bring ruin to our planet! Now do as you're bid, officer!"

Koparr seemed offended, "With all due respect Chancellor, you're not in charge of the guard force. Although I respect your position, I'll not just arrest people on your say so." He turned to Calegg, "What's going on?"

Dolegg started ranting and raving, threatening Koparr's career, his life. Anything he could come up with to have his own way.

Koparr ignored him, as did Calegg, who responded to Koparr's question, "I believe my father is acting in the best interests of the Empire and may actually be in their pay. My captain here," he pointed to me, "has just offered 15 senlar per Suldr, as I told him that is closer to their true worth. My father refused, and said he could only accept four senlar, as per the terms of the Empire's agreement, which seemed very odd."

"That is odd," Koparr said, turning to Dolegg, "You actually turn people's money away, when our people struggle so badly?"

"That is not all they came for; they are attempting to put our whole planet at risk by trying to take Torax as crew members," he said, trying to deflect from the accusations thrown his way.

I worried how Koparr would take this revelation. He turned back to Calegg and raised a questioning eyebrow.

Calegg shrugged, "We came to trade, but also to offer some of our people a chance to become crew on the fastest ship in the galaxy. When I told my father this, he outright refused, saying it would destroy our people by reducing the miners available, and that unless we were trading, we should leave immediately."

Koparr looked angrily at Dolegg again and pointed a finger. "Out of respect for your son, I have put up with you, but long since have I had my own suspicions. I'm taking this matter to Moulagg," Koparr said authoritatively, then spoke to one of his squad. "Guparr, go and bring Moulagg. Tell him it's urgent, and I will consider his debt to me paid."

Guparr nodded at once and ran from the room. The other guards had relaxed their weapons slightly, and in a gesture of good faith, I slipped Havok onto my back, although he grumbled at the lack of action.

Dolegg began ranting again. "You're finished for this, Koparr!" he said as he began to head for the door, "Let me know when Moulagg arrives and we will have a discussion about your future."

"You're not going anywhere, Dolegg. Currently, you're on the cusp of arrest yourself."

"You can't hold me; you do not have the authority," he retorted indignantly.

"Of course I do, Dolegg. If this goes badly, then I know how much trouble you can cause for me. But I believe you won't get away from it this time. You think I'm the only one who suspects you're double-dealing, taking pay from the Empire? It's long past time your foot was removed from the necks of the Torax people!" he said, angrily. He turned to face Calegg, "Are you willing to defy your father in court?"

Both Ember and I looked to Calegg. I knew it was a big request, yet he didn't hesitate.

"I most certainly will. I left because he's a mean spirited, selfish, man, and now I've come back, he's even worse."

"Very good, Calegg. So, why did you come back again?

You said something about a crew?"

"I did. My friends here have a large spaceship and a desire to build a crew."

"A crew for what, though? What are your objectives?" Koparr asked, eagerly. His men also seemed to hang on Calegg's every word. He was about to answer when Ember kicked him.

Calegg let out a yelp, turning to Ember, "What was that for?"

"I'll admit I don't know everything going on here, nor do I wish to offend anyone, but your father," she said nodding to the fuming Dolegg, "seems openly hostile to us. How much information do you want to divulge in front of him?"

Calegg nodded thoughtfully, Koparr responded by looking dubiously at Dolegg, and replied,

"Yes. I understand your point."

I whispered over to Ember, "Divulge? Aren't you getting better with your words?"

"Yes. I am, and it's called a vocabulary you dumb fucker," she whispered back, smiling sweetly back at me.

We were stirred from our little conversation by Koparr speaking up. "I'd like to say that there will be plenty of takers to join your crew, depending on your purposes. I might even be tempted myself."

"You're a traitor to your people," Dolegg snarled.

Koparr just laughed, "Ha. Good one, Chancellor. Really? Coming from you, that's brilliant. Just take a seat and we can sort all of this out once Moulagg comes."

Dolegg quietened and sat down at his desk pretending to be busy. Ember and I sat back down, too. Koparr watched me as I did. "That axe is a marvel. How did you get it into your hand so quickly when we entered? And how does it move when you sit? For that matter, how is it even attached to your back?"

I smiled softly, "He's a marvel, indeed, and I take no credit for the things he can do. He's an ancient sentient weapon who has decided to help me out."

Koparr looked at me like I was mad. I saw Dolegg looking over with a gleam of interest in his eyes.

"That is some story for a weapon. Whatever the truth, it is a fine weapon."

"That is the truth," Calegg said, "Havok, the, er, axe has spoken to me."

"Ha, ha. Very well. Whatever the case, keep a close eye on it. Many people would eye such a weapon covetously."

Havok laughed in my head at the thought of someone stealing him.

"Don't worry, Koparr. I guarantee Havok would be one of the hardest weapons in the universe to steal."

"I'll take your word for it," he said, then fell into conversation with Calegg. From what I could hear, it was mainly about the good old days. Seemingly, they had been close friends.

It took a while, but finally Moulagg arrived. He was an older Torax with a similar bulk to Koparr and a commanding appearance, or rather a 'don't fuck with me if you know what's good for you' appearance. "Koparr, Dolegg!" He boomed. "What's going on here then?"

"I brought the guards in to arrest these off-worlders..."

"And his son," Koparr added, helpfully.

"...they threaten to destabilize the fragile peace we have with the Empire," Dolegg continued, riding over the interruption.

Moulagg laughed at that, "Peace?"

"Dolegg rejected an offer for a fair price on the Suldr

from his own son and the captain here," Koparr added, pointing to me.

"What was the fair price?" Moulagg asked everyone.

I answered, "I offered 15 Senlar per Suldr, and my offer was refused. The Chancellor informed me he can only accept four."

Moulagg's eyes went wide, "You refused more money, Dolegg?"

"We are only permitted to sell for four senlar, as per our agreement with the Empire. My hands are tied, and I don't intend to hide money from their auditors."

Moulagg went from a mildly terrifying, cool, calm alien to just downright terrifying in a second.

"An insulting agreement, which you signed for some insane reason, Dolegg! Apparently, for all of our own good. I can't remember there being any stipulations on not taking more money for our Suldr. Aside from that, please explain why you would try to have your own son arrested?"

"He is a traitor. Bringing these off-worlders here with the intention of smuggling our people from the planet. If the Empire discovered why they were here, only trouble would follow."

"We hoped to find willing crew members," Calegg added, calmly.

Moulagg acknowledged Calegg's statement, then turned to Dolegg again. "Let me get this straight. You tried to arrest your own son and his captain for offering more money on our only export, and offering a genuine route for our people to leave this planet?" he said, eyes almost popping out of his head with the intensity of his gaze.

"It is best that our people do not leave the planet. I say

again, only trouble will follow," Dolegg replied, calmly.

"Damn it, Dolegg. There are no rules against leaving. They have just crippled our ability to leave and have slandered us across the universe. This could be a step to start making things right with the people of the galaxy; show them we're not the animals we have been made out to be! But you try and prevent it?" He let out a loud huff. "I cannot tolerate you any longer. I am calling a council of judgment on you. Until then, you are under house arrest!"

"Are you serious, Moulagg? You want to go down this route with me?" Dolegg replied, a mix of anger and bewilderment, "You know this won't go how you expect it to, don't you?"

"You're a damned, shit-eating worm Dolegg, and all I can do is try. Koparr, please escort Dolegg to his home."

Koparr and his men did as asked, leaving us three remaining in the cool room with Moulagg.

"Come on then, young Calegg, tell me everything."

Calegg looked sheepishly at me and Ember.

"Go ahead," I said.

Calegg regaled Moulagg of everything that had happened since he met us. Plus what he knew of our history. It was strange hearing our story from someone else's lips who'd been there. And strangely empowering.

When he finished, Moulagg spoke to Ember and me, "So, you've no prejudice against the Torax?"

"The opposite, having befriended Calegg," I said.

"You understand that you'll be viewed in a certain way if you have Torax crew members?"

Ember flashed a confident smile at Moulagg, "Our aim is to have many crew members. It seems there are plenty of races in this galaxy that are mistreated. Providing they're good people, we'll have them all. And if we can collect as many as possible, perhaps we'll be able to change a few of the injustices going on."

"That's a lofty desire. To be honest, it sounds more like a death wish going against the Fystr and the Galactic Empire while making enemies of the Mazltor."

"Go big, or go home," Ember said. I was happy for her to take this conversation on. She was generally more articulate than me, at least when she wasn't being acerbic.

"Well, if you're judged by the caliber of your enemies, then you're judged highly. I'm inspired by your attitude and will help you pick our toughest, most level-headed warriors. I hope you look after them and help ease the oppression the Torax live under."

"I promise you, we'll try best on both counts. It's a tough galaxy out there, and we want to make it a little better if we can," she replied, and Moulagg nodded.

"There is one problem though," he said.

"Yes?"

"Our customs are entrenched in our minds, and no Torax will follow an off-worlder if you cannot beat them in single combat."

"What?" Ember said animatedly, "That's bullshit. Calegg follows, and you can't expect Shaun to fight every crew member."

I was glad Ember summed up everything I thought.

"We'll crush them all," Havok said in my head.

"Thanks, bud," I replied.

Moulagg, obviously unable to hear Havok, continued, "Calegg is not a warrior. It's not his way. Our warrior caste follows an exacting code. You will only have to fight the strongest among them, whoever that may be. I believe that even if you were to simply put up a good fight, they'd still follow you. Do you think you can stand up against one of our warriors?" he asked, turning to me.

Ember was about to refuse, but I answered quickly, "Sure I can. Why not! I'll do it, Moulagg."

Moulagg looked surprised, but continued, "It'll take a few days to find out who wants to go and who should get to go. Where will you be staying?"

"In this damn heat, I think we'll be best off heading back to the Uprising until everything is set up. Just send word and we'll bring the ship down to Torax to collect the Suldr and our new crew members," I said with a wink. Moulagg nodded and Calegg spoke up.

"Captain, may I have permission to stay planet side? I've a few things I'd like to catch up on, and I'll need to be here for my father's impending charges."

"Of course, Calegg," I said, patting him on the back, "But next time you think you can get more crew members, inform us of any customs that involve a brutal challenge."

"Oh, yes. I'm sorry, I never even thought about that. But if it's any consolation, I have ultimate faith in you." I nodded acceptance to the troublesome Torax, then addressed Moulagg again, "Um, so, what weapons are expected in this battle? I can't really use guns, but I'll face anyone with my axe," I said, trying to gain clarity on the rules of this fight.

Moulagg's eyes raised a little. "We don't want deaths; the bout will be weaponless of course."

"Oh…," I said, and felt my stomach drop a little. I felt invincible with Havok, but without him I really wasn't sure of my abilities. Yet I had committed now, and I wasn't one to back down from the trouble my stupid mouth got me into. "Makes sense," I said casually.

"You're a peculiar human, but I think I like you. I look forward to seeing your bout."

"Yeah, I look forward to it, too," I said stupidly, as I couldn't think of another response.

Calegg and Moulagg led us back out into the stifling heat and walked back with us to the landing shuttle.

We were both worse for wear again by the time we made it back to the docking bay. Moulagg looked worried. "Will you be able to fight in our heat, if it has this effect on you just walking to your ship? I can try to arrange a Cool room for the match if you need it."

"Oh thanks, man. Cooler will definitely be better for me. This heat is insane."

"We'll ensure there is somewhere cool to fight, Shaun. I'll keep in touch over comms and let you know when to come back down."

"Great. Now I'll see you guys later. I want to get this damn door closed."

"Ha, ha. Yeah, sorry Captain," Calegg said.

"Goodbye for now, humans. It was a pleasure to meet you both," said Moulagg.

"You too, Moulagg. See you both soon. Oh, and stay out of trouble, Calegg."

He grinned as the door closed.

C3

Brains or Brawn Shaun?

Both Ember and I were relieved to get off Torax. Returning to the Uprising was a piece of cake, as the landing craft had its own return function. It was simply a case of pressing a button.

We went straight to the bridge, where Elyek was waiting for us, eyes questioning. "So, how did it go? You're back faster than I thought you would be. And without Calegg?"

"He had some catching up to do. Apparently he has a few friends down there, as well as one particular enemy," Ember replied.

"An enemy?" Elyek raised an inquisitive eyebrow.

"His father. A total wanker," I answered this time, "tried to have us arrested for poaching people from the planet. Luckily, one of their guards was a good friend of Calegg's. Anyway, long story short, his father is now under house arrest and awaiting trial for being in the pay of the Empire. While Calegg is working with the Torax head of security to gather some badass fighters for us."

"Wow!" Elyek exclaimed. "As always with you guys, a lot has happened in a short space of time."

"Yeah, and it's hot as hell down there. We're gonna stay on the ship until they've arranged our Suldr shipment and who'll be coming with us. Then we just need to head down and pick them up." I gave a tired smile. I had omitted the part where I had to fight the strongest, toughest Torax they could find in a duel. Not to worry though, Ember was more than happy to fill in that particular blank for me.

"Shaun has forgotten to mention that he's agreed to an unarmed fight with the biggest, toughest Torax they can find. Because he's a bloody moron."

"Hey! I thought you had confidence in my hurting-people skills?"

"I do, mostly. That you won't have to fight in that heat has certainly made me a little more confident. But there's a difference between general carnage, at which you excel, and a stand-up toe-to-toe fight with a trained warrior who's probably the toughest Torax on the whole damn planet."

I was about to reply, but Elyek started speaking.

"I did not realize that was part of their culture, although many war-like races insist on combat trials," Elyek said, then added, "If that is what we have to do, I'm sure Shaun can do it even without Havok. How is your unarmed combat, Shaun?"

"Um, should be okay. Though I should probably go and constantly train until I have to go back down there."

"Yes. That might be wise, now I think about it. You did not fare too well against the Ang-bor when unarmed," Elyek said with a concerned look.

"I'd just been shot! My damn arm was literally hanging off, Elyek!" I said, throwing my arms in the air in exasperation, "I killed a bloody Gro-bar with one knee!"

"You did, Shaun. I trust you to win," Ember said, turning from disgruntled to soothing as my anger got the better of me, "I suppose you did what you had to do to get our crew. And I'm sorry for winding you up about it. I just didn't like that we didn't talk about it beforehand."

"Sorry. I should've discussed it with you, but I didn't want to look like I was scared."

"Yeah, I get that. But next time, realize that you're in a position of authority. You can calmly deliberate your choices without losing face," Ember said.

"Okay. Fair enough," I replied, then turned to Elyek, "While it's fresh on my mind, is there anything we can do to help with the heat? Even walking to whatever room they've set up for the fight will be grueling. I don't want to be knackered before I start."

"Other than a full environmental suit or acclimatizing you to the temperature, I do not know of anything specific. Veiletians are able to tolerate a wide temperature range, so it is not something I have looked into in any detail."

"Okay. Well that's a bit shit. I suppose I'm gonna have to recreate the heat. Perhaps I should've stayed on Torax."

Havok spoke to me, "I might be able to help you to acclimatize, Shaun. It should work similarly to when we trained your muscle growth, hopefully."

"Thanks, Havok. We'll have to give it a go," I said back, but then had to explain why I had gone quiet.

"Havok thinks he can help me with getting used to the heat, so I've agreed to give it a try. Now, I'm going off to get something to eat, and then *train*."

Ember followed me out, while Elyek went back to monitoring the ship's systems.

We sat and ate a ton of steak, potatoes and greens in silence, our still-battered bodies craving the sustenance. Ember finished first. I felt like I could have kept eating for eternity.

"So, what are you planning to train in?" She asked.

"Kickboxing. What do you think?" I answered.

"I knew you'd say that. But don't you think you should be training your Mental Skills? Like you said, you broke that Gro-bar's sternum and the other guy's neck. I think Combat Skill-wise and physically you're as good as you can get in a day or so of practice. Don't neglect the whole arsenal of mental powers at your disposal, especially in this heat. I tried navigating my body from the Mindscape down there, on the way back to the ship, and it helped a lot."

"That'd be cheating!" I said in mild outrage at the thought.

"No it's not, you melon head. This fight is between you and another, and the skills you each have. These mental abilities are part of who you are. You'd be an idiot not to use them, Shaun. Oh... wait. That's right, you are an idiot!"

"And you're a sarcastic so-and-so, but you don't hear me going on about it," I said as I stormed off in a mood to the training room.

A few minutes later, Ember followed. "What's up with you, fuck nugget?"

"Dunno. Maybe the heat got to me," I smiled, tiredly.

She nodded, "You know I don't think you're an idiot, right?" she said gently, "I just like fucking around."

"Yeah, I know. I'm well aware of my strengths and weaknesses now, so your words don't hurt at all anymore. Although I can still occasionally be idiotic," I laughed.

"Can't we all," she replied with a friendly punch to my arm. "So, you gonna train up your other powers a bit? You keep saying you're bad with them, but you're not really, not at all. I think you may have been trying too hard in the past, or just expecting too much."

"You were so much better than me, straight away," I said, sullenly.

"Yeah, but I had higher Mental Clarity, which as we've been over a number of times now, makes everything else easier to do. Plus, I'd say you were better than anyone else on the ship, bar Ogun. I mean, seriously Shaun, you're the first human to transcend. And that was with a Mental Clarity of two percent!" she chuckled.

"Maybe, but it just doesn't feel natural to me."

"Of course it doesn't. I'm sure when you first started walking as a toddler it didn't feel natural either, but look at you now, walking around nearly as well as a normal person," she grinned cheekily.

I didn't find it funny. I sat there with a sour face on.

"Let me put it another way," she said, "We're in a strange new life, filled with aliens of all kinds of skills. Now, let's say you were a Veiletian and your friend could go invisible for an hour, but you could only go invisible for 45 minutes. Would you stop going invisible and just throw away that huge advantage you have over other races? You don't have to answer by the way, it's a rhetorical question."

My answer died on my lips.

"One more thing, before you accept what an absolute dipshit you're being. Torax can shoot fire at you and go supernova. You can't fight that shit with a well-executed right hook. What if the Torax comes into this fight thinking they can use their powers? They probably will. What will you do then? Apart from returning to me as a Shaun shish kebab."

"Okay! For god's sake, Ember. Okay! You've made your

point. Thanks for pointing out my stupidity yet again. I'll train my friggin' mental skills."

"Good," she said, a satisfied expression spreading across her face, "Now, we should focus on your Cognition Room again."

"Ugh! But that's literally the most boring thing to do."

"Seriously, Shaun. We're not going through this every time."

"What if greater Mental Clarity means I start running away when the odds are against us, like Ogun did?"

"That hasn't happened to me, and I know without a doubt it won't happen to you. It doesn't matter if your mind is as clear as a bell, you'll still have your own authentic personality. You're not Ogun, and never will be. You're an obstinate shit, and I love you for it," she gave me a heartwarming grin and I relented, laughing at her description of me.

"I'm fighting fairly, though, I'll only use my powers if my opponent goes to use theirs. But no matter what, I promise you I'll win. Keep Havok close, I may need his healing afterwards."

"Fair enough. I understand a little. I'd personally go straight in and freeze that fucker up, like an ice cube. I realize that's not exactly your style."

Over the next ten hours, we worked on clearing my Cognition Room. We cranked up the heating to match the planet's surface temperature. Ember was right, as long as we were in the Mindscape, we were more or less impervious. We went to see Elyek a few times, stopped for snacks, and generally just let our bodies recover from the heat on occasion, but rarely for longer than ten minutes at a time.

Havok told us that new blood vessels were being

formed, and he was assisting in their growth. I didn't know what he was talking about, but he assured me it was a good thing.

With the clearing, we were getting quicker and quicker all the time, pretty much throwing shit, on the shelves to the beat of Havok's wild and heavy music. I'd even say there were a few hours in which I began to enjoy it. When we stopped, on Ember's command, we were just under halfway through the room.

"Let's check your Mental Clarity now. Then we should get something to eat and rest up a little, ready to crack on with training some of your mental skills. Otherwise, we won't have time to sharpen you up."

"Okay, boss," I said, glumly. Although I knew she was right, I could have done with a bit of kicking-the-shit-out-of-a-training-bag for an hour, just for a change of pace.

Entering my Interface Room, I was pretty impressed by the changes:

Name: Shaun Sutherland
Age: 29 GY
Transcendence Level: 101
Strength: 203/1000
Agility: 74/1000
Speed: 108/1000
Intelligence: 46/1000
Constitution: 210/1000
Wisdom: 15/1000
Mental Resilience: 60/1000
Mental Clarity: 42%
Potential: 99%

"My level is 101! My Wisdom and Constitution went

up, too!" I shouted and over-enthusiastically jumped into the air with a fist pump.

"Welcome to the one hundred club, Shaun. And now your Mental Clarity is *nearly* as high as mine, you've no excuses for being useless anymore."

"I'm over the moon with it. But why is my wisdom so shit still? It seems to be related to Mental Clarity, but yours is much higher, even though we're close on Clarity now."

"I imagine it's because I've actually used my Mental Clarity to make informed decisions on occasion, whereas you haven't."

"Oh, right. That could be it, you cheeky bitch."

"Don't worry. We'll get you using your head, rather than your muscles. More interestingly, why has your Constitution gone up so much? Let me check on mine," she disappeared from my Interface Room as soon as she finished talking, which was annoying.

I moved back into my normal state to find her there, smirking. "I'm level 101, too. My Constitution has also gone up by ten. I wonder if it's the heat we're working under?" She said.

"That's great! And yeah. It must be why. What a fantastic side effect, we will have to see if we can keep that up."

"Maybe train with low oxygen?"

"Probably cold too, we will probably have to go to a cold ass planet at some point." I laughed.

"More than likely. Now come on, let's go to the canteen."

We went and filled up on food. Still just meat and veg for me, yet again. It was starting to get boring fast. I was beginning to feel the need to have some more exotic choices programmed in. Although I didn't think a curry would be a good choice right now. Afterwards, we went back to the gym to train.

"The main thing I think you'll need to work on is seizing your opponent," Ember said, standing a few paces away from me, "Now, seize me."

I did as asked, quickly morphing into her Mindscape, then moving into her Nerve Center. I felt through the room in order to find the nerve bundles that operated her legs and arms. Once finding them, I took a grip and thought about paralyzing those limbs. With that done, I came out of her Mindscape to check. She had a wry look on her face.

"Well done, Shaun. It took you long enough, didn't it? I'd have had you killed while you messed around in there."

"It took a while to find which nerve bundles did what."

"You're supposed to be in a fight! Just grab everything, and think paralyze," she kicked out of my control, subsequently getting her movement back. "Now, try again. But this time try to appear directly in my Nerve Center, then do as I said, because I'm gonna come over there and kick you in the nuts as soon as you close your eyes."

"What? No. Don't do that!" I squawked, indignantly.

"You can easily stop me. Just don't fuck around. Okay?"

I took a few deep breaths, then did exactly as she said. Without hesitation, I fully concentrated on appearing in her Nerve Center, rather than the corridor. Then I paralyzed anything I could get my arms around, which turned out to be everything. I really didn't want to take a shot to the nuts. Coming back to normal state, I saw Ember lying on the floor, not two paces away from me, locked up solidly. Again, she freed herself from my control. I suppose this was good practice for her too.

"Brilliant!" she laughed, "Again, all you need is the right incentive. How did it feel? Any easier with the work we did in your Cognition Room?"

"You know what, it was actually a lot easier. Thanks, Ember."

"I've noticed that the clearer your mind, the more time seems to pass when you're in the Mindscape, like a small time dilation. It becomes more obvious each time I improve. At least I don't think it's an effect on time."

"I had noticed. Yet another thing Ogun never told us about. So you think it's just your brain's ability to process shit faster?"

"I can't think of any other reason for it that makes sense, so yeah."

"Well, whatever it is, it's really cool. I'm glad we've practiced it a little, but in a fight like the one I'm about to have, I don't want to paralyze someone's body completely. They'll die, won't they?"

"There's a simple solution to that. Get in there, paralyze everything immediately, and then go through what you don't want paralyzed. We both need to get used to what nerve bundles do what, so we can do it as second nature. I've been going through my own quite a lot."

"Thanks for making me do this. I actually do feel much better about it."

"Good. I'm glad. Now, come on. Let's keep practicing. I want to go over telekinesis again with you, as well."

I found telekinesis was so much easier, and I could also see why Ember was clearing her mind in her spare time. The leaps and bounds you could make with your skills were remarkable. I could now do all the tricks Ember had done with the balls, but better than that, I could lift my ass up from the floor by about ten feet, easily. Although horizontal movements were still precarious, I could do it.

We trained for quite a few more hours. When we were done, we invited Elyek to have a meal with us, and later offered to watch the bridge while they got some rest. Elyek refused, insisting they didn't need to sleep in the same way we did, and would take a few hours after we had slept.

I won't lie, we were both dead on our feet to be honest. I really needed to rest, and I imagined Ember would have felt pretty much the same. We went to bed, too exhausted for anything other than hugs. I was out like a light in minutes.

When I woke up, Ember was gone. A minor pang of worry shot through me, but I stifled it. We were safe on our ship. All was good. I still got ready in a hurry and made my way to the bridge. Ember was there alone, messing with a hand terminal while draped over her chair, eating an apple.

"An apple? I hadn't even thought to get fruit from the FSU."

"Yeah. They're yummy too! You should go get one," she replied.

"Nah, I don't really like fruit too much."

She gave me a black look in return, and said no more about it.

"So, what's happening?" I asked, a little confused.

"I got up a few hours ago and took over from Elyek. I'll continue until they wake, then I'll come and help you train some more. First, how about you go and get us some breakfast. I was just eating this until you woke your lazy ass up. I could really do with a proper breakfast. After that, you could go and train until I get there. Then we'll get to your favorite job of all, clearing again. It's by far the most important thing for us to do, and the further we go with it, the more I see how important it is. It's probably the one thing Ogun should have had us doing once we transcended. I don't think he knew half as much as he pretended to."

"Who knows what he was thinking. But fuck Ogun, we can look after ourselves just fine," I said, before heading to the canteen to rustle us both up a fried breakfast. I was strong, and I held off on the fried bread. Putting the breakfasts on a tray, I grabbed a jug of coffee too. Ember seemed to be pleased with my choice, as she tucked in with relish.

After breakfast I went to the gym. Although I had been told to work on my Mental Abilities, I really felt the need to get my heart pumping. I did a 20-minute burst of exercise, consisting of a combination of calisthenics and bag work. I'd worked up a grand old sweat by the time I'd finished and happily moved to working on levitation. Though I was loathe to admit it, I was glad Ember had talked me into practicing. With a fresh mentality toward it, the skills were coming easier.

Ember joined me after a couple of hours. I was more than happy to start our clearance once more. We cranked the temperature right back up while we were working hard in our Mindscapes. It seemed an excellent way to acclimatize my body to the excessive heat, without even having to be there to suffer it.

By the end of the day, the mental cleansing, and the duress our bodies had been under from the heat, had taken an uncanny toll on us. We were absolutely exhausted.

There remained around one-quarter of the original mess left to store away, and I'd hit level 103. My Constitution had moved up another 15 points, Wisdom another five and Mental Clarity was sitting at 64%. I was a bit confused by that, but I'd probably just overestimated how much stuff had been there to tidy originally.

I was now ahead of Ember on level and Mental Clarity, and I felt bad for her, I'd have to make sure that I returned the favor after this combat. For now though, I just needed to rest. We expected the call to come tomorrow for my fight.

Not for the first time these past two days, I wished Calegg was here to offer advice on Torax fighting styles and customs in duels such as this. It would have been great to spar with him too, in preparation. Not to mention it would have been fun to kick the cheeky bastard's ass a bit.

I woke before Ember the next day, full of nervous energy. We had acclimatized to the galactic 27-hour clock, but it was still mighty odd to me. Rolling out of bed, I jumped straight in the shower. The proper one, too, not the goddamn powdered one. Despite respecting its convenience, I still didn't trust that piece of shit after my horrific ordeal at its hands on the Thoth.

By the time I got out, Ember was stirring. Opening her eyes, she looked at me with a puzzled expression. "You okay, Shaun? You're never up before me."

"Yeah, totally. Just a bit pumped to get on with today."

"It's going to be okay. I may have understated my confidence in you the other day, but I've no doubt whatsoever that you'll comfortably get through this."

"Well, thanks for the confidence. It means a lot."

We got dressed and went to see Elyek. When we arrived on the bridge, they were sitting nursing a cup of coffee.

"Sorry, Elyek. Do you need to go get rest before we make our way down to the planet?"

"Not at all. I have only just awoken myself. It was nice the other day to have the responsibility of watching over the ship taken away, if only for a few hours. We have talked about it before, it's really a just-in-case scenario that we need to have someone here at all times. Plus, with regular cups of this fetid drink, I feel like I could stay up forever. I hated it at first, but I have discovered that the more I drink it, the more I have found myself looking forward to my next cup."

"It gets you like that," I agreed. "Do you want anything to eat? I think we're gonna grab something. I expect to hear from Calegg, soon."

"No. I'm not hungry, thanks," Elyek replied.

Ember and I went to the canteen. No sooner had we grabbed some scrambled eggs and toast than Elyek's voice came over my comm.

"Captain. Calegg has just called and requested we make our way down to the planet as soon as we're able."

"Coming Elyek, do you want anything from the canteen?"

"No, I'm fine thanks."

Without further ado, we scooped up our plates and coffees and headed to the bridge to enjoy our breakfasts with Elyek, as they took us down to the planet for an ass-kicking lunch.

C4

No Havok, No Problem.

Within an hour we were landing on Torax again, scrambled eggs a distant memory. Elyek handled the ship expertly. Admittedly far better than Calegg, but that was of little consequence. We were a team, all that mattered was that we worked together and did our jobs.

When we landed, Moulagg, Koparr and of course Calegg were there, waiting for us. Calegg came over and, to my surprise, hugged me before speaking.

"Everything is set, and we've 30 of our best Torax warriors ready to serve. They'll follow you without question, if you defeat the leader. He's ferocious, but he's also very excited to be part of our crew, as are all of the others," he spoke in a whisper as he leaned in conspiratorially. "Put on a good show. That's all that's needed. They're all more than happy to be coming along. We have 30 willing crew members, and they're all top Torax warriors."

"That's good to know, Calegg old buddy. I don't really want to hurt anyone too badly. Nor get hurt too much myself," I laughed. "Now, lead the way, and let's get this over with."

Moulagg spoke next, "Unfortunately Shaun, I was outvoted by the council on the location of the duel. This whole endeavor has turned into something of a spectacle, and the whole city wants to be involved. I hope you can handle the heat here. I have at least been able to get you a cool dressing room. I am sorry this has grown to be quite different to the arrangement you originally agreed. I will understand if you wish to bow out. No honor will be lost, as the environment strongly favors our people. However, as long as you put on a performance, everything will be okay."

"Well, I can't say I'm happy about it, but I won't back out," I turned a little angrily to Calegg. "Why didn't you tell me about the venue in the extreme heat?"

He shrugged, "Wouldn't have made any difference. I knew you'd still do it, and I've true faith you'll perform admirably, and even if it was a real fight, probably win, somehow."

"Okay... Thanks then, I think?"

Calegg patted me on the back as I shook hands with Moulagg and Koparr, then we set off to my seemingly fixed fight.

I still didn't want to do this, and the fact that it was fixed made it worse in some ways. To make matters worse, I'd gotten myself incredibly worked up, and now I'd have to massively rein in my bubbling adrenalin.

The arena was like the rough, stone-hued Colosseum of ancient Rome. Although it lacked the fine architectural details, there was no doubt it was an important building to the Torax. Judging by the mass of bodies streaming into the entrance, I had the feeling that this was a spectacle not to be missed.

I was still hotter than Satan's ass crack. I was coping much better with it than last time, and those increases to my Constitution were a godsend. But it still wasn't comfortable by any stretch.

Ember, Calegg and Elyek were told by Koparr to follow him down a corridor. I quickly handed off Havok to Ember.

"You've got this, Shaun," Havok said cheerfully, then added, "If you get fucked up, I'll just come over and sort you out."

"Thanks, pal. You're a real blessing," I replied, genuinely strengthened by his words.

"Don't sweat it, Captain," Calegg said, giving me an over-the-top wink.

"I find it hard to do anything else but sweat on this planet, Calegg."

He laughed in response, while Ember hugged me and said quietly, "Just hurry up with it so we can get going."

Surprisingly, those few words of nonchalant confidence empowered me the most. They all followed Koparr, while Moulagg beckoned me in a different direction.

We entered a sort of changing or training room. The first thing I noticed was that it felt noticeably cooler than outside, as promised, which I was very relieved about. When the door closed behind us, he turned to face me, a serious expression on his face. "I won't lie, Captain Shaun, I don't know how tough you are. Calegg said that with your axe you're damn near unbeatable, but he was unsure what you could do with just your own body. The group I've picked out for you will do our people proud, and they're very keen to go with you. So much so that our top man, Calparr, who you'll be fighting, is happy to fight to a draw with you. That'll appease everyone's sense of honor. You'll just need to put in a good showing. If it turns out you're the better fighter, then I'll ask you not to put a beating on him. He's going into this fight with the spirit of cooperation. Is that okay with you?"

"Absolutely!" I exclaimed. Immediately afterwards, I realized I sounded like a right wet lettuce. "I can handle myself, but I don't know your Torax capabilities. I really want to get off on the right foot with your people and not be kicked to shit. Or wallop your guy all over the shop," I added, hopefully explaining that I wasn't scared.

He nodded, seemingly satisfied with my response.

"I'll leave you now and take my seat. Wait for the gong, next head through that door. It won't be too long a wait." Then, he left.

I sat down on one of the stone benches that lined the wall, and waited in anticipation. I sat there for what seemed like an eternity, but it was probably only five minutes. My nerves were frayed to shreds. Even though I had learned the fight would be a fix, even after everything I'd been through.

A noise sounded, but I didn't know if it was a gong or not. I didn't even know what a damn gong was supposed to sound like. I sat there in uncertainty for a minute, wondering what to do. Finally, I got up and crept over to the door and peered through. There was a tunnel leading to a bright, sandy area. I'll be honest, I didn't want to go out there in front of all those people, or leave the relative cool of the changing room.

I could just make out a Torax, standing on a sandy surface, staring down the tunnel back at me, and thought *fuck it*! Let's get this show on over with. I strode purposefully out of the room and down the tunnel with all the confidence I could muster. The Torax I was about to fight, stood like a statue watching me. I noticed he was a few inches taller than me when I finally made it to the center of the arena. And he was stacked with athletic corded muscles.

"You are not what I expected from a Fystr. You are a runt. It seems I may not be leaving this planet as I hoped."

I was taken aback by his stinking attitude, but perhaps this trash-talk should be expected. So I went along with it, "I'm not a fucking runt. I'm a six-foot-four man!" I replied, then realized that was not a trash-talk reply, and I just sounded like a whiny dick.

"Oh, wow. Congratulations! Are you really a Captain? Or was he too scared to face me and sent a pathetic little proxy?"

"Don't be too much of a dick dude, or I'll have you scrubbing toilets on the Uprising for the entire time you're serving under me."

He raised an eyebrow at me, and a very vague smile tugged at the corner of his mouth, "So, there is a spine in there. Good, I will enjoy breaking it over my knee."

"Big words. I'll remember them, when I'm squirting out the undigested remnants of a chicken vindaloo in my private toilet,"

He looked at me with complete confusion.

"It's a spicy Earth food that makes your craps extra soft and stinky. You'll know what I mean when you're scrubbing away with a kids toothbrush and..."

I was disturbed from my verbal diarrhea by an uproar from the crowd.

I looked around to find out the cause of the commotion. Another Torax had come onto the sand and was striding over. This fucker was closer to seven-foot. As he approached, his voice boomed out, deep and commanding.

"Calparr. I also wish to serve this captain. Since I am the undisputed champion of Torax, I challenge this weakling instead. Now, leave us. The results of our battles are known."

The Torax, known as Calparr, turned back to me and said, "I am sorry, friend. I would have taken it easy if it was necessary and I would truly have liked to come with you, but Maukarr here is the best warrior in our land. His ruthlessness is well known. I cannot dispute his claim to fight, though I doubt his motives are true."

"Quiet whelp and be gone. You are not worthy to stand here," Maukarr snarled.

Calparr had one last thing to say to me before he went, "He is Dolegg's man. He is here to kill you." With that said, he walked away, leaving me to the mercies of this monster.

There was further uproar from the stands. I looked over to see that Calegg, Moulagg and Koparr were all shouting at another group Torax, mainly elderly and seemingly in positions of power to my eyes. They included in their number an extremely smug looking Dolegg. I caught sight of Ember, who was visibly overheating, but who remained as cool as a cucumber. She smiled her beautiful smile, and I felt confidence surge in me once more.

I felt a calm descend. I felt better and more focused. I had come out to face someone who was intending to throw the fight. I didn't dwell on why that would be, or why it had made me more nervous than I felt now. I turned to face my new opponent. Of course I could beat this guy. I didn't always need Havok, did I? I'd beaten Rodger with one blow, I'd beaten the Gro-bar in Ipsis with one blow, and I snapped that other guy's neck with a little jerk of my arm. I was strong as hell, and I fucking had this.

We stood waiting for the commotion to die down and

get a decision on whether the contest should be allowed to go on, when I thought, 'Fuck this. Let's get on with it.' After all, it didn't really matter who I fought. We were here for a reason. "Hey! You big, ugly bastard. Let's fucking dance." I raised my guard.

His face stretched into a feral grin. Without hesitation he came at me with a series of well-aimed, controlled blows. I wasn't shocked that he was fast and strong, but I was surprised by his discipline. I blocked all of his blows and was now very aware the big bastard had a lot of experience fighting.

The crowd was wild, cheering every blow. I chanced a quick glance at my friends. The arguments had stopped, and everyone stood transfixed on my battle. I continued to defend against Maukarr, without returning a blow. I could have but I thought I should test him out a bit first. He kept coming forward, throwing kicks and punches, all of which I deflected. He began to speed up, his frustration becoming apparent as his form began to deteriorate. This was actually going to be easier than I first thought.

Finally, I decided to make a move because of the heat. Without Havok, I was going to tire fast. I slipped past a right hand from him and fired off a lightning-fast jab of my own, catching him cleanly on the jaw. I could see the speed and force of my blow had completely shocked him as his head rocked back. I followed up with a right hook, which sent him sprawling backwards onto the dusty floor. I was annoyed with myself a little for not respecting my own abilities enough. I should never have been so nervous; I was a bloody good fighter. With all the strength and agility I'd built up, with my new physiology, I was kind of a big deal.

Maukarr got up quickly, rage now tempered with respect as he brought his guard up a little higher. Moving towards me again, there was a wariness to his movement this time. Not giving him a chance to press for an advantage, I threw a weak jab at his head. He blocked it easily with his guard, but it was never intended to do any harm. Next, I faked a straight right to his midriff. He reacted to the bluff quickly, dropping his guard to cover up low, and leaving his head wide open. I whipped out a full strength, lightning-fast left hook, connecting sweetly with the side of his head. It was a near perfectly executed blow, the only problem being that I caught one of the horns on his head, which was much harder than expected. While he went stumbling off to the side, I gave my hand a little shake out, 'cause fuck me that hurt.

Bringing my full attention back to Maukarr, it was a relief to see he was seriously rocked from the blow. While he did recover more quickly than I'd have liked, I could tell the fight was now won as he changed his tactics for a third time, probably realizing that I was quicker, more skilled and far stronger than expected. He now focused on using his sheer size and brutality to overwhelm me.

He threw a left, missing but pressing relentlessly forward with it and managing to score a glancing blow on me with his giant right hand. He seemed to be renewed from that small success. Unfortunately for him, it was part of yet another small play from me. I fell back from the blow, but it was intentional. As I moved backwards, I jumped and pushed a straight kick right through his guard, crushing his nose to smithereens. He fell to the ground, clutching his face. I would argue the fight was over at that stage; I had completely outclassed him. However, the cheating motherfucker began glowing as he unsteadily got to his feet.

I looked over to find Moulagg and the others shouting again. Dolegg smirked. But, not as wide as Ember as she tapped her temple at me. I nodded back over to her. She was right, I'd beat him like a drum in the physical matchup, now I'd strum his fucking nervous center like a damn guitar. Looking back at him I saw for the first time what happens when a Torax goes supernova. It was a fucking terrifying sight. A heavy covering of flames coated his entire body. I could only see a vague shadow of the alien inside.

He started walking towards me, raising an arm, then the bastard shot a damn fireball at me. I rolled out of the way and backwards to give myself some time.

I'd spent too long goggling at his transformation and put myself on the back foot. I jumped as far back as I could, while simultaneously going into my Mindscape. Once there, I levitated my body ten-feet away from him. I quickly went into Maukaurr's Mindscape, directly in his nerve center, and I dove on his nerve bundles, instantly paralyzing him – and hoping he wasn't burning me alive outside. With that done, I relieved his internal organs and his mouth. Afterwards, I morphed into my own Interface Room to see my handiwork.

He was frozen to the spot. I raised the piece of shit off the ground for dramatic effect, before I went back into his mind, "You went too far with the fire, you fucker," I said. I saw the shock on his face, and smiled.

"Were you supposed to kill me?" I asked, while looking at his mental display. I saw him imagining killing me in multiple ways and Dolegg coming to see him. There were no words, but one thing was certain, he had intended to kill me. "You're fucked now, mate."

Leaving his Mindscape, I came back to my Normal

State in the sand circle. It appeared that hardly any time had passed, so I was satisfied with my work. It had felt like a good minute or two that I was busy. I was still levitating, so I had to think about moving back down to the ground. Amazingly, unexpectedly, I dropped. I had sensed I'd done well, but that was for the audience to decide. I think I'd gotten away with it. The now-extinguished, giant Torax hung suspended in the air, unable to move or react. I left him there while I took in the group of Torax leaders with my gaze. I addressed the now silent crowd.

"Is this enough!" I shouted. "Have I won yet? I beat him with fists. I beat him with powers! Are you all satisfied," I screamed, "Or do you require his death, as he required mine?"

"You have done enough!" Moulagg shouted back. "We apologize for the criminal actions of the traitor, Maukarr. He should not have used his powers and has brought further shame to our people. And to one who would treat us as equals!" He addressed everyone in the stadium.

I walked over to the barrier where my friends had moved down to greet me, while Moulagg continued his speech. "Not only will 30 of our warriors come with you now, should you ever need the services of more Torax going forward, you need only ask. We are indebted to you for this grievous injustice."

"Thank you, Moulagg. But I don't hold the Torax accountable for that abomination's actions." I thought about him dropping to the floor like the sack of shit he was, and freeing him from the paralysis. Again it worked. I was really cursing not spending every waking minute clearing my mind at every opportunity, now. My control over the powers had been unreal.

"Fear not, Captain Shaun. We will not be lenient with his crimes."

I looked over to Dolegg, and he was a pale color. I didn't understand why he seemed to be here in an honored position, but I didn't give a damn either. I wanted to get my new men and the Suldr, then get the fuck off this oven of a planet. Calegg would tell me anything I needed to know later.

We left the arena, and I refused any offer of celebration, food or entertainment. I wasn't alone in wanting to get straight back to the ship and out of the oppressive heat. Moulagg came along, as did Koparr, who was apparently coming with us.

We discussed the plans they had in place to discreetly move the new crew off the planet, which madly involved crates being loaded onto the ship. It was weird, and I felt a little uncomfortable putting people in crates like they were animals, but I just let them get on with it. To be fair, I wasn't comfortable with animals being kept in crates either, but there you go.

By the time I'd had a shower, the Torax and the fire gems had been loaded aboard the Uprising. We were ready to go. Moulagg was here still, so I spoke to him briefly, "Just so you know without a doubt, it was Dolegg who ordered Maukarr to kill me. I hope you manage to deal with that poisonous shit-stain. He's a curse on your people."

"Don't worry, Shaun. He may still roam free at the moment, but that won't last for long. I am onto him now, as are a few others. There are clearly some of the Council members in either his pay or the Empire's. But I will be sure to root them all out. I also have friends."

"Well, good luck Moulagg. We'll be back, and if we can, we'll offer more aid next time."

"I look forward to it, Shaun. Ember," he nodded to her, "look after yourselves. Until next we meet."

"You too, Moulagg, you too," Ember replied.

With that, we left Moulagg and Torax. I wasn't sad to see the back of that hellhole.

C5

Caught at Last

We flew away from Torax at a fairly leisurely pace. All in all, it was a job well done, even close to how I thought it was going to go. I just hoped our next plan, to find some Veiletians, would be a little easier. At least this time it was only me in any danger.

We were heading to a Veiletian enclave – as Elyek had described it – hidden on a moon that was habitable only because of the domes that had been erected to stop everyone floating off into space. For once, speed was not essential. It was more important that we got to know our new crew mates.

The addition of the new Torax crew members had certainly added a fresh dimension to life on the Uprising. I was getting to know Calparr and Koparr very well. They were both good guys. We could see great potential for the Torax to be useful members of the crew, so we did some focused sessions with the few laser-rifles we had on board in the training room. They were mastering it all just fine; the rifles were little different from the ballistic ones they had been used to, in the sense of simply aiming and pulling a trigger. Calparr ran training drills with them, which gave Ember and me plenty of opportunity to hone our own skills, although we did join in with them now and again.

Calegg taught a few of the quicker-witted Torax how

to operate the various ships and weapon bays. One of our main concerns, up until now, had been that despite having six weapon bays, there would not be enough crew members to man these, should we be attacked. Ten in all showed some aptitude in learning the basics of the controls, although I could see Calegg becoming frustrated from time to time. Fortunately, Koparr seemed to take to it like a duck to water, and he became a full-time bridge crew member.

By the end of the fourth day of travel, I felt as though we were all getting on well. I'd even remembered everyone's name – mostly – and obviously there was a much better atmosphere than on the Thoth. Which was really fantastic, considering what happened next.

We were blithely Sunday driving through the stars, when out of nowhere a small fleet of large vessels appeared around us. "Dunno who these guys are, but we should fold the fuck out of here," I shouted at Calegg.

"Shaun, we have to wait for the drive to power up!" Calegg snapped back at me, clearly frustrated, as he set the folding drive to charge.

"We should keep that thing on standby *at all times*," I snapped.

"We have been through this, Captain," Elyek said calmly, "You can't have it charged until you're ready to use it. There is around a 30-minute window..."

"I know that, Elyek. Not now. Can we escape with our standard engines?"

Before Elyek got the chance to answer, Ember shouted, "We have an incoming communication. Shall I let it through?"

"Shit, shit, shit!" I said.

Ember took that as a yes, or didn't care and wanted to

hear the message herself.

A gruff voice came over the communications panel, "Uprising, power down your engines now. This is the Commander Gerdu of the Galactic Empire's military police. We have reason to believe you are transporting a large number of Torax on board your ship, and that you intend to use them in military endeavors. This goes against article 42837, section 185 of the Galactic Law Mandate. Again I say, power down your engines. Surrender the Torax for re-habitation, and yourselves for questioning."

"Someone must've sold us out," Ember said, killing the communication.

"It'll have been my father. An attempt to regain his power, no doubt. He's already sold his race out once. He absolutely would do it again," Calegg added, in a state somewhere between panic and sadness.

"None of that matters. What matters is that we stall them long enough for the folding drive to charge," I said, then pressed the comm to talk, "Hey, Commander Gerdu. We only have Suldr. And one Torax crew member, who's our pilot."

"It is not your pilot of which I speak, as well you know. You have exactly 30 Torax warriors on board. Now, power down your engines and prepare to be boarded."

I switched the comm off. "Elyek, or Calegg. Same question as earlier; can we outrun them?"

"We can outrun their ships, but we cannot outrun their weapons," Elyek answered, dejectedly.

"Shit! Then if we can't outrun them or stall them, can we at least fight?"

"They have military ships, Shaun," Elyek explained, like they were talking to a child. "They are built specifically for space battles. Uprising is an explorer class. While it does have an impressive array of combat systems and could potentially take out one of these juggernauts, it definitely couldn't take out all four of them. That would be simply impossible."

"What should we do, then?" I asked the room loudly. There was a part of me that was just furious that all my newfound Mental Clarity didn't give me any help whatsoever in this situation.

I was surprised when Koparr offered what I thought was a good solution, "Let them onboard the Uprising and we will kill them all."

I was so used to there being just Ember, Calegg and Elyek with me on the bridge, I am embarrassed to say I forgot he was even there. I looked to the others to gauge their response to Koparr's plan. Ember shrugged, Calegg looked hopeful, while Elyek shot the plan dead with their usual knowledgeable cool head. Unfortunately, I didn't hear what they said, because they spoke at the same time as Havok made his thoughts known, and I couldn't concentrate.

"Yeah, let all those motherfuckers on. Let's kill us some Galactic military guards."

I sent back an acknowledgement to Havok to wait a minute before asking Elyek to repeat themselves.

"If we kill the borders, they will just destroy us. And if we let them attach their anchors, we won't be able to jump. This is not a viable plan. Sorry, Koparr."

Sighing, I opened up the comm again, "Commander Gerdu, we'll allow some of your men on our ship,"

"Excellent. I'm glad you have seen sense. Prison is, after all, still better than death. Now you need to stop your ship first so we can anchor to it."

"You'll have to give us a little time, Commander. My crew are at odds with my orders. A few minutes please."

"You have five minutes to stop, then we will open fire. I hope you understand, we will not be giving you the 15 minutes it takes to warm up your folding drive."

The comm went dead after that bombshell, and I paled. "For fuck's sake! They know our plan," I ranted, "We're totally fucked."

No one had anything to offer, until Calegg piped up, "Can we board their ships?"

"No. They will kill us as we cross," Elyek said, and I had to agree with their assessment.

"We've no choice to either surrender or fight on the run, then," Ember summarized for us.

"Which aren't choices at all. But we haven't come this far by surrendering," I added.

"Captain! Another two ships have appeared," Calegg announced, "They're just up ahead and advancing straight towards us."

"Fuck... shit... double fuck... Bastard!" I screamed in frustration, "Well, we're really fucked, now. Aren't we?" I seethed to no one in particular, "Get them up on the screen, Calegg. Let's see if there's a way we can get past them. We only need to evade death for... How long now, Elyek?"

"Nine minutes, Captain."

"Nine minutes," I repeated, "We need to wait until the last possible minute to bolt any which way the coast is clear. And make this ship dance like it's high at a rave."

I received some uncomprehending looks from everyone, apart from Ember, who smirked but shook her head. She never liked my metaphors.

Calegg shifted the view to directly ahead of us to encompass the two large, fast-moving ships coming to join the fuck-the-Uprising party. They were familiar. Hope soared within me, but Ember shouted first, excitement tinging her words, "No fucking way! Shaun, is that…"

"I bloody hope so! If it's the Fystr we're double fucked with a cherry on top. See if you can contact them, Ember."

She smiled in return. "No need. They've just contacted us. Here," she said, pressing a button.

"Uprising," came a familiar voice over the radio, "if you attempt to escape again, we will shoot without hesitation. Please hand over the criminal known as Elyek, and you can be on your way."

She quickly jabbed the button to talk back over the comm. "Astrid! Don't shoot! It's Shaun and Ember. We're already in enough damn trouble as it is."

"Ember?" Astrid's voice came back, and the sound of shock was clear to hear, "But how?"

"Now isn't the time to discuss it, but you can't have Elyek. They're a good person and a valuable member of our crew. Their only crime is that someone wanted them as a slave."

"That doesn't matter, really. It was just a job to make ends meet. I'd far rather have you and Shaun back safe."

"We are safe-ish," I shouted into the comm, "but these guys surrounding us are not our friends. Fancy helping your old race mates out?"

"Sure, we'll help Shaun. We aren't exactly making friends out here. We've already run into our fair share of trouble with the Empire, too. How do you want to do this?" Astrid's cool voice came back. I felt like jumping around like an excited kid. I was so happy we had a chance to get out of this. But I couldn't really do that at the moment.

"I'm no Sun Tzu," I responded, "but I would like to not be surrounded when shit kicks off. How about you and the Seshat each take one of the two ships between us. We'll fly over next to you, while firing on a third, then we can all concentrate on the last ship together."

"Sounds as good a plan as any," Astrid said, "I will communicate with Rufus and let you know when to pick up the pace."

"Okay, great. Thanks, Astrid. And it's nice to hear you again," I said.

Ember shouted, "Hi Astrid. See you soon, hopefully."

"It's amazing to speak to you both again, we have much to talk about I imagine." Then her comm went dead.

"Okay, everyone!" I said, far too energetically, totally pumped from the arrival of a lifeline. "Koparr! Call up the best crew for the weapon stations, and let everyone else know we're under attack. I imagine some crazy shit will probably start happening. Elyek and Ember, you can man the other two weapon stations. Calegg, when you get the word from the Thoth, don't hesitate. I need you to get over there, yesterday."

I received strange looks from everyone, other than Koparr who was busy. I didn't know why, until a little Havok in my head implied a reason, "Go, Shaun. You're bossing this situation. I think I even got a little chill, and that's not possible."

"Thanks, Havok," I replied.

Ember quickly spoke to me, "Nice work. Just what we all needed," she patted me on the shoulder and moved over to her weapons terminal. At that moment, several Torax poured into the room, and without hesitation went to an empty weapons terminal.

"Last thing before this starts," I said firmly, "you all need to pick the same ship to fire on."

"The green Destroyer with 856 on the side. It's the weaker of the two ships," Elyek explained. I looked at the screen and could see some markings on the hull, but they didn't translate as numbers, or anything remotely understandable.

"You got it, Ember?" I asked quickly.

"Yes, you fucking idiot. I know what color green is," she snapped, and I couldn't help but smile at her.

The comm flashed a notification. I answered it immediately, like the idiot I am, assuming it was Astrid. It wasn't. It was the Empire Commander Gerdu.

"Your five minutes are up. I will say once more, stop or we'll fire."

I cut the comm with Gerdu. "Elyek, get me Astrid quickly."

As second later Astrid's voice came through, "Shaun?"

"We've got to come now, Astrid. They're going to start firing," I left the line open, and without awaiting a response from Astrid, looked over to Calegg. "Hit it, dude!"

He didn't hesitate, and we shot off like a bullet. Thankfully without a command from me – because my mind was frazzled – everyone began firing on the target of choice. The Galactic ships started firing only a second after, along with the Thoth and the Seshat. We got hit by a barrage as Calegg didn't even try to weave, just putting all the ship's power into our speed.

It took less than a minute to reach the Fystr ships. Calegg pulled a stomach-wrenching maneuver around the back of the Seshat that helped draw some of the fire off the battered Uprising. It was a bit shit for the Seshat, but

I approved of it all the same. We needed that brief respite; we had taken far and away the most damage.

When we came out from behind the Seshat, we continued our attack on ship 856. To my awe, the two Fystr ships had already destroyed the first two ships and were proceeding to attack the last two. With the Thoth helping us attack the 856, it took seconds to finish them off. We both switched targets for the last time, and that was my first real space battle over and done with.

We were victorious... somehow... by the biggest stroke of luck ever. I was actually beginning to wonder whether there was a hidden Luck stat. Had the universe taken pity on me for my shit luck as a young lad? I realized everyone was cheering and looking at me, expectantly. I'd totally phased out. My Mental Clarity was great now, so why the fuck was I still phasing out? I wasn't sure. Habit, perhaps? Whatever it was, I needed to start getting my shit together. Ember was hugging me now, which I returned, happily. Elyek joined in, followed by Calegg, then there was just a big crush of Torax bodies, seemingly wanting some victory-hugging action too. I felt like the hole in a donut.

Astrid was still on an open line, and shook everyone out of... whatever the fuck that just was. They all began to move back to their weapon stations, apart from Ember.

"Are you guys okay? That was pretty intense, and you took a fair old walloping."

"Thanks, Astrid. And yeah. We're all good. Thank all the galactic gods – if there are any – that you came along when you did. Even if it was to kick our ass, too."

"I'm happy we were able to save you, after we abandoned you on Xonico."

"Yeah. I suppose you owed us that one," I laughed, "Though now we probably need to go get some repairs. I just hope that the word doesn't spread too quickly about what happened here. We should get the fuck out of here, now. Do you have a jump available?"

"No. We just used it to catch you up."

"Damn! Sorry. That's okay. Are you alright just following us? There should be safety in numbers, at least," I said, when a thought hit me, "Astrid! Where is the Hunter ship? And for that matter, where the fuck is Ogun?"

"I think we both have long stories to tell. Let's move well away from here, like you said, then perhaps we can have a good talk about where you've been, and where Ogun has gone."

"Sounds interesting. Okay, Astrid. Speak soon." We ended the communication, and Calegg moved us off once more.

C6

Friend in Deed

Once we were a few hours away from the site of the battle, I arranged with Astrid to have a private conversation. We were able to set up a video conference from mine and Ember's quarters. Astrid had set it up privately from her quarters. Apparently, it wasn't hard to do. Still, Elyek was a bloody lifesaver when it came to anything to do with computery thingamabobs.

Now, Ember and I sat waiting for the connection to link up. It went from blank to sort of fuzzy for a second, then a close up of Gus's head appeared on the screen. He looked up, "I think that's it. Hey, Shaun, Ember. Can you see and hear us?" he asked.

"Yeah, Gus. Great job," I grinned, like a cat that got the cream. It was hard to describe just how much I missed Gus and Mick, despite my anger at being left to die. They were genuine friends and had risked their lives alongside me, and for me.

"My god you guys!" he said, head still filling the screen, "What, in the actual fuck, are you even doing here? We thought you were dead. We even had a little funeral for you, and everything."

"Oh, right. Well, thanks... I guess, Gus," I said, not really knowing how to respond to that. Not only had they had a funeral, but it was probably the most words Gus had ever said in one go, unprompted. He must have been really happy to see us.

Astrid's voice came from behind Gus's screen-consuming head. "Gus. Come and sit down, so we can all speak."

"Sorry, guys. Got a little overwhelmed there." He went and sat on a long couch next to Mick and Astrid.

I opened my mouth to speak, but as so often happened, Ember beat me to it, "So, here we all are. You deserting motherfuckers!" Ember said, angrily.

The three couch mates looked taken aback, but also guilty. Hell, even I was shocked by Ember's outburst. I thought she was over the moon to see them all again. They began to try to mumble responses, but Ember cut them short with a raucous laugh, "You guys, I'm just fucking with you. We never thought we'd see you again. I'm so happy."

"As are we, Ember," Astrid said, relaxing slightly. Mick and Gus's faces lit up again.

I still didn't get a word in though, because Astrid started talking next, a serious expression once more on her face, "I promise you, once it is safe, we'll get you back on the Thoth where you belong. You're not being held against your will, are you? I'd assume not, as you've been allowed to talk with us."

Ember and I looked at each other. "Um. We won't be coming back to the Thoth, Astrid," I said.

"What! Why on Earth not? You seriously want to fly around with random aliens, all of them wanted by the Empire?" The confusion was clear, not just in her face, but in Gus's and Mick's also.

"Okay, two things we need to get cleared up. Firstly, we are all the enemy of the Galactic Empire. Two, this is our ship. And it's the fastest in the galaxy."

"It's your ship?" Astrid said, patronizingly.

"Sure is. Now, you've said enough for now, I think. So, let me ask you a question. Where the fuck is Ogun?"

Astrid's eyes dropped. Mick and Gus looked at each other, worriedly. Finally Astrid spoke, "He left us. He took the Hunter ship and just went."

"No way!" Ember said, pissed off. "He just left you all in the middle of the galaxy? With no help or support?"

"Why are you surprised, Ember?" I said, "He did it to us, twice."

It was the normally laid-back Mick who spoke next, "After he left you two behind, he wasn't the same. We managed to fight off two Hunter ships in a pitched battle, and escaped the Fystr who came to Xonico for us. Once clear, he went to his quarters and stayed there, barely speaking to anyone. After nearly a week of isolating, he came out and announced that he wasn't worthy to lead us. The following day he had disappeared with the Hunter ship."

"What about the crew of the Hunter ship?"

"He called them over the day before and anchored the ship to the Thoth. We had no idea what he was planning. It was done very cleverly," Astrid added.

"Typical. That seems to be his style," I said, although I was beginning to feel a little bad saying it. With my increased clarity, combined with my improved ability to see the bigger picture, I could now see Ogun hadn't acted selfishly. It just hurt to be expendable.

"I'm upset," Astrid continued, "but I have our people to care for, so I focus on that."

"So, what the hell are you doing next? What's your plan?" I asked, hoping they would be interested in joining us on a more permanent basis.

"Trying to survive. We've managed to pick up enough

contracts to buy synth crates and fuel. Though it's damn near impossible to look after two huge ships and 150 people on the scraps we've had. Elyek was worth a thousand senlars to us. Would've kept us fueled and fed for a couple of weeks, at least," Astrid said. I could see the stress on her. I noticed the other two looked frazzled as well.

Ember and I looked at each other again. She smiled a little, while I tried to keep a poker face. "You thinking what I'm thinking?" I asked her.

"Yes. I am, Shaun… Astrid!" Ember said, questioningly, looking from me to Astrid, "What exactly is your overall plan?"

"I really am just trying to keep everyone alive. There's no way we can ever go back to Earth, and we aren't welcome here either. To be honest, we are just floating without direction or clue." Mick nodded in agreement. Gus was fiddling with a handheld terminal.

"I have a proposition," Ember said, dramatically.

Astrid looked confused, "Okay?"

"Shaun and I have actually set up a company. We're called Uprising and our goal is to build a mercenary army. We'll be taking the best military contracts we can find, and hopefully attract more warriors along the way. The more new recruits we can attract, the bigger the jobs we can get, until we're a force to be reckoned with. The question is, will you join us? Though I must make it clear from the beginning, Shaun here is our leader," Ember said, patting my shoulder.

I didn't know what response to expect from Astrid, but it definitely wasn't that she'd start laughing her ass off. The expression on her face as she looked at Gus and Mick in disbelief irritated the fuck out of me. As if to say,

'Are these guys serious?' Thankfully, Gus and Mick didn't share the same reaction. They looked tentatively interested. She finally calmed and turned her attention back to us, "Nice one, Ember. I don't know if you're taking the piss, or if you're serious and just delusional."

I could feel Ember's rage building. She was about to turn our 'Join Uprising' pitch into an irretrievable argument. I had to step in, even though I was just as pissed off myself with Astrid's rudeness.

"Astrid, I like you, I do. But take a little care. I'm the leader of the Uprising, and I offer you the same as Ember just has. Before you respond, take a moment."

"I don't need a moment, Shaun," she butted in aggressively, "Do you have any idea how much stress I'm under? How much Ogun has dropped on my shoulders? Grand dreams are great, but life in this galaxy isn't built on dreams. It's built on money and power. I have none, and you have less. While I respect you both and what you've done so far, I don't think you appreciate the demands of looking after so many people. Can you even guarantee work for us all? NO! You fucking can't. So stop dicking around. I've already lost 1000 senlar for letting you keep Elyek, but that puts the Seshat and Thoth in real dire straits. We've put all our resources into hunting them down. Now we need to find something else, quickly."

Ember was practically vibrating with indignation at Astrid's words. I don't know if it was my improved stats, but I could understand where she was coming from. As a rarity, I managed to get in before Ember could start shouting, though I could see she was now fuming with me for interrupting her twice in a row.

"Fuck me, Astrid. You've made this so much harder than it had to be. Just join the Uprising and you won't have to worry about surviving, only growing stronger," Ember was about to jump back in, when I held a hand up to stop her. "We're going to look for more crew members for work and for repairs to our ship. If we can't find work, we can look after you all indefinitely until we do. Just wind your neck in and accept the proposal. It's not like it can hurt you any, by joining with us."

"Do you have any idea how much it will cost to look after us?"

"Yeah. Around 500 senlar a week. You just told us," Ember snapped, finally getting a word in.

"Yes. Exactly! We've had to sell things from the ship just to cover our basic needs."

"We can cover you," I said without emotion.

"How? How do you even have that ship? We left you on a backwater shithole to die, yet here you are months later, thousands of light-years away in what basically looks like a sports-car spaceship, offering to cover our bills? How much money do you have?" she asked, finally starting to come around.

"More than enough. Join us. Help build this army, or we can go our separate ways. If you do choose to leave, we'll even give you 5000 to help you out," I offered.

Ember glared at me, "Five thousand? You goddamn cheapskate!"

"I want them to join, don't I? I'm hardly going to throw a million at them. They'll just fuck off!"

"We won't leave!" Mick shouted, "We believe in you both."

Astrid was looking between us and Mick, frantically. Finally finding her words, "You could give us a million?"

"Easily," I said, "but I'd rather give you a chance at a future and a way to eventually help Earth."

She let out a massive exhale of breath, "Goddamn it. I'm in! I can't handle this responsibility anymore. All of these people's futures in my hands, and I've got nothing. We're just slowly dying out here."

"That's cool," Ember said, "Dipshit here is the man for that job. He's too stupid to realize when he's beat and always seems to come out the other side better off. Just hang onto his coat-tails like I do, and somehow everything will be okay."

Mick and Gus broke into laughter at Ember's description, with Mick saying breathlessly, "One of my last images of you, Shaun, is telling me to levitate you into a massive mob of armed aliens. I said no, and you just charged them anyway. So I threw you up and you came down like a tornado. Apart from Gus here, it's possibly the most beautiful thing I've ever seen."

"It was spectacular," Gus said, laughing even harder.

Astrid looked puzzled, but a small smile lit her face, "To be honest, Ogun told me there was something special about the two of you, and though I liked you both, I just couldn't see it. I felt like he had put you above me in all but name. Turns out, he was right about you, and now here I am, putting you above me!"

"It's not like that, Astrid," said Ember. "But we want to build a fleet. You'll need to continue looking after the Thoth. Shaun will basically just guide our overall plan, as we actually have one. The only difference is, now you don't have to worry about supplies. It'll give you some breathing space to think. You're one of us. Don't worry, he's not going to start lording it over you, or I'll kick his ass," she laughed.

"I thank you for your kind words. You haven't even met Rufus, the Captain of the Seshat, yet. He's a good guy.

I hope you'll make the same allowances for him as you would for me. I'm sure he'll be happy to join once he knows that I've agreed. He also is aware of the high regard that Ogun held you both in, and will probably respect that more than I do."

"Before Ogun left, he told us both that he'd made a huge mistake leaving you. He believed that you in particular, Shaun, could have been the difference in our war. I just thought you should know that."

"It doesn't matter anymore. Ogun has gone. And honestly, I'm just buzzing to have you on board. The Uprising grows stronger."

"We're glad to be on board. You've no idea how stressed and depressed everyone is here."

"Quick question," Ember asked, "How did the Thoth pay for things?"

"We've a sort of ship's bank. Computerized of course. We wouldn't want to be carrying thousands of coins about, Fystr or Galactic," Gus interjected.

"So, when you buy things, you do it through transfers, rather than currency?"

"Exactly. Why do you ask?" Gus replied.

"Gus. I need you to talk to Elyek and arrange a transfer of funds. We'll transfer some senlar over, just so you'll be okay in case anything were to happen to us, or we got separated. Just keep it in the account. We'll cover any expenses going forward," Ember said, then pressed her personal comm and asked Elyek to come to our room.

Astrid grinned, "Sorry, who's in charge?"

"Ember," I said, returning the smile.

"Shaun, but he forgets things. A lot," Ember replied smugly at almost the same time.

"Not anymore, I don't, Ember. You may remember I'm

ahead of you in Mental Clarity, now."

"Well, whoop-dee-doo for you! Would you like some help carrying that massive fucking head of yours around, instead? Perhaps I'd be better suited helping with that job?"

"Ha, ha, ha," I drawled. Luckily, I was saved from going any deeper down this rabbit hole by Elyek's arrival.

"Hey, Ember. How can I help?"

"Once we've finished this call, could you talk to Gus here about transferring some funds between us and the Thoth?" Gus nodded. Elyek smiled and waved at him. Ember continued, "Say 100,000 senlar to be shared between the two ships? They're part of the Uprising now."

"Oh, that's great news. Of course I'll do that, Ember," Elyek turned to Gus, "Hi, Gus. I look forward to working out the details with you."

"Hey, Elyek. Me too," he said, sheepishly; his quiet, unconfident demeanor returning at the arrival of a stranger.

"Good. I'm glad that's covered. Now, Shaun. Why don't you tell Astrid and the boys our plan?"

She had my head spinning. "Right. Yeah... We're, er, we're going to a planet,"

"Moon," Elyek corrected, "The moon of Tanath. It is named Arus."

"Yeah. What they said," I indicated Elyek with my thumb, "We're hoping to pick up more Veiletians. They're the race of people that Elyek here is from. They're really fucking intelligent, if Elyek is anything to go by. And they've got the ability to go invisible. Apparently, there's not many of their kind left, but I'd imagine that would be hard to gauge, right?" I laughed. Though I'd clearly misjudged my audience, since my laughter was a solo endeavor. "Anyways, they're highly prized as slaves, which is why they're secreted away around the galaxy. Another injustice I wouldn't mind sorting out in the fullness of time.

"For now though, if we can get them on board with us, we're going to be so much stronger. We've just gained 30 Torax, and trust me when I say that those fuckers are tough! They're laser-resistant and can turn into balls of fire. But even they are pretty much kept as slaves on their own planet. Which is something else we hope to address as we develop.

"First, we need to focus on strength. If we can get a decent military contract, we hope to mop up a few mercenary groups who aren't part of the *big two*," I finished.

Astrid responded immediately, "I don't know what you mean by the *big two*. But you seem to have a plan, and money, so that's good enough for me."

"Cool, then. We'll leave Gus and Elyek to sort out the finances," I said, making ready to leave.

"Not so fast!" Astrid shouted, taking us all aback, "Before you go, I want to know how the hell you're here... like this?" she gestured with her arms. It didn't make any sense, but I knew what she meant.

"I'd like to know that too!" Mick added.

"Me three!" cried Gus.

I shrugged and set about telling them the whole story. Occasionally, Ember stepped in when she thought I'd got something wrong. Even Elyek added some choice details and perspectives on occasion. The three humans on screen sat dumbfounded at the tale we wove together.

When we had finished, their amazement was obvious. Typically, only one question was asked, and that was from Astrid, "So, how much did you get from the bank? Elyek's five million would be amazing enough. Although it's clear you've got a lot more."

"Uprising Inc. has approximately 60 million senlars," Elyek said.

Both Ember and I turned to look at Elyek in disbelief.

Astrid laughed, "Thanks, Elyek! These two would never have told me."

"No, we wouldn't," Ember said, half smiling, "You'll be wanting new clothes and everything now."

"No. I don't want anything; I'm simply happy to be part of the Uprising. And thanks for having us."

C7

Brighten Up!

We traveled for just over a week before we approached Tanath and its moon, after making two depressingly short jumps with the folding drive; we now had to stay within the Thoth's and Seshat's capabilities. We were just under a day away from the moon using our standard engines. Again, it was a slower pace than we would have done with our ship alone, but I'd have to stop whining about that. It was what it was! And having another 150 friends out here did, kind of, negate that disappointment.

I asked Elyek to sort out the video links to the other two ships, so I could have a meeting with Astrid and Rufus. I'd had a comm link with Rufus on the way to give us time to become acquainted. He came across as a good man, steady and calm. And he seemed incredibly happy with the new situation; apparently, our merger had caused a massive increase in morale on his ship, which was always good to hear.

We had the meeting in our room. There were plans to be made and things to discuss. Astrid popped up first on our screen, then the screen halved as Rufus and his quarters appeared.

"Hey, guys," Ember said to start off proceedings, "How are you both doing?"

"Great, thanks. This last week has been a breath of

fresh air," Astrid replied, "People are starting to have ambition once more, rather than just desperation."

"Yeah. Same over here. It's just the little things, like the noise level in the canteen. Now, there's the constant buzz of chatter in there at mealtimes, rather than the low intermittent groan of people grumbling," Rufus added.

"That's really great to hear, guys. Hopefully, we can make it even better for everyone once we've been to Tanath," I said, happily.

"I thought we were going to Tanath's moon?" Astrid replied.

"Oh. Well, we are. But afterwards, we're going to go to Tanath to pick up work. We don't know if the Uprising has been marked as a wanted vessel after the Torax incident. Elyek assures us we can get repairs on Arus, the moon, and run less of a risk of being stopped or checked there," Ember explained.

"Why would the moon's inhabitants be any less likely to stop or detain you than the planet? That seems rather odd," Rufus asked.

"From what we know, the moon is kind of a smuggler haven. According to Elyek, its existence is well known by the Empire, but they turn a blind eye to it. I'm sure it's convenient for them on some level to allow such places to exist and remain unmolested," Ember replied.

"I can't imagine politicians are any less a bunch of lying wankers in space than they were back on Earth. Nonetheless, that's where we're going," I added.

"So it makes sense for one or probably both of you to go to Tanath, as we will need a lot of supplies, I'd imagine. But it's the only viable option for picking up some mercenary work.

"While you're there, make sure to fill your cargo hold

with an extra full load of fuel and synthesizer supplies, and anything else you can think of. We should be able to get what we need for the Uprising from Arus."

"Sure thing," Rufus said. "We really do need a stop off. Everything is running dangerously low. It'll be nice to have some back-up supplies, as well."

"Hey. While we're on the subject, do you guys have any more of these uniforms? Because mine has taken a fair hammering. I know it's self-repairing, but it doesn't seem to be doing it very well anymore. It's started to look pretty jaded."

"For someone who has achieved so much, it's surprising how little you know. We can make as many suits as we've supplies for," Astrid said, a wry grin on her face.

"Really. How so?" I asked. I was used to brushing off the insults of assholes, even if I did like those assholes... Ah, shit. Stupid inner monologue! That's not what I meant!

"We've a textile synthesizer, similar to a food synthesizer," Astrid continued, and I was happy to be brought out of my head.

I thought this was supposed to get better after I had increased my Mental Clarity? And if it was just down to a personal mental deficit, I thought the game had fixed all that shit? There was a lot I still didn't know or understand, but one thing was for sure, now my Mental Clarity had increased, I suddenly had an appetite for learning. I wanted to know exactly what the fuck was going on in every facet of my life, and in this stinking fucking galaxy. I realized I had once again gone off into my own little world. Everyone was looking at me, waiting for me to respond. "How much raw material do you have?" I asked, thoughts and plans springing up in my mind.

"Quite a bit still. We haven't had any reason to use it

that much. In fact, funnily enough, I think you probably accounted for around 80% of what we had used, anyway," Astrid replied.

"That's actually pretty funny. But seriously. Could we make uniforms for the Torax and Veiletians, too?"

"We may need to stock up a little afterwards, but sure," she answered.

"Can you make it fireproof?" Elyek said dryly from my side. It was a valid point.

When Astrid responded, it was with uncertainty in her voice, "Oh. I'm not sure. I mean, I think they're pretty fireproof anyway, as standard. To be honest, I've never used the machines before. I'll give Gerome a quick shout. He's the whizz in that department."

"Yeah. That would be great, because fireproof-ish won't be good enough for these crazy bastards. They need their uniform to be totally fireproof, like chuck them in the Sun and pick them back up a week later kinda fireproof."

"Okay, one moment," Astrid said, and spoke into her comm.

A second later, I'm assuming Gerome picked up. We heard his voice, "Hey, Captain. What can I do for you?"

"We've a request from Shaun to make some completely fireproof uniforms. Can the textile printer handle that?"

"Um, sure... I think. I'll have a look at what options are available. From what I know, we may need to acquire specific materials to do that."

Astrid looked at me questioningly.

"Great!" I said, "Find out what you need, and when you're on the planet, pick it up. We should arrange and issue new, official Uprising uniforms to everyone. The

Fystr are kind of our mortal enemies. Wearing their uniforms kinda takes the piss out of what we're supposed to stand for."

"Yeah. You actually make a really good point. I mean, we've worn them purely because of their functions and durability. It's a bit of an insult to continue to wear them if we don't need to. It feels right that we should create our own identity," Astrid replied.

"Yes, I can definitely agree to that sentiment." Rufus added. "I had honestly never even thought about it, but now it's been mentioned, I feel dirty just wearing this thing."

Ember patted my arm, "Yeah. We should definitely get rid of them."

She was just about to continue, when Gerome's voice came through the comm.

"Sure I can do that. Forward me some designs. I already have everyone's size. I'll start printing them off as soon as we have a decision."

"Two for everyone!" I shouted, so he could hear me over the comm.

"Sure!" Gerome shouted back, "Though I might need more materials for that."

"You're going to get everything you need. As for the style of the uniforms, stick to the same as we have, only with a new logo and the Uprising name." I said.

"And a different color! This color is shit, I don't like navy!" Ember shouted after me, then she spoke at a normal volume, "Any suggestions on color, guys?"

Rufus shrugged, "Gold?"

"Green! A nice dark green," Astrid said.

"If I had to choose a color, I'd go black, like a panther," I winked at Ember. She smirked but also blushed slightly.

"That leaves you with the deciding vote, Ember," Astrid said.

"We can have all those colors if you like, guys. Trust me, I can combine them to have us all looking *fabulous*," Gerome announced.

"I'm happy with those colors, I would have picked black, so Shaun has already done that for me. I can't wait to see what you come up with, Gerome."

"Keep it cool though, I don't want to look like a bloody Christmas tree," Rufus added. I had to agree with the sentiment. The 'fabulous' statement had me slightly concerned, too.

"I'd like to see a sample before you churn out over 400 of them," I threw in. I wasn't floating around in the best ship in the galaxy wearing a shit uniform.

"I can't wait to look *fabulous*," Ember said, prompting a smirk from Astrid.

"Right. Enough about bloody clothes, for now," I snapped, "We'll work on a design, and you guys can, too. Put the word out across the ship if you like, and we'll choose from the best ideas."

"Should make it a competition," I heard Gerome's voice again over the comm.

"Ah, Gerome. You're still here. Welcome to the captain's meeting," Ember said, sarcastically.

"Oh, right. Sorry! Gerome out."

I shook my head, smiling at the ridiculousness of the last five minutes. "Back to business, guys. Once you have what you need on Tanath, and that includes a good job for us to take on, meet us over on Arus," I said.

"Okay, Shaun. Are you sure you want us to split up? Seems unnecessarily risky. You know like in a horror movie, where you scream at the TV 'No! Don't split up!'"

Astrid said.

"It's going to be fine, Astrid. Don't worry. We're practically on the same planet, anyway. Plus, we'll be in constant contact with one another; we can do hourly check-ins if you like? Obviously not us personally, but we can get set up some kind of system."

"You clearly haven't seen the same horror films as me, then. But yes. We'll aim to set up a system of constant communication," she replied.

Ember jumped in after I had finished, "Astrid, I think we can all agree that splitting up is a stupid idea. However, we don't have any choice. The Uprising is potentially a target after harboring Torax. Not to mention those ships we've destroyed. The Thoth and Seshat are not, nor are you, linked with us. You need to get us our next job, and we need to go to a smuggler moon to kidnap a load of Veiletians. Let's just get this fucking done. Hopefully, life will be easier once we do."

Astrid looked affronted, but smiled, "I suppose we have few choices here. So, I'll agree to source mercenary work, providing we remain in constant communication. If we don't hear from each other, we'll know quickly that something has happened and come to your aid, or you to ours."

I nodded acknowledgement. "And once you're finished up, we'll meet up on Arus. I think we could do with a face-to-face meeting."

"Yes, Shaun," said Rufus. "It's been quite the stroke of luck running into you again. We were at our wits' end in this strange place. I felt mounting any kind of retaliation upon the Fystr to save the Earth was worse than impossible. Now, I feel like it is just improbable, but I'll take those odds."

"Well thanks, Rufus. I know how you feel. Hopefully, if we keep going in the right direction, improbable will turn into easy-peasy." I took some weird looks for that, but it was to be expected, "Okay, with that said, I think we've a good plan going forward – for now. Keep in touch with any developments on Tanath, and we'll do the same."

"Will do, Shaun, Ember. See you soon," Astrid said.

Rufus gave us a thumbs up, and their screens went blank.

I heaved a sigh of relief.

"What the fuck's wrong with you?" Ember enquired.

"These meetings are stressful!"

"How? You just sit there talking shit, like usual."

"It's bloody terrifying! Astrid and Rufus are like the most powerful humans there are. And I've just waltzed in and started telling them how things are going to be. You do realize that takes a toll on me? Don't you?"

"I know you're a fucking idiot, Shaun. For a start, you're the most powerful human there is. *Fact.* And only you would be worrying about that shit. However, I'm willing to concede that thinking about new uniforms was a really nice touch, it hadn't even occurred to me," Ember said, "I can't wait to get out of this piece of shit, I'm sick of it."

I leaned in and gave her a peck on the cheek. "You still look amazing in it."

"Behave yourself," she laughed, "Now, go and captain this ship, will you?"

C8

Hide and Seek

We landed the Uprising on Arus without a problem. Initially, it seemed like our ship might have been recognized when landing control took a lengthy pause before letting us dock. But nothing further had been said. It may have just taken a while to find us somewhere to dock considering the unusual layout of the moon's habitable areas. By which I mean over half the moon was covered in large transparent domes. We also mentioned we needed repairs, so perhaps they had to arrange a particular bay for that. That was Calegg's problem to deal with. We had our own task to do.

"Elyek, Calparr! Are you ready?" I asked.

The massive Torax nodded. Elyek just stood patiently and waited for us to leave the ship.

As usual, we all carried weapons, only mine was ridiculously obvious. Although I had wrapped Havok up in some cloth, there was no mistaking the massive weapon perched up on my back.

Upon leaving the ship, Ember spoke with the dock supervisor. She tended to deal with this aspect of our lives more and more. I don't think she trusted me not to get ripped off, and she was probably right. Especially since we were rich now. I was happy not to have to think about every little thing alone, and believed Ember was definitely why I never completely stressed out, like

Astrid and Rufus appeared to have done. Well, her and Elyek. Calegg, not so much, but I did like the asshole.

Next to the supervisor stood a looming guard with a massive, brutish, blue, ridged face. I knew him straight away to be a Grobar, and I felt a little surge of pride at being able to recognize and name an alien. As Ember began asking about repairs and supplies for our ship, the Grobar guard eyeballed Calparr and me, sizing us up.

"Calparr," I nudged the big Torax, "if you're ever fighting one of those ugly bastards, here's a quick tip. Their sternum reaches down to about here," I pointed to my navel area. "If you're expecting to drop one of them to their knees with a body shot there, you're more likely to break your own hand."

"Interesting, Captain. Thank you for sharing this knowledge." It was never easy to tell exactly how Calparr felt about any subject, but I could see the gleam in his eye when we talked about combat.

"You're part of the family now, Calparr baby. We've got to be able to kick everyone's ass!"

He looked at me like I had four heads – I know, it's supposed to be two heads, but there were more than a few aliens out there with two heads, so that saying didn't work up here. Anyway, I digress – he was glad of the information.

After Ember finished her haggling, we moved off, following Elyek. They seemed to know exactly where we were going.

The moon wasn't open to the elements like any of the other planets we had been on, and it was surreal to be walking inside these habitation domes. The whole place had a very industrial feel about it, with a lot of the buildings, and even sidewalks, made of metal. As we walked along, I checked out the people passing by. If I hadn't already been told of this place's special function as a base for less-than-lawful activity, I think I would have guessed it soon enough. Everyone wore powerful-looking weapons and grim expressions. There was an air of degradation and danger permeating the whole domed city. It had a cyberpunk feel to it that I didn't really care for.

"Hey Elyek, how much further?" I said, feeling uncomfortable. I knew we could fight our way out of anything here – probably. But I was getting a sort of itchy feeling, like we were being watched.

"We are heading to Epsilon Tunnel, Captain, which is around a 100 yards away. Then, we must go through a number of other zones before reaching our destination. My people are at the furthest point from a docking bay, for their own safety. Did you not listen to the plan I laid out back on the ship?"

I looked over with a fake offended expression, "Yeah. I just meant how far to the tunnel." I hadn't listened to a word.

"Well, I'd say five minutes. No more. Then, approximately 40 minutes on the transport tube to the dome we need."

"Super. Can't wait," I said, lamely.

Calparr ignored me, while Ember quietly asked, "What's up, Shaun?"

"I dunno. Just got a bad feeling about his place. I feel like we're being watched."

"Well, I trust your instincts. Saying that, we can't really do much about it. We'll just have to stay extra vigilant."

"Yeah. You're right," I said, eyes flicking from side to

side, watching everyone as intently as I could. Then it dawned on me that I probably looked a lot like Crazy Eyes in the Sopeka pen all that time ago, so I stopped and tried to calm down a bit.

"Yeah, Shaun. I don't know why you're getting overly jumpy. We're tough cookies," Havok said in my head, and damned if it didn't make me chuckle.

"Do you even know what cookies are, Havok?" I responded playfully.

"I know you eat them, and I know we're all tough cookies in our little group, here."

"Fair enough, pal. Fair enough."

Elyek cut our conversation off, exclaiming we were at the Epsilon Tunnel transport hub. A long, hotdog-shaped, windowless capsule was hovering in a metallic furrow. I couldn't see how it was suspended, so in my head I opted for magnets. Not that it mattered any more. I didn't understand one percent of the shit I saw these days. I had hoped gaining Mental Clarity would help, yet it turns out a clear mind doesn't mean you just suddenly know stuff, like I hoped it would. What it did mean was that anything I saw and learnt from now on should actually stick there. Theoretically, I should have much better retention and be able to use that going forward.

I was brought out of my usual meanderings by Ember saying, "What now, Elyek? Do we need to pay for tickets, or something?"

"No. They're free to ride. We just need to get on."

We did as bid and stepped on to the big, metal hotdog through one of eight sets of doors. The instant those doors closed, we were off like a rocket.

It was a pretty cool experience, and I felt the sense of being watched fade. That was until we had to get off and cross over to another hotdog. As soon as we were back in the open, my senses flared up again. This continued to happen each time we changed tubes. The final hotdog wasn't in the transport hub of this dome; we had to head back, out onto the streets. The differences in the outer habitation domes were remarkable. Clearly, the very lowest of the low eked a living out here. It had me concerned for what conditions we would find the Veiletians living in, if they were yet another tunnel away.

Although I knew the Veiletians were very secretive, I was not prepared for the next transport hub location. Elyek led us down a scruffy, trash-ridden street and into a derelict-looking building. It could have been mistaken for a dilapidated factory unit if it hadn't been so small.

Once through the doors, we were led down some stairs up to an empty desk. Elyek walked over. They lifted a necklace, which had been invisible only seconds before, from their neck and over their head, and placed it down on the desk.

"These people are the best of friends. I will stake my life on their honor," Elyek spoke to the air in front of them. I was quite proud of the fact that the penny had dropped for me already; there was obviously an invisible Veiletian behind the desk. Whoever they were, they were being a wanker, because they didn't answer. Just as I had that thought, I heard a bolt unlock from the door behind the desk. Out walked a fucking Veiletian! I felt tricked.

"Elyek! How amazing to see you again. We heard reports that you had been taken as a slave for an owner on Weka Four?"

"Nuwista. It is good to be back here once more. I had been held as a slave; however, these fine friends rescued me from that life, and we have had quite the adventure since. May we be permitted passage to the haven?"

"You have vouched for them, so you may all pass. They remain your responsibility."

"I accept that. May I request one addendum? My captain here would never intentionally harm or endanger our people; regardless, he is an Onnekus and his path to positive action is not always direct."

The Veiletian, known as Nuwista, gave me a long, hard stare, "I will let the eldest know, and it should be taken into account if anything untoward happens."

"Thank you, Nuwista, I hope to meet again before we leave," Elyek said.

"Me too. I am truly overjoyed that you were not taken," Nuwista replied, while pressing a button to reveal the doors of a hotdog.

"Cheers, Nuwista," I said as I went through the doors. Everyone followed me, with Elyek finally entering and the doors closing. This hotdog was smaller than the others that we had been on.

Entering the Veiletians' hidden dome, the difference was stark. There were not as many people about. The place was immaculately clean, and more like a small town than a city. There was no one around at all; it felt like a ghost town. Elyek took the lead once more, leading us through half-a-dozen streets before we reached the gates of a large mansion-type building. It even had stone in its architecture, which was odd, as everything else we had seen so far was metal and glass.

"It's so much quieter here," I whispered to Ember. "Plus, I don't feel like I'm being watched anymore."

"We won't be seen here," Elyek offered, having overheard me. "The rest of the domes in Arus have an extensive security network, despite the fact that it is a smuggler's moon. However, there are a few dark domes where there is the utmost privacy. Now, before we enter, I feel I must warn you again. We'll still have to be vetted to enter the Elders' Headquarters.

"I will continue to do all of the talking. It would be unwise to make a communicative mistake here. This is one of the largest enclaves of my people, outside of the Veil itself. Most are unwelcome, as it is a highly secret location. As I have said before, my people are often hunted and captured as slaves. Please act accordingly. They will be distrustful of you. Do not take offense."

"Sure, Elyek. We wouldn't want anyone putting their foot in it, would we?" she said, while giving me a sarcastic look.

I shrugged.

With that said, Elyek pressed a panel set into the thick gate column. A voice quickly answered from the panel's speaker, "Elisialor Yekandistripolisiumar. Could you please state your business here?"

"This was once my home. I have come with my captain and two of our most senior crew members. We would like to offer a number of our people the chance to serve on board our ship, the Uprising, as paid and respected crew."

"You were declared as a slave. Are these your new owners?" the intercom said.

"No. They rescued me from slavery. They are the best of people and we should be honored to be part of their plans."

"Plans to enslave us all, perhaps?"

I could see Elyek getting very frustrated, despite holding their cool very well. The back and forth continued, and after much deliberation from the intercom, along with persuasion from Elyek, the gates finally slid open. They revealed a lush, well cared for garden, with even the odd small tree here and there; although the trees had a clinging-on-for-dear-life look about them. This was the first greenery we had seen on this strange moon.

We followed Elyek up to the main building. Veiletian guards stopped us at the doors. These were the first Veiletians I had seen other than Nuwista – and Elyek of course. They were clearly of the same race, but they couldn't have been more different; where Elyek was slim and relatively short of stature, these two guards were both stocky and around six-feet in height. The guards exuded an air of strength of menace that Elyek did not possess.

"We are here to speak to the Arus council," Elyek firmly stated.

"They are waiting for you, Elisialor Yekandistripolisiumar. Your friends here," he said, waving at us with disdain, "may wait in the seating area." He indicated where we were to go.

"I was about to protest, then remembered I'd already been warned to leave this entirely up to Elyek. So I just nodded blithely.

Elyek turned to us. "Just take a seat for now. I will go and put forward our offer. Better they do not think I am being coerced by you in any way."

"Fair enough," I obeyed, then turned back to the guards. "You got a visitor toilet anywhere?"

They both scowled at me, then resumed their stony-faced stares straight ahead without answering.

I was about to say, 'I'll just pee up the wall then', when Elyek spoke again, "Shaun! You agreed you would not incite trouble."

"He can't help himself. Don't worry, I'll keep a better eye on him," Ember replied.

"What?" I said, exasperated. "I only asked for the toilet." And I was glad I hadn't added the rest now.

"It's the way you do it, Shaun. Let's go and sit down. Anyway," Ember said, "you're a big boy, now. You can hold it in for a bit." She smirked and took a seat, while Elyek headed off following one of the guards.

We sat there, bored, for over an hour. I chatted to Calparr, although he wasn't a massive conversationalist, not like Calegg anyway. Ember didn't seem particularly chatty either, for some reason. Havok only wanted to talk about killing all the Veiletians if they started any shit, and that he was sure he could still see them when they were invisible – which I could tell was total bullshit. In the end, I decided to go to my Cognition Room to tidy. I was almost there now, and a little bit of work here and there was bound to help, so Ember told me.

Finally, I was brought out of my meditative state by voices. Elyek was back, and the Council wished to meet me. 'Oh goodie,' I thought, then whispered to Ember, "Hope this goes better than with Calegg's dad." Elyek whipped their head around and gave me the stink eye.

We entered a large room, and like the outside of the building, it was quite classy. Especially when compared to the rest of the rough-ass moon. The four of us were led in front of a table holding six Veiletian elders. "So, you are the Captain of the Uprising? We hear that you set young Elyek free from captivity that you yourselves held them in."

"Well, it's not quite like that. They were being held as a prisoner, and we..."

The elder rudely waved away my explanation. It annoyed me, but I tried to remember that this entire race had been treated terribly by the rest of the galaxy.

"And now you have one Veiletian under your control, you wish to have more to use as you see fit."

"What? No. That's bullshit" I cried. I received a warning glare from Elyek. Ember looked like she was doing her best to hold a retort in herself.

"Sorry for that outburst," I said, "We need a crew. There're a lot of arseholes out there in the galaxy, and when we meet someone as cool as Elyek who is kind, considerate and helpful, we want them on our crew. We want our new crew members to work with us, and hopefully make this shithole of a galaxy a better place."

"We can all have grand dreams, my boy. The reality is that we will not risk our rare and precious people on a fool's crusade."

"Okay! Not your boy, for starters. I know your people have had a crap time of it wherever you go, but that wasn't me or any of the crew on the Uprising. You're hiding out on a little dome on the arse-end of a shitty little moon, filled with smuggling shit-stains. I would like to change that. I want to back the Torax, and I want to help my own people, and anyone else who's abused by powerful people, just because they've grabbed for power first, then used it to shit on everyone else."

"Lofty ideals," said a different Veiletian elder, "That does not alter the fact you still intend to take our people into danger and put them at further risk. By serving your individual goals, what makes you different to anyone else who seeks to use our people?"

"My goals?" I asked with a confused expression. "So, you've really no aspirations to be free of the oppression that your people suffer under?"

"Very good, Captain. We do not seek to put our lives in danger."

"Righto. Well, good luck with that when you're extinct, or completely living in servitude. Does every Veiletian feel that way, or just the old ones?"

That prompted another scolding look from Elyek, which I waved an apology for.

Even Ember gave me a look of, 'why the fuck would you say that?'

Another Veiletian elder spoke, but they had a wry smile on their face, "As we have talked, I have watched the interaction of you and your crew members. It is interesting to say the least. I would go so far as to say you have been advised by Elyek on how you ought to behave, judging by the berating looks they give when you are rude. I see you acknowledge this and try to be better. This leads me to two questions. Why would Elyek care so much to help you in this way? And why would you hold Elyek in such high regard to acknowledge the advice and signals given?"

"Elyek is a crucial, senior member of our crew. Four of us originally formed the Uprising, and we are all equal partners. I'm basically a figurehead for the four of us. We're a solid team. If it wasn't for Elyek, we would never have achieved all we have."

The elder nodded and turned to Elyek. "Do you feel this is a true reflection? Are you valued as an equal?"

"Absolutely, Prefector Kalika. We work as one team."

Prefector Kalika turned back to me. "Will you treat other members of our race as you treat Elyek?"

"Probably not," I said, and before I could continue, the gasps interrupted me. I received a myriad of different expressions. "Come on! I hadn't finished what I was saying.

I'll treat them all with respect and look after them as best I can while they are with us. Even so, Elyek is like my best friend; we have a bond, and I care for them like a close family member. That's all I meant."

Prefector Kalika had a smile on their face, while the other five still looked like they were processing what I had said. "I, for one, give my blessing for you to recruit further Veiletian crew members. No more than ten for now, until we see how it works out. If you return here in the future, we can discuss at that point whether others would like to join you," Kalika turned to the rest of the council. "What say you all?"

There was a chorus of agreement, although some voices still sounded unconvinced.

The Prefector turned to face us. "All agreed, Uprising. We will have a group of our willing people ready for you to talk with tomorrow at the earliest. It will provide an opportunity to discover if they would prove a good fit for you, and you for them."

"That's great news. I promise they'll be looked after to the best of our capabilities."

"That is all we ask. Now, will you be returning back to your ship for the evening, or can we offer accommodation here?"

There were sounds of further grumbling by the other elders, but fuck them!

"Oh, yeah. That'd be great, thanks. It's rough as toast out there on Arus, and we don't want to run into any trouble while we're here, if we can help it."

"Very well. I will have you escorted to the guest rooms."

C9

Best of both Worlds

We were shown to some pretty nice rooms, each with a table and chairs, a dresser and a very comfy-looking bed. Ember and I shared one room. Calparr had his own next door.

"Is your room acceptable?" The Veiletian who escorted us asked.

"Yes, it looks very comfortable," Ember replied.

"Excellent!" they said, seeming genuinely happy. "Now I must inform you that while you stay with us, visitors are expected to remain in their rooms. Travel around the house or grounds unattended for any reason is prohibited, for our own safety more than your own. I am sure you will understand."

"Well that's not great news, but we do understand," Ember said for the both of us.

"Superb. Meals will be brought to your rooms three times a day. The next meal will be in around four hours. If you require anything else, don't hesitate to contact the house staff, using the communicator located on the wall just inside your door."

"We will, thank you." Ember replied.

"Very well, I shall leave you to relax now, the Veiletian said, and with a quick bow, turned and left.

"Well, this is going to be boring as shit," I said, throwing myself on the bed. "We've signed ourselves up as prisoners for the night and… Oh, god!" I cried, my blood running cold. "Oh, what have I done!"

"What's the matter, Shaun? Spit it out!" Ember said, looking concerned.

"You've seen what Elyek eats, right! Are they going to feed us that shit?"

Ember let out a laugh of relief, "Yeah. That's not good, but seriously, Shaun. So what if it's rank and we have to go a few extra hours without food. We'll be back on the Uprising by tomorrow afternoon. I thought you'd beaten your obsession with food?"

"I've beaten my obsession with bad food. But I need to eat a lot, and I don't want to be eating whatever the fuck was in Elyek's bowl, and that's just how I roll."

She laughed at me, "Well, don't worry about boredom. I've got just the thing for you to pass the time."

"Yeah?" I said, suddenly eager. I had the feeling I knew where this was going, and I was happy about it.

"Let's declutter my mind. We did a lot on yours, and I'm feeling a bit left behind."

"Nope! That isn't what I was thinking about at all! Though I have to agree, I do wanna get that out of the way. I'm fucking sick to my core of clearing stupid shitty Cognition Rooms out," I said with feeling.

"Me too, a few good pushes and we will be there. It's not like there's much else to do. Might as well make the most of it." She clapped her hands, then zoned out. With a heavy sigh, I followed her into her Mindscape.

We worked for the rest of the day in Ember's Mindscape, going well into the night, and stopping only for the evening meal. It was some kind of orange soup. While surprisingly tasty, it was still a pointless bowl of soup.

I was thankful it came with plenty of bread. Elyek must have put in a word about not bringing us anything too weird. I couldn't complain, as long as I didn't know what was in the soup – it could have been the produce from a space squid's penis, for all I knew.

It must have been near midnight when we finished up in Ember's Mindscape. There was only around ten percent of the room left to go. She had started at 48% Clarity, having gone up even more from the last time I'd seen it. She was obviously making a lot of effort in any downtime. I felt a little guilty because I wasn't doing the same. We had a quick check of her stats before we hit the hay, and were a little baffled that her Clarity was lower than we expected.

Name: Ember Davison
Age: 25 GY
Transcendence Level: 103
Strength: 81/1000
Agility: 110/1000
Speed: 100/1000
Intelligence: 45/1000
Constitution: 116/1000
Wisdom: 59/1000
Mental Resilience: 210/1000
Mental Clarity: 70%
Potential: 83%

"Seventy fucking percent! That's pure pig-shit on a dinner plate. I should be around 90, for sure!"

"Clarity growth seems to be slowing down the more we clear," I replied, just as equally concerned. "I thought mine looked lower than it should've been after our last stretch of work in there."

"Oh, yeah. Now you mention it, I suppose it was a little off. Come on. Let's get some sleep and we can crack on with it in the morning. I want to try and get that last bit cleared to see what happens."

"Totally. Mine too, when we can."

"I'm fucking sure yours too! We also need to get your Wisdom up somehow; I just hope it doesn't affect whatever invisible Luck stat you have."

I didn't reply, just laughed, and jumped into the bed.

When I woke, Ember was sitting in one of the chairs at the table, eyes closed. I supposed this meant we were getting back to it then. With a sigh, I lay back down and closed my eyes. "Havok, old pal. You gonna give us some tunes?" I said to Havok before I entered Ember's Mindscape.

"Sure thing, Shaun! You should never work without blasting out some inspiring songs about obliterating the enemy like bugs!" he replied, happily.

"True that, dude. I really need to check if the Thoth or the Seshat have any banging Earth tunes. I love what you play, but I wouldn't mind mixing it up a bit with some of my old favorites. Bit of Zeppelin would be awesome!"

"I'll listen to anything you want me to play, Shaun. I need some new songs in my repertoire. I'd be interested to hear what you listened to on Earth."

"We'll have to get a bit of Slipknot in there, too. I think that'll be right up your street, though it might go down like a lead balloon with Ember," I chuckled.

"I can't wait!" Havok said, before we both morphed into Ember's Cognition Room.

"Bloody 'ell. You've been busy!" I said, looking at her almost empty room.

Ember spun around in shock, then looked sheepish. "Oh, yeah. I woke up about two hours after I'd fallen asleep. I couldn't get back off, thinking how close I was. I need to know what the fuck happens next, Shaun." I could hear the desperation in her voice.

I grinned at her, looking at what remained of her piles. "We should have this done in an hour, I'd say. Come on, Havok, Hit it! Something fast and upbeat."

"You got it, guys."

We both plowed back into Ember's room, going faster than ever to get that shit done, once and for all. Less than an hour later, Ember stood reverently holding a broken tennis racquet, the last item in the room. A tear formed in the corner of her eye. "I'm not going to lie, this is a huge moment for me. So sorry for getting a little emotional."

"You don't have to be sorry. This is a huge fucking deal!"

She walked over to the shelving unit and slammed it down happily. The shelves instantly disappearing to be replaced with a small, empty shelf and a screen hovering above it. We looked at each other briefly in surprise, before turning back to the screen. It displayed a file icon for each of the years of Ember's life on one side of the screen and on the other side was a list, the first item of which was a broken tennis racket. She opened up one of the file icons and 12 new files appeared, categorized by month this time. "Weird that it's in months, I would have thought it would be some weird galactic measurement."

"Could be just because it's in your head, and it's how you measure stuff." I replied.

"Almost insightful, till you said '*stuff*', Shaun, but you're definitely getting there." She said before turning to continue selecting file Icons. They reduced down to weeks, then days and finally hours. At the bottom of the page was a line of text.

Rebuild mind-database: 0% complete.

She groaned, "Well, this is about as overwhelming as a tsunami."

"Yup. Looks about as much fun as shitting out bricks sideways."

"Well, I'm not going to let it get me down. I'm still happy with what we've achieved. Let's go check my stats, huh?"

"Yeah, I'd be interested to know the result of all this," I said, following her to the Interface Room. The only change that appeared was to Clarity, as expected. It now sat at 75%.

"I have to say, I'm pretty fucking annoyed about this, Shaun. I feel like my own mind has really misled me."

I couldn't help but laugh, "Yeah, it's super shitty, but still a massive step forward. Don't worry about it Ember, we always knew we'd have to do inventory at some point."

"It's going to be painstaking. How the fuck am I supposed to remember what I did at a specific hour when I was four?" She held her head in her hands.

"Hey, seriously, you're not thinking about it the right way. I bet you can remember so much more now than you ever could before. I sure as shit can."

"Yeah, I can, but not that much, it's impossible."

"It's impossible _now_, but I know I could organize a lot of it into years. Once we've done that, our clarity will be better again. Then we can focus on each year, starting with the most recent ones."

She looked at me with a confused expression. "Well shit on the table and call it a steak Shaun. You're absolutely right, you fucking closet genius!"

"Yeah, I know. So what do we do now? Do we know when anyone's coming for us?"

"Later today, I'd imagine. As for what now, were gonna smash the shit out of your room 'til we're called for."

"Ah shit, I knew you'd say that," I grumbled. Thankfully, I was saved by a knock at the door. A Veiletian was standing there, holding a tray with two bowls of a cream-colored soup, a pile of bread and two glasses of water. This time the soup had a small, green garnish on top. "Here is your breakfast. Elyek asked me to inform you that it will be much later today for the meeting with the elders. If you wish to go to the training rooms at any point, or have any other needs, please don't hesitate to contact us."

"Oh, okay. Thanks," I said, taking the tray. "We'll think about it. Is Calparr okay?"

"Yes. He contacted us last night and asked to be shown the way to the gym. He took his breakfast there this morning. He is much happier training than sitting in his room."

"Oh, that's good. I'm glad he's doing well. Thank you."

When the Veiletian left, I carried the soup over to the table for Ember. "I'll warn you; it looks even less appetizing than last night's meal, although it has a garnish this time. I'm hoping it's cilantro. That stuff really makes the flavors pop."

Ember took a spoonful of the soup with the green sprig in it. "Bleurgh! No, it's not. That shit tastes like soap."

"Right. I'll take the fucker out, then," I said, removing the offending article. To be fair, the soup tasted like shit, too. We both left a lot of it.

"Well, Shaun, it sounds like we have most of the day to wait around," Ember grinned. "So let's scrub the last bit of stupid out of that head of yours, eh?"

I'd like to say that the day passed in a blur, but it really didn't. It was a long, arduous, boring day, and I refuse to talk about it anymore. You'll just have to use your imagination for this little five-hour window of misery. But the main point is that I finally got my shit mostly together. The inventory screen popped into existence, and I was damned relieved. I depressingly had four more years of files than Ember, which sucked balls.

"Shall we start the inventory then?" Ember asked.

"Absolutely no fucking way! I'd literally rather get eaten by a troll. You can do yours if you want, and I'll just lie on the bed and meditate on getting back to the FSU for a decent meal."

"I actually agree with you. But you're not just lying there. We'll do some training instead. I want to see what 75% Mental Clarity looks like in real life."

"Yeah, okay, that's fair. As long as it's levitation first, that's the main thing I want to improve on. I'm not too bothered with telekinesis at the minute."

"That's fine by me. I want to excel at both," said a now smug Ember.

We went through a series of levitation practices that were limited by the height of the room. We were both doing far better than ever before. It was pretty exciting, all told. Apparently, Havok didn't agree. Nonetheless, he did offer an amazing insight: "So, guys. I'm watching you fumble about like fat, pink babies on the floor. It's embarrassing, and a little depressing. Jotun never looked like you guys when he flew. Still, he did know a lot of stuff you don't."

"Flew?"

"Well, that's what it looked like when he did it. When you two do it, I don't even know what it looks like. But I'm thinking, is there a way to link up your eyes to your External Interface room, then you don't have to fuck about like you're doing."

"I don't think there is, pal. Ogun told us it was just about increasing Mental Clarity to the point we could operate in the two places at once."

"What if I told you that's a common misconception encouraged by the elite, like Jotun, to give them an advantage over other Fystr? Now, I only think this from what I picked up from being around Jotun. I definitely know he didn't operate like you guys do, or most other Fystr for that matter. It's part of what made him so formidable. He never even told his fellow crew members about it, because he didn't want the competition. He wanted to be the best and kept many secrets."

"Really?" Ember said. Before Havok had a chance to respond, Ember continued, "So, Havok, you know I like you, right? But I have to ask, why the fuck are you only telling us this now?"

"I like you too, Ember, and it just never fucking came up before," Havok replied, deadpan.

I had to laugh.

"Fair enough. But if you can wrack your brain and find any other vital information like that nugget, then *please* let us know."

"I will do, Ember. I guarantee it. Jotun developed the ability about 900 years ago. I was still very young in my sentience; not a lot made sense to me in those days. I vaguely remember the knowledge was given to him by one of the Fystr elite. But I do know that the Fystr have a very rigid class system, and much is kept from the lower classes."

"It seems ingrained in their culture to keep people down as much as possible," I retorted.

"Not surprising, really," Ember said. "Growing is tough, especially when you've achieved what the Fystr have. It's probably just much easier to keep people down than continue to develop yourself."

"My old coach used to say, 'Blowing someone's flame out doesn't make yours shine any brighter'. Which sounded great, until he spoiled it a bit by adding, 'Unless you're in the ring, then you kick the living shit out of their flame'," I chuckled to myself.

"Very funny, Shaun. So, how are we going to learn to link our Interface Room with our eyes?"

"I don't know, just try, I suppose," I replied to Ember.

She spoke to Havok instead, "So, you think he somehow just overlaid his internal vision over his actual vision? I'll have a try." She closed her eyes to enter her Mindscape. I loved how hungry she was to do well with the Mental Skills we had developed. As I sat there watching her though, I instinctively knew that she had gone about it the wrong way. Why would you need to close your eyes? That's just backwards. If you wanted to improve your eyesight, then the opposite would be true.

I decided I'd try to levitate. However, instead of going to my Interface Room, I just imagined what I had seen in there being projected through my eyes. It barely made sense to me, just you get a certain feeling when you're in that room; you have much greater peripheral vision. Nothing happened at first. I did feel a weird sensation, a slight tingling in my eyes. I focused on that feeling, trying to push life into it, then something happened. Nothing dramatic, only I felt my vision begin to slowly broaden, spread out almost. I knew I was on to something, so I forced it to the point that it actually began to hurt. I thought of the time when I had transcended, and that pain led me to, sort of, the next level. With that in mind, I knew this was worth doing. As long as I didn't get kicked out of my body. I suspected that I wouldn't, and I trusted Ember to find me somehow. I forced onward. Feeling a snap, my vision disappeared altogether.

"Shit, Havok. Help! I'm blind!"

"What do you mean?" he asked.

"I can't see a damn thing, Havok! Help me, dude! I've got too much I still wanna see!" I said, panicking.

"Shaun?" Ember's voice sounded from the darkness. "What's up? What's wrong with you?"

"I'm blind. I can't see anything!"

"I know what blind means, Shaun. Now, what the hell did you do? Havok, can you do anything?"

"I'm looking now," Havok replied, "There doesn't seem to be any damage. I don't know what's wrong."

"Shit! Oh, Shaun. What have you done? Can you see anything in your Mindscape?"

"I never thought of that," I said, quickly jumping into my Mindscape. Relief flooded me as I could see again, in the Mindscape at least. Ember appeared next to me. "I can see in here," I told her. "Let's check what my Interface Room shows."

Upon entering, we saw the large screen that usually let me see what I would view through my eyes. My heart sank when I saw it was black. "Oh shit, what have I done? I'm blind."

"Wait. What's that in the corner of the screen?" Ember

said, pointing out a very small, flashing, blue line of text in the bottom corner. She was over to it before me and began to read it out, "'Visual update in progress. Merging visual functions. Estimated time to completion, 2 minutes and 39 seconds.' Oh Shaun, I think you're gonna be okay, you insanely stupid, amazing man. It looks like you've done it again! I'll wait to see if you're okay, first. Then, you need to tell me what you did."

"Thanks for hedging your bets, Ember."

"I'm hardly going to risk going blind just because you did, you idiot. Let's just see how this plays out."

We were down to a minute left on the timer. "I'll just wait in here. I'd rather be able to see," I told Ember. The vision screen flashed to life, once more showing the room we shared in the Veiletian compound. It looked the same as before, and I was relieved.

I went back to my normal state. My vision was back, albeit weird and disorientating. It reflected the same powerful vision of the Interface Room but more... so much more! I could see nearly everything in the room. It was like my memory of the room had combined with my senses. It was fucking weird, awesome and totally natural all at once. I could now appreciate that I'd never have been able to do this with my Cognition Room as a shit-tip.

"Hey, Ember. This is pretty cool," I said to her expectant face.

"So, how do you do it?" She asked impatiently.

"Imagine you want to levitate, while at the same time picturing what you can see when you're present in your Interface Room."

She closed her eyes.

"No. Keep them open," I instructed.

She tried once and failed to replicate the feat. Frustrated, she said, "I need them closed. I can't imagine seeing something without closing my eyes. I can only see what I can see,"

"Keep trying. You'll get there. I felt a tingling at first. Look out for that."

She continued to try with her eyes closed, so I decided to see if I could levitate without my Mindscape. I tried, and only started floating up in the bloody air! I'd only bloody done it! This was amazing.

I brought some objects into play, raising them up in the air. I was still unsteady, but I had jumped massively in terms of my ability. Havok broke into my thoughts: "We can adapt our fighting style now. I should be able to drink more souls already."

My mind put the brakes on, screeching to a halt. "You're fucking with me, dude! Drink more souls?"

"I can see how that sounded a lot worse than I intended. I was trying to be cool, and admittedly I normally am, even if I do say so myself. Although I accept that I may have overstepped the mark a bit there. Let me rephrase: I can already see how we'll be a much more effective fighting force. Our enemies will fall before us, which will benefit us both. Was that any better?"

I couldn't help but laugh. "Yeah, man," I slapped my thigh, laughing my ass off. "Seriously though, if anyone else heard you say that there'd be some worried people around. Keep the soul drinking on the down-low."

"I will, Shaun. Now let's see some more of your *ARSE* skills."

"My *arse* skills?"

"Yes, ARSE! Your ability to Affect Real Shit Externally with your mind."

"Havok, old pal. That acronym was both brilliant and shit. But I appreciate the effort, and we'll continue to use it."

"Shaun, I accept that my acronym was shit, only how do you know what an acronym is?"

"Beats me, Havok. If I was to take an educated guess, it quite possibly has something to do with the clearing of one's Cognition Room, thus gaining vastly improved re-call speeds and memory capabilities. Unexpectedly, my vision takes into account that which I've seen and im-poses it upon my projected images with what I assume is near to 75% accuracy."

"Oh no, Shaun! You're talking like you're clever. Please stop it. You're ruining your charm."

"Whatever you say, Havok. I think you're probably right. People have an expectation of me, and I wouldn't want to disappoint them," I laughed "But I see and under-stand so much more."

"Good. Keep your burgeoning intellect well hidden. You're much more fun like this."

Ember came around just then and I switched my focus back to her as she began to speak, "No luck. I don't know what the hell you did. Has it allowed you to do every-thing without going into your mind?"

"Well, I think so. I've not done much yet."

"How are you going to get me this skill, Shaun? You're not getting ahead of me."

"Ha! You've already tried once, and she wouldn't lis-ten. This is going to be an interesting conversation," Havok said.

"Fuck you, Havok."

"If only."

"What? That doesn't even make any sense!"

"She's looking at you, waiting for a response."

I quickly moved on, "Ember, it's like I told you. When I did it, I just thought closing my eyes would be the opposite of what I wanted to achieve, so I thought about how it would feel to overlay my Interface Room with my real vision. I won't lie, it involved a little pain, but now I can kinda see everything around me. Focus on what I said, until you can feel like... I don't know, like they're actually trying to merge together. It hurts in the way transcending did. Only you just have to force through it."

"There has to be another way. I'll try it out again though." She kept her eyes open, staring at the wall. I saw her wince in pain.

"Keep going, Ember. You can do it," I encouraged.

I actually sensed the moment that she broke through; I don't know whether it was a look on her face, or a change in the aura around her.

"Shit! This is freaky-deaky. I'm blind as a bat. I'm going to check in my Mindscape to make sure everything is as it should be." I left her to it. Within about three minutes, she was back in her body. "Here it comes, Shauny baby. Eyesight level two, on its way," she paused for a moment. "Oh, wow. This is weird. It feels right, though."

"It's pretty cool, huh?"

She didn't reply. She suddenly levitated over to the far wall of the room. It was a little ungainly, but it was fast. Within an instant, she was back next to me. "Shaun, you're a goddamn genius. I don't know how you do it, but keep doing what you do!"

Before we could practice anymore, there was a knock on the door. I answered and found Elyek standing there. "Ah, finally! Are we to be freed from our prison?" I said, smiling at them.

"It was not a prison. You were allowed to go to the gymnasium, were you not?"

"You know prisoners are allowed to exercise, right Elyek? At least in Earth jails."

"You were not held as prisoners, Captain."

"I know, Elyek. I'm only messing around."

"Oh, okay. Enough of that now. We should go to collect Calparr. It's time to vet our potential new crew members. He should be in the gymnasium."

We went for Calparr and found him doing pull-ups at an extraordinary rate. "Hey dude, time to go." I said.

"One moment. I'll grab my things," he said, then returned a minute later looking fresh as a daisy.

As we walked along the corridors, I spoke with Elyek. "I really don't know much of your people, other than what you've told me, so I hope you're okay to conduct the interviews for the most part. You know what we're looking for, and probably how to spot someone unsuitable from your race. At least, much better than we ever could."

"Of course, Captain. It would be an honor to act in this capacity, and it also makes a lot of sense."

Ember gave me a pat on the back. "Well done, Shaun. It's always a nice surprise when you use your brain for a second. Keep up the good work."

I growled internally, feeling her tone was a tad patronizing, but quickly let it go, taking it in the good humor Ember intended.

C10

Come out to Play

Arriving in the hall, I was blown away by how many Veiletians were in the place; it was crammed. Once we arrived, the loud clamor of multiple voices dropped, to be replaced with silence and stares. It got uncomfortable quickly, so I smiled and waved, with a cheerful, "Hey, everyone!" Amazingly, this didn't help. If anything, the awkwardness grew.

"My people!" came the commanding voice of Prefector Kalika bellowing to the roomful of Veiletians. "Is this how you make a good impression on those who bestow you the opportunity to become a crewmate on their prestigious ship? You have been greeted. Do not be so discourteous as to not return that greeting."

There was a palpable atmosphere of shame and embarrassment from everyone I could see in the room, as a disjointed chorus of "Good day to you all" rang out from – I assume – everyone's mouths.

We continued our way to the front of the room, where the elders sat. "Hi again, everyone. So, what are we supposed to do now? This all feels a little awkward," I said, addressing mainly Kalika.

"Take a seat at the table and interview everyone who wishes to go with you. Make a shortlist. The people who still wish to come with you after the two-way assessments will be matched up with your shortlist. From there, we'll have a good idea who is to be recruited," Kalika replied.

"There are like, 300 people here. This could take days," I said, dismayed.

"Then it will take days. We must not rush these choices," added another of the council members who had spoken yesterday, but had not given their name.

"Right. I'm not sure that's going to work for us," I said, turning to address the crowd. "Everyone! I'm glad you are all thinking of joining us. We would be proud to have you all with us. Alas, that cannot be at this moment in time. In the future, we hope to have more ships, and even a base from which to run the Headquarters of the Uprising. Our vision is that more of us can work together to make this galaxy a safer place. With that in mind, I have a few specifications to find the most-suited candidates.

"You know what we plan to do. If you really want to be part of that, make your way to the right side of the room. If you're just here to find out more about us, or are unsure if you even want to join, go to the left side."

People began to move. Havok chuckled in my head.

"This is preposterous and not how things are done here. Everyone is given a fair chance," one of the council members complained. It was taken up by a few others.

"Sorry, guys. I'm not meaning to be rude. We just have to be realistic here. We don't need people who are unsure of themselves, or of being part of the Uprising," I said quietly, then turned back to the crowd. It had parted, leaving only around a hundred gathered on the right-hand side; great for sorting, but annoying that so many had come essentially to waste my time.

I continued, "Brilliant, thank you. Those on the left

may leave." There was a grumbling of discontent as people began to file out. I really had no idea what they expected to happen. The elders were complaining again, too. I just blocked them out. This was potentially for everyone's benefit.

I glimpsed Kalika and saw she had a small smile on her face, which was good, because I intended to continue with my sorting. "Okay, everyone else. Now, I'm really sorry we have to cull your numbers; the council has only permitted us to take ten of you, until such a time as we can prove our good intentions and behaviors towards Veiletians. I must ask you once more to split into groups. As it stands, we're going to be a mercenary group, so can you please divide to the right side for those that are competent fighters, and over to the left side for those who are not confident fighters."

A stream of deflated, dejected faces flowed to the left side of the hall, leaving around 30 in total who considered themselves as skilled in the art of fighting. "Right," I smiled. "Of those of you in the remaining group of fighters, whoever has medical knowledge and abilities, come stand by the desk to be evaluated."

Four came up to the desk. I spoke with them as a group. "Are you still happy to join the Uprising after what you've heard so far?" They nodded in unison. "Excellent. If you can all go to speak with Elyek, they will carry out the final stage of vetting and answer any of your questions." They walked over to Elyek, who looked taken aback, even though we'd agreed to it earlier.

"You 26 remaining, raise your hands if you have any experience of being part of a ship's crew with expertise of your own."

Eighteen hands went up.

"Excellent. To the rest of you, I'm very sorry we cannot recruit you at this time. We have our shortlist of candidates. Thank you for coming, and when we increase our capacity in the future, we hope you can join us. We'd love to have you on board.

"As for those who are left, please form an orderly line to speak with Elyek." I sighed, turning my attention to the councilors.

One of the councilors spoke: "You have treated our people with great disrespect. I am beginning to rethink if any should be allowed to leave with you." He was encouraged by nods of agreement from the other council members. All except Kalika, who remained silent.

"I haven't got the time for time-wasters, when there are those who genuinely want to come with us. I don't want to take people into war zones who cannot fight. I need people with fighting skills and expertise to operate a ship. If you think any of my filters were unfair, or disrespectful, then I don't really know what to say to you to change your opinion. I can only discuss thoughts and opinions that have a basis in reality."

The speaker was about to begin an angry retort, when I cut him off. "I'm also curious as to your relationship with your own people. I hadn't realized you were an oppressive governing body."

"What!" he spluttered, "That's outrageous. How dare you!"

"Hey, hey, hey," I said, calmly raising my hands up in a submissive gesture. "It was you who said you'd not allow your people to travel freely, which, by the way, nearly all the other council members seemed to agree with.

"Don't be too saddened. I hear it's almost impossible for power not to corrupt, even for the pure souls of

Veiletians."

There was a gasp at that statement. Ember glared at me. Havok laughed his ass off. I think I must have overstepped the mark. Thankfully, Kalika intervened and saved me from my own mouth. "I'm sure Councilor Mirlek misspoke. We do not, in fact, prevent our people from exercising their freedoms. We only seek to protect them from the cruelties that various other members of the galaxy wish to inflict upon our race. Despite that rather indelicate sorting of prospective candidates, I do see the merit in its efficiency. I am also impressed that you have handed over the finer details of the interview process to our Elyek. You seem to be at least aware of your own shortcomings. I find myself both insulted and impressed by your straightforwardness. Perhaps, an ally who is so direct will be beneficial to our Veiletian council, who are by nature, indirect," Kalika chuckled.

"Listen, we're happy to be your ally, but I have to ask: can we take everyone that's left after Elyek's interviews? I promise we'll look after them like our own. We will return when we can so you can see they are safe and happy to continue as part of the Uprising crew."

I could sense angry responses building in various councilors. Again, Kalika calmed them down. "It is not what we agreed, Captain Shaun. However, there really isn't any valid reason to begrudge this request. Although you will have to move in smaller groups, and you must promise to care for our people. We are placing much trust, and dare I say hope, that you can help change the fortunes of the Veiletian people."

"I totally promise that. And thank you for your faith in us."

"I hope so," they said, thoughtful.

I felt an increase of pressure on my shoulders at our exchange of words. With that agreed, I wandered over to the corner where Elyek was conducting the interviews. I sat in a chair listening to them speak, but staying out of it as much as I could. I didn't want to seem overbearing.

To their credit, Elyek didn't mess about either; they made it through the interviews in 20 minutes. After the last person, they turned to me. "Excuse me, Captain. I have gone through all of the candidates, and it is a strong group. I have written down some of the basic strengths and weaknesses of each individual. From this, I will help you select the most suitable from the list."

"Could you not pick six from this group?" I asked.

"No. It is going to be a tough process to whittle it down, I'm afraid."

"No need then," I smiled, and spoke to the remaining group. "The good councilors here, have just given me permission to offer you all a place on board the Uprising. Welcome to the gang!" I said, happily.

"Glad to have you all with us," Ember shouted joyously.

Calparr just nodded stoic acceptance, which was cool, as well.

Looking at the group of Veiletians, their expressions ranged from pleased and excited to sudden nervousness. And they should be nervous, I thought, we definitely weren't a pleasure cruise ship. "So, all that's left for you to do is make ready to leave. We won't hurry you all on this. We understand you'll have loved ones that you wish to say goodbye to and personal affairs to take care of. Still, if you could give us a rough idea on how long you think you'll all need before you leave?"

No one spoke for a moment. They all looked almost

afraid of me. Finally, one of them plucked up the courage: a small Veiletian with vibrant red hair said, "I can go today if you wish. I keep a few possessions that I can grab quickly."

This started a cascade of replies. Many said today. A few said tomorrow. No one said longer, from what I could hear.

"We can wait until tomorrow, then. If that's what suits?"

"That may be unwise," Kalika said. "When we originally agreed on ten recruits, it was actually for a good reason. So many cannot traverse Arus together: that would make a huge space filled with invisible Veiletians. Accidents would occur. The most we normally take out at one time is ten citizens. We can increase that number a little, but 22 people, invisible or not, would prove impossible to hide."

"Gotcha. That's a very good point, elder. Well, how about we take 11 back with us to the ship today and collect the other 11 tomorrow?"

"I could stay behind and take the others tomorrow," Elyek interjected. "It will be nice to spend another night here. I never thought I'd see this place again."

"Sure. Of course," I said. "That sounds like the perfect compromise."

"Yes. We would be satisfied with that division and plan," Elder Kalika said, then added: "Sort out among you the 11 who will go today."

Ember and I spent the following hours in our room. I wanted to be out of the way while those coming with us got themselves prepared. The following days would be spent trying to remember everyone's names, so as not to be a dick. Luckily, the Veiletians had quite a bit of diversity among them in appearance. Their looks ranged from masculine to feminine, while some, like Elyek, were completely in between and you really couldn't guess. Unless of course your guess was androgynous, when you'd be bang on the money.

I was overjoyed when someone came to get us. Apparently, everyone was ready to leave. Back in the hall there were 11 excited Veiletians, six grumpy councilors and a worried Elyek. "Are you going to be okay getting back? I hadn't thought about how you would navigate back to the ship when I suggested you leave without me," they said with noticeable concern.

"We will be fine, Elyek," Ember said soothingly. "Shaun and I have near perfect recall now, anyway. So, don't worry about it."

"Yeah. We know everything," I joked, trying to lighten the mood.

"No, you damn buffoon," Ember interrupted. "We can remember anything we see, providing we store it correctly. Remember?" she explained, removing any levity.

"Yeah, Ember. I know."

She shook her head, "It's going to be fine, Elyek. Our new crew members will be able to guide us if we get lost."

"Yes. You are right of course. I was just suddenly concerned. I know you will be fine."

"We'll see you tomorrow, Elyek. Don't sweat it," I said, clapping them on the shoulder. They seemed to relax a little before returning the goodbye.

After that we all set off out of the compound. To my surprise, all of our new members turned invisible when we reached the compound gates. Even though we had already been told that would happen, it still set my nerves a little on edge. Off we went for the transport tubes.

C11

Pain in the Arus

Traveling across the Arus habitation domes with 11 invisible strangers was a totally weird experience. I kept worrying that I would bump into one of them, which was a ridiculous concern because they were able to see fine. Not only that, but they could also somehow see each other. That bit didn't make any sense to me though. What good would invisibility be if everyone could still see you? If they were Veiletian anyway. I would have to ask Elyek next time I saw them. Although to be fair, I had just gained a load more Veiletians who were going to be part of our new family, so I could probably just ask one of them.

I snapped out of my daydreaming, ruing the fact that all this evolving hadn't stopped my mind from occasionally going to the far end of a fart and back again. Looking around as we walked, I noticed that I did in fact recognize where we had passed through. I hadn't felt like I'd taken in any more detail than I normally would have on the way here; and in general I would often get from one place to the next without noticing or remembering a damn thing about the journey. But this time it appeared that the information had been stored by my subconscious. "I can clearly recall these places we've passed. This is awesome, Ember. It's going to make life a lot easier."

"Yeah, it's cool. The idea that I'll never forget another thing fills me with a confidence I've not felt before, if you know what I mean."

"I think I do know. It's like finally feeling in control a little, not just blindly staggering through life, following impulses."

"Wow, Shaun. You've pretty much nailed it. Finally, your intelligence is able to stretch its legs, huh?"

"No matter how much you've improved, you still love sticking the knife in," I said back to her.

I noticed Calparr trying to ignore our exchange but failing. His facial expression indicated he must have thought we were both bonkers.

When we came up to the first commercial moon tube, I felt a pang of nerves. I didn't know how this was going to work with our convoy. I mean, how was I even supposed to know if they were all aboard? Thankfully, the carriage we entered was pretty empty, so I dared a careful whisper, "Is everyone on board?"

A series of invisible hands touched my arm. I was freaked the fuck out by it, but also more than a little amazed that my now-more-mature subconscious was able to count those touches, and confirm everyone was present. I felt like I was about three different people some days. Stupid Shaun, evolved-alien Shaun and, when Havok was in my hand, gods-be-damned-berserker Shaun.

Ember was looking at me questioningly.

"Yeah. They're all here, Ember," I said, answering her unasked question.

"Good. This is really fucking odd."

I nodded and smiled in answer.

Calparr remained stoic.

We got off the tube at the next stop and headed over to the next platform. A tube arrived within seconds. I continued to chat amiably to Ember, while trying to also engage Calparr, when a small whisper sounded in my ear, "We're being followed, Captain."

I obviously didn't know who said it, but replied with a quick, "Thanks."

"You get that?" I asked my two visible companions.

Calparr gave a nod.

Ember shrugged and said, "Yup. Let's just keep moving. There was always a chance someone would spot us and have a problem."

Our conversation dropped off a little bit, but still no one confronted us as we swapped tubes yet again. It wasn't until we reached the central hub, located where we were docked, that I really even became aware of our pursuers. We had a long-ish walk to the ship, and I saw the occasional person watching us suspiciously. It was not long before it came to a head. The next street corner we turned was quite empty, apart from a group of eight aliens in front of us. They wore moon base security uniforms. They were clearly hired for their thuggish demeanor. "Stop there," snorted the leader. He reminded me strangely of Bebop, with small horns at the side of his mouth and a wide ungainly nose, or rather snout. The overall result when coupled with his size was that of a mutant warthog. His pals were no smaller.

"Why?" I asked, slowing but not stopping.

"Because you're under arrest," he said, hefting his plasma rifle into a more threatening position, and I had to admit that it was an impressive looking bit of hardware.

"Hey, you fat fucker! We've got places to be and this

whole moon is a criminal's wet dream. So, how about you do us a favor and fuck off?" Ember gently suggested from my side.

"We're going for diplomacy, then?" I asked her.

"Shaun, like you told me so long ago, in a fantasy world far away, these arseholes aren't here for friendly chit-chat. Capiche?"

"Yeah. I know that," I huffed. "But let's at least find out what they want first."

"Meh! You might have a point," she smiled, which I loved. Under attack on an alien pirate moon, and Ember was still giving everyone shit with a smile on her face.

"The three of you need to stop moving forwards, now! Stop or we will shoot your legs out from under you." He must have been under orders not to hurt us if he could because he looked like he really, really wanted to. I was impressed with his restraint; I knew how annoying we could be.

"What do you want?" I sighed. "We haven't got all day."

"Oh, but you have. At least until you're executed for attacking galactic spaceships and taking Torax from their planet."

"That wasn't us, dude! Honestly, we wouldn't do anything like that. Now, come on. Out of the way." I made a shooting gesture, while at the same time asked Havok to come around in front of me. He happily obliged with a maniacal laugh as his cover fell away from him.

"Oh, baby! It's my favorite time of the, EVER! Let's chop some shitheads up, Shaun!"

"We will, Havok. Don't you worry about it."

Bebopaloobop raised his gun to shoot, as Havok slapped into my palm. "Put it down now, or I'll put you down!" he snarled.

Everyone else was a second later to the party, but now this whole section of Arus was bristling with death-dealing devices. Remembering we were being followed, I took a quick look over my shoulder to see who was there. Four more armed aliens had their guns trained on us. Feeling concern for the Veiletians, I spoke in a hushed tone. "Hey, guys. I want you to clear the area. I don't want you to get hurt, and it's going to be messy."

"Damn right, it's getting messy," Havok announced to me.

There was no answer from the Veiletians.

"Guys?"

"Looks like they've already made that decision, Shaun. Now, fucking focus will you," Ember snapped at me.

"Hey, it's okay. I've got this. Stay behind me and defend yourselves against those guys. I'll cover you as best I can. If you can get somewhere safe, do it."

"Their weapons are plasma; they will only tickle," Calparr smiled. "Ember should take cover between us."

"Sounds good to me. These open pitched battles aren't really my thing. You know, not being bulletproof."

"Are you three stupid? You won't make it out of here alive. Now, drop the weapons."

I didn't answer. I just started walking towards him again, Ember behind me, Calparr behind her, weapons raised facing the enemy at our rear.

"Last chance!" the guard shouted.

Havok actually giggled in my head as he charged himself up. Blue plasma flaring to life over his crescent moon blades. Then all hell broke loose… just not the kind I expected.

"*Noooooooo!*" Havok screamed after deflecting the first

shot.

Gushing torrents of blood began pumping out of the severed neck arteries of all of the guards in front of us, almost as one. It was like some kind of sick art display as it sprayed all over the street in the panicked death throes of our attackers. I turned to see the four behind us in a similar disposition. "Fuck me! Was that the Veiletians?" I said to Ember.

"My kills. They took my kills!" Havok cried in my head.

She looked at me wryly. "Of course it was the Veiletians, dumbass. Now, let's get moving. This is not going to go unanswered."

"You're right. We need to get to the ship, fast." Running now was probably our best option. So, off we went. I just had to assume that the Veiletians were with us.

I brought Calegg up on my comm. "Hello, Captain," Calegg said, respectfully.

"Hey, Calegg. We're comin' in hot, as usual. We were attacked on our way back; Arus guards, apparently."

"Oh, shit. Are you all okay? Do you need us to come out and help?"

"No. I think a bunch of Torax kicking ass would turn this little scuffle into an intergalactic incident. Just fire up the engines. Get ready to fly as soon as we're aboard. Shit, are the repairs even complete?"

"Yes. Luckily, they were complete around two hours ago. I'll have everyone ready in case we've no choice but to come down and help out... oh, Captain. A group of guards have just appeared on the gantry to the ship. Shall we deal with those, at least?"

"No, Calegg. Thanks for the heads up but we can sort that out. See you soon, and be ready to get the fuck out of here. As soon as that door goes up, I want to be like a well-baked shit, shooting out of Arus."

"No problem, Captain. Piece of cake, yeah?"

"Yeah, Calegg," I said as a shot fired by my head. I ended the communication just as we entered the final street leading to the docks. Plasma fire crackled through the air. I had to deflect the occasional shot from hitting me, and Ember seemed to be developing a knack for deflecting plasma fire herself.

Calparr, however, couldn't give a fuck. He had a thin veneer of fire over his skin and just fired back merrily as plasma shots fizzled out on him. Looking round, I saw more uniformed guards appearing from adjoining streets. We were doing okay, but it was turning into an absolute shit-storm. "Not far. Come on!" I shouted. I fell back to make sure Calparr and Ember were in front of me and I could deflect incoming fire. As for the Veiletians, I could offer no help. I just hoped they were looking after themselves.

Arriving at the docks, the gantry to our ship was blocked by enemies, just as Calegg had said. Our recent Veiletian recruits had already hit them hard and were making promising headway, as bodies slumped in rapid succession as a result of deadly surgical incisions. Havok and I couldn't join them in their fight, or we'd probably end up killing them as well, which was to be avoided.

Those approaching from the street were only shooting selectively now, in fear of shooting their own men. When the occasional shot did come in, it was ineffective. Havok was up to the task of covering us all. Not that Calparr needed it. We put ourselves behind a wall of various boxes and crates on the dock: siege tactics. And then the real fun started.

Calparr was standing up, shooting carelessly into the

increasing stream of bodies coming to apprehend us. Ember was demonstrating some sick telekinesis skills. Within a few seconds, cargo boxes were whizzing around the dock at a terrifying speed. I did some good work throwing the odd box about, hitting a few people here and there, but Ember was working with style. I chuckled as I saw one guy running away from a floating box. He tripped over, rolled a few times and just as he was getting back to his feet, Ember dropped a heavy crate on him. He was squished like a pancake, and blood exploded from under the box. That last bit wasn't so funny, nonetheless it was effective.

The numbers were starting to drop, yet more still came. After about five minutes of carnage, I was relieved to hear the voice of a Veiletian next to me: "The way is clear to the ship, Captain."

"Thanks," I said to thin air, noticing the pile of corpses. These Veiletians were hot shit. I gave the call, "Come on, guys. Time to bounce."

Ember hurled her two remaining crates at two different groups. Calparr started moving backwards, firing unrepentantly. Once we were all ready, we ran as one to the ship, the door dropping to give us all access.

As soon as it closed behind us, there were a few mild tremors, indicating the ship had started to move. I leaned against the door, grinning my ass off, glad to be back on the Uprising.

"Well, that was fun," Ember said, smiling as well. "You guys are insane!"

"I second that," I added, as the Veiletians began to materialize in the loading bay.

"Oh, shit. Some of you are injured," I cried. Three were bleeding. On the plus side, I was glad to see all 11 recruits were here.

"It was in service. We are happy to have been of use to you, Captain." The voice was that of the one who had spoken throughout our journey and fight; the same bright-red-haired Veiletian who had been ready to go immediately from the Veiletian enclave.

"Thank you for all of your help," I replied, genuinely impressed with what they had achieved, and the dedication shown on the way.

Ember spoke before I could say anything more. "We'll have time to talk later. For now, I'll take them all to the Medical Room. Shaun, you go and see Calegg. He could probably do with some moral support."

"I will. But we've done the hard bit. Flying away should be a walk in the park."

C12

When in Doubt, Delegate

It was no fucking walk in the park getting away from the Arus. It turns out the smuggler's moon had an array of impressive artillery to call upon. Also, fun fact: Torax can sweat. I'd previously thought it impossible, having never seen it before, but there were literal rivers running down Calegg's head and face. He looked like he was carved from granite as he stood arched over his control panel flying the ship. Even so, we seemed to have coped relatively well, with other Torax gunners occasionally crying out that they had scored a hit.

There wasn't much to say to the crew. We just had to get the fuck out of there as quickly and safely as possible. I patted Calegg on the back. "You're doing great, Calegg," I said, then loudly spoke to the rest of the bridge crew. "You guys are doing great! Keep up the good work."

I went into my office; I trusted them to get us out of there. My mind had now flipped to concern for Elyek. They were stuck on the moon that we were running away from at full speed. There was only one option I could think of, and that was to ask Astrid to pick up Elyek and the others. I fiddled with the comm on my desk a bit, bringing up a line to the Thoth. A crewmate I didn't know picked up the line, but thankfully was able to pass me through to Astrid.

"Hello, Shaun. Is everything okay?"

"Not really, Astrid. We're fleeing from Arus with all speed. We're probably gonna have to make a jump if we continue to be pursued."

"Oh, I see. We'll come and assist."

"No. That's not what I need at the minute, we should be fine. However, we have another problem. Elyek and 11 new crewmates are still on the surface. They're not in any danger, as far as I know, but we can't get to them. I'm hoping the Thoth won't be on anyone's radar yet, so can you pick them up?"

"Of course, Shaun. We're just finishing up here. Rufus has found what we think is a fantastic contract, well paid. I'll fill you in with the details later."

"That's great, Astrid," I said as the ship rocked violently. I just managed to keep my feet. "By the sounds of it, our escape is taking a turn for the worse. We're going to need to jump. What's the direction of this contract?" I asked desperately.

"I'm not sure Shaun, I'll just check," Astrid said with concern.

"No wait. Just ask your pilot what coordinates the Thoth would use if you were going to our destination. Preferably somewhere relatively isolated too, please."

"Sure, Shaun. Bear with me a moment." The comm went silent, the ship continued to move erratically. As much as I wanted to pace, I took a seat before I had an accident. My mind was ablaze with scenarios and concerns, so it was a relief to be brought out of my cyclical thoughts by Astrid's voice.

"Hey, Shaun. I'm sending over the coordinates for the jump directly to you. Good luck. We'll see you soon."

"Great! Astrid, thanks so much for your help. I'm really grateful fate has put us all together again."

"Me too, Shaun. We're a team, so you don't have to thank me for doing my job. Now, go and get safe."

With that, we ended the link. I quickly brought Ember up over the comm. "Shaun?" she answered as a question.

"It doesn't seem to be getting any easier for us, Ember. We're gonna have to make a jump. I've just spoken to Astrid, and they've agreed to pick up Elyek and the others. The Thoth and its crew won't be marked, as we now seem to be."

"That makes sense. I've been chewing over leaving Elyek back there, even though I knew we wouldn't have left them there forever. Well done for getting that sorted out."

"Thanks, Ember. It's a relief, for sure."

"How will the Thoth and Seshat find us if we jump? I mean, I know they can track us, but if we do a full jump, that might take them days, if not weeks."

"Ah, yeah. Don't worry about that. They've found us a job. I'll explain later. Their pilot has just sent over some coordinates in that direction. Somewhere quiet in the area. So we're gonna use those coordinates."

"Brilliant thinking, Shaun. You're impressing me in more ways than just your jammy-bastardness lately. Keep it up."

"Will do," I said, "Now, gotta go get this jump sorted out. See you soon."

"See you, Shaun. I'll come along in a bit." She left, and I missed her immediately. She always loaned me a lot more confidence in myself than she rudely took. I jumped up out of my seat. I had shit to do. I needed to get the space-folding drive charging quickly. As I walked out of the office, I saw Calegg hadn't moved an inch. Everything was just as intense as I left it.

I was about to tell Calegg to sort out the folding drive when it hit me that he was 110% focused on getting us out of here, and couldn't do this alone. And Elyek was not here. To my shame, I had no clue how to switch the fucking thing on and had never bothered to learn. I smashed the buttons on the comm on my bridge chair for Ember. "Do you know how to turn the bloody folding drive on?" I cried desperately over the private channel.

"No, sorry Shaun. We should probably do something about that *soon*. I'll ask the Veiletians, now. One of them might be able to help."

I frantically paced by my seat, praying one of them might be able to help. A flood of relief washed over me when four Veiletians came running in only seconds later. "Hey, guys!" I greeted them eagerly. "This is the folding-drive control panel. We need to set it charging to escape. I also have coordinates to enter. It takes 15 minutes to charge, so time is precious."

"We'll work it out, Captain. Have no fear," the confident, red-haired Veiletian replied. I won't lie, I was a little happy they were among those who had turned up. They had been amazingly useful so far. They all moved over and began looking over the terminal. They talked quickly and quietly among themselves.

To my surprise, it wasn't the red-haired one that took charge at the panel; it was a tall, slender Veiletian, fingers flashing like lightning over the screen. "There!" they said proudly. "It is charging."

One of the other Veiletians now moved to the panel, gently shifting the other out of the way. They began to go through the panel at lightning speed for a short while, a calm in the storm. Finally, they looked up. "I can reduce the charge time. Regrettably, this will cut the power to non-essential parts of the ship. Unless you have any other sources of power?"

"Do it! But I don't think we've any other sources of power, other than fuel. Is that any good?"

"Suldr!" one of the Torax shouted over.

"Oh, shit! Of course, I didn't even think about that. We've a load of Suldr fire gems."

"They will do, perfectly," said the Veiletian now at the terminal. "We should use the ship's power for now. Then, we can replenish what is used with Suldr."

"Okay. How much time can you take off the charge rate?"

They didn't answer; just began tapping at the screen again. The lights began flashing. Speaking eventually, they announced, "I've re-routed power from the ship and bypassed the safety measures to prevent overcharging the drive's cores. We now have five minutes until we can make the jump."

I nodded then opened the file on my chair. "Here are the coordinates to put in, guys," I said.

The one who had set the ship to charging came over and then hit a few buttons in quick succession on my terminal. "There! All done. It's set," they said, sounding smugly satisfied.

"Don't you need to enter them in the folding-drive?"

"No," they looked at me oddly. "The captain's terminal has a direct line to all of the systems on the ship."

"Oh, right," I replied, a little embarrassed – I had a lot to learn.

"Don't worry, we'll get you up to speed, Captain."

"Oh, thanks. That'd be great. If you guys can offer any

other help on the bridge, I'd be more than grateful."

They nodded and moved back over to the folding-drive terminal.

With that problem sorted, I went back over to Calegg. I was torn. He was clearly under a lot of strain still, but I wanted him to know we appreciated his efforts. I put my hand on his shoulder, then removed it quickly. It was seriously fucking hot and actually burnt my hand. I noticed then that the sweat had stopped, to be replaced by a barely visible steam rising off him. I attempted some words of comfort: "You're doing great, dude. Thanks for your efforts."

He didn't respond. Yet I knew he had appreciated my words, as his look of intense stress seemed to change slightly into resolve.

At that moment, I felt completely impotent, a total fraud. All these people saving our bacon, and there I was, wandering around like a lost fucking lamb, burning my hand on a damn crewmate's shoulder. "Shaun, *you've* brought these people together. *You've* organized the escape with your telepathy. And *you've* arranged for Astrid to collect Elyek, while coordinating efforts on the Uprising," Havok said, uncharacteristically soothingly for him. My hand was already healed thanks to his ministrations.

"Thanks, man. I don't know if you're right, but it was nice to hear," I responded, just as a massive impact shook the ship. Everyone was reeling from that one. We felt a series of smaller hits as we continued our hasty withdrawal. At that point, it didn't feel like we were going to make it. A second big impact, and the power cut out; only the dim emergency lights remained on. It seems I had overestimated our ability to get away from the moon.

Calegg turned to me, horrified, "I've lost controls. We're dead!"

Our screen to the outside had gone blank, as had everyone's terminals. The Uprising was a sitting duck. We all looked at each other, almost saying goodbye with our gazes.

"Uh, hey everyone," a Veiletian said, "I'm really sorry but this is my misjudgment. I may have miscalculated how much energy would be drained from..." The folding-drive suddenly kicked in. Blackness descended.

Once the jump had completed, those who hadn't been seated now picked themselves up from the floor. The Veiletian randomly continued speaking, as if nothing had happened "...drained from the ship in the process."

"You mean, we didn't lose energy because we'd been badly hit?" I groaned, still disorientated.

"I thought it odd, because our shields were still holding," Calegg said.

"Luckily, our enemies also thought we were finished from their assault," the red-haired Veiletian added.

"So, we've jumped. Yeah?" I asked.

"Yes!" The Veiletians all said together, joyously. One of them asked for the Suldr to recharge the ship's functionality for efficiency.

I sent them off with a couple of the Torax gunners to get what they needed. As they left, Ember was just arriving on the bridge. "Phew! Well, that was fucking close," I said to her, then had a mild panic attack, "Shit! We didn't let Elyek know what the plan was! They won't know to contact the Thoth. And can Astrid even get in touch with them?"

"Don't worry, dipshit. I sorted all that out. All we need to do is recover and wait for them to arrive tomorrow.

Okay?"

I let out a huge exhale of air through puffed out cheeks. "I'm getting too old for this shit," I said, deflated.

"You're potentially immortal. You'll never get too old for this shit."

"You know though, I've just done to Elyek what I berated Ogun for doing to me. I ran and deserted them."

"Don't be stupid. They're in a Veiletian enclave, where they're safe and comfortable. In fact they actually used to live there. And we have a ship that's far safer to travel on than ours going to pick them up exactly when they're supposed to be picked up," Ember offered.

"Thanks for trying to justify it Ember, but I ran. Whether or not it was for the right reasons, I left one of our best friends and crewmates behind."

"Well, you were too hard on Ogun anyway, maybe this will give you a bit of perspective, you dipshit."

I laughed at her reply, "Yeah, it has. I feel like an asshole."

"That's fine Shaun, you are an asshole. Now stop moping and go see Calegg, he looks like he could do with some attention."

I responded with a shrug, then walked over to Calegg. Poking him with a finger to make sure he had cooled down, I then grabbed him in a hug while singing his praises. "Great work my friend. You sure saved our bacon."

"That was so intense. I hope we never have to do that again," he replied as we broke the hug.

I turned around to the others. "Really well done to everyone! That was a great team effort. Does anyone know how bad the ship is?"

"No," Calegg answered, "We won't be able to tell until

all the systems come back online. I totally thought that when the systems went down, we'd been hit bad and that had caused the power cut. If it was just the folding drive taking power, then hopefully the damage isn't too bad."

"I bloody hope so." Just as I finished speaking, the lights sprang to life, followed by the terminals.

"Brilliant. Calegg, tell me how bad it is? No, wait… tell me how good it is?"

Calegg scanned his screen for a few moments before looking round to me. "It's actually not that bad, Captain. Hardly anything got through the shields, and what damage there is, is negligible."

"Fan-fucking-tastic! Thanks again, Calegg."

"Yeah, Calegg. You did amazing," Ember added as the bridge doors opened, admitting the four Veiletians and their two Torax escorts.

"You too, guys. I doubt we would've escaped if it weren't for you."

They looked surprised by my addressing them.

"Yeah. How the hell did you know how to speed the folding drive up like that?" Ember asked the Veiletian who did it.

"I didn't know of this ship's drive, but I do know that any charging technology can usually be sped up – although it is not always safe to do so. I checked through the drive's option files and settings. It was risky, but I had felt it was worth trying it to escape. Thankfully, you had the foresight to stock all that Suldr we found hanging in your cargo hold. A really lucky coincidence."

"Yes, it was. Now, after you've helped to save the ship, I really need to learn all of your names. I believe the best way to do that is over dinner. I don't know about you lot, but I'm famished." I turned to Ember. "Canteen, dear?" I asked, holding out my arm.

"Why of course, Captain. I could eat a damn horse myself," Ember replied, linking my arm. We exited towards the canteen, followed from the bridge by the Veiletians and a few Torax. Calegg just slumped down in his chair, as did Koparr.

Sitting around a large table in the canteen, the four Veiletians, Ember and I had steaming food of varying descriptions. I looked at the Veiletian folding-drive speeder-upper. "What's your name then?"

They stuttered a little, showing more discomfort under my direct scrutiny than they did when we were under attack. "It's Wulek, Captain," they finally replied.

"Pleasure to meet you, Wulek." I turned to the one who had initiated the drive-charging. "And your name?"

Again there was discomfort. "I am Hwista," they replied.

"Hwista, huh? I was expecting you to have *ek* in your name, after Wulek and Elyek."

The red-haired wonder who had been so useful throughout spoke next. "We have a few common suffixes among our people: 'ek' is perhaps the most common. I am Acclo, by the way."

"Thanks for that, Acclo. Great to meet you, too," I turned to the last Veiletian. "And finally, your name?"

"I am Miraek. Thank you for bringing us along, I haven't had this much fun in forever!"

After only ten minutes, I found myself liking all of these Veiletians very much. They were helpful, useful and quirky. "Hey, Ember. I think we should get these guys as bridge crew, straight away. There are a few workstations normally free, although I'm not going to lie and tell you I know what any of those stations do. These four are quick, clever and capable," I said in her mind.

Ember responded in my head. "Totally agree. We can even ditch a few of the Torax from the gun stations if need be. There are a couple of them who are more useless than you up there."

"Thanks so much for the kind words, dear. And that's fine. As long as it does not cause too much ill will. To be honest, we need to have people on the bridge the whole time. We can arrange shifts, so as to keep the majority happy. Although our priority is to have the best people on the bridge, even if it means hurting a few feelings," I said, then quickly added, "Before you say it, I'll still need to be on the bridge: useless or not. At least until you've deposed my tyrannical rule."

She actually snorted out loud at that, causing the Veiletians to zero in on her with their gazes.

There was nothing more forthcoming from Ember, so I plowed ahead, speaking aloud. "Miraek, Acclo, Hwista and Wulek, I've already mentioned how impressed we were with your work. We want you on the bridge crew. We'll work out shift rotations over the next few days. Preferably when Elyek comes back. They know the lay of the land better than me around all that business."

"That's because you're just a tyrannical mascot," Ember slipped into my mind, which threw me from my thoughts.

They all nodded enthusiastically at the prospect, which was good.

I really had fuck all idea of what to do with these different groups of people, other than to instruct one of their more skilled members to train the rest and report to one of us. It had all seemed to be working fine so far. Nonetheless, we were potentially heading towards a war zone. I might need to polish up on my leadership skills.

We relaxed, chatting amiably with the Veiletians, then decided to turn in. But before I could do that, I had to make sure we had someone to cover for Elyek. "Any of you energetic enough to work alongside Calegg? We need a fast learner to pick up the pilot functions. Calegg will need to rest soon, and we need cover until Elyek gets back." Although in reality I was thinking that I'd like to pull Elyek away from piloting all together to focus more on managing our increasing numbers of personnel. We couldn't do it before because we didn't have skilled-enough crew to take over piloting duties, but now we could.

They all willingly jumped at the chance.

Nodding, I hit the comm. "Calegg, mate. I'm sending the Veiletians Miraek, Acclo, Hwista and Wulek back to the bridge. They're all competent pilots but unfamiliar with the Uprising. Show them the ropes, then once you're satisfied, they can go unsupervised. Give your steaming ass some rest."

"I'll be fine, Captain. Don't worry about me. I can hold the fort."

"Calegg, I'm not asking you, and I'm not trying to replace you. You'll always be the main pilot of the Uprising. It is your right, earned a hundred times over. But we all need help sometimes. Now, do what I bloody said. That's an order!"

"Yes, Captain," he said, wearily.

"There you have it. Good luck with Calegg, guys," I said, standing up. "Now, I'm gonna catch some zeds."

Ember stood with me. "See you all in a few hours," she smiled and waved, and we went to our room.

"What a day!" I said as I fell to the bed. I had no intention of getting undressed, showered or anything.

"Yup. It's been yet another epic one." She got into bed alongside me, draping her arm over my shoulders. You aced it today. It's amazing to see you grow and find your way to making the right decisions, with barely a clue as to what you're doing. You're the best fucking mascot a mercenary army with delusions of grandeur could ever wish for."

We both chuckled at the ridiculousness of it all, falling into a comfortable silence, swiftly followed by sleep.

C13
Waiting Game

When we awoke the next day – although in our current existence, day and night literally meant sweet fuck all – Ember and I went to the bridge. I was relieved to see Calegg had gone to bed, as had Koparr. I was also impressed to see all of the weapon stations were fully manned by either Torax or Veiletian crew members. It was a strange feeling; I felt really proud to have a full bridge.

I noticed only Hwista and Acclo were on the bridge. The other two must have gone to rest in order to swap over. Made good sense. Acclo saw us first and came over. "Captain, as we have more crew members, I took it upon myself to allocate people to positions. Elyek can make any necessary adjustments when they return, but here is what I propose. Hwista there is piloting the ship. They're excellent, much more accomplished than me. I'll be good enough in a pinch; I am a fast learner. In the meantime, I am acting as they copilot using the next workstation, which is purpose-built for the task."

"Cool. I saw Elyek over there quite a few times. That explains it."

"It does, yes. I have made sure all of our weapon stations are manned, as we have many enemies. We are heading into dangerous territory, are we not?"

"Yip, we are. Totally agree with your foresight," I replied.

"There are various simulations that the weapon users can run through. They are like games. Miraek found them hidden away and has ensured they are accessible with ease, so now on-duty weapon operators can practice with these tools.

"With your permission, we will run nine-hour-shifts on all systems. Although I believe Calegg will be piloting for 18 hours. Correct?"

"Correct." I replied.

Acclo leaned in conspiratorially. "Hwista is a far superior pilot."

"Funny story, Acclo. Elyek has the greater expertise, and yet Calegg remains our chief pilot. Maybe while you're all co-piloting, you could iron him out a little."

Acclo gave me a confused look. "Shouldn't we have the best people for the job?"

"Once upon a time Ember and I were stranded alone on a planet, no money, no friends, no pilot.

"Calegg was a ship engineer who could fly a little. He got us off the planet, and has managed to save us a few times since. He is solid, reliable and a founding member of the Uprising. As such, he'll be given the respect he deserves."

"I can see why you are keeping him as pilot. Although I disagree with your decision, I appreciate the loyalty you have shown to your comrades. On reflection, I think it means more." Acclo paused, looking as though they were processing something. "I find I agree with your decision after all. I will make sure Hwista and the others support Calegg as much as possible. It does bring up another matter, the engineering terminal. Some of the Veiletians with us are competent engineers and should be of use. However, Calegg also operates that terminal while piloting. Although that may have been your only option prior to our arrival, it seems foolhardy for Calegg to continue being stretched too thin. I hope you don't mind, but I have set up a roster system that covers all of the positions on the ship. I have not filled in every position, as I am aware that we may have more Veiletians coming on board."

"More humans too, potentially," I informed them.

"More humans?" Acclo said, cocking their head to one side.

"Sure, like me and Ember. We're going to bring some of them onto the Uprising from the Thoth and Seshat, and possibly put a few Torax and Veiletians on each of those in return. Providing people are happy to go of course; no one has to go anywhere they don't want to. We just felt it would benefit each ship to have a diverse crew, and to appreciate what each race has to offer."

"Yes, this does make sense." A look of concern crossed their face. "The four of us who came to the bridge won't be going anywhere?"

"No. I'm more than happy to keep you guys here. I'm thinking, maybe the others who are not as emotionally tied to the ship are gonna be amenable to moving ships?"

"Yes. I'm sure they will be fine with that, provided they are treated as fairly and respectfully as they would be here."

"You make a valid point about how people are treated. I know for a fact there are some knob-heads among the humans. However, I'll give the ships' captains explicit instructions to ensure your people are treated well. I'll also ask you to liaise with the others of your race to get a feel for how they're received. Let me know if there are any problems and I will fix them."

"That is good to know, but there is only so much even you could do. You don't operate capital punishment, do you?"

I laughed. "Good god, no. But let's just say I fucking despise bullies. Understand one thing, the Uprising is about standing up to bullies. Anyone caught abusing their place will be given the same treatment they see fit to dish out."

"I hope that is true. I have seen many abuse their power, and it has been ignored by those above them."

"I can only act if I know about it. As long as I'm made aware, I'll deal with the issues that arise, personally."

"I'll take you at your word, Captain," Acclo said, half-bowing.

"You should too," Ember said from my side. She'd been unusually quiet until this point. "This lunk once ruined his entire life to stop someone being bullied, yet he still seems to have made it his calling. Some people never learn," she smirked.

"I think I have seen and heard enough to put my trust in Captain Shaun," Acclo replied.

Ember nodded, and continued to talk. "I'm really impressed with you making a roster for our bridge crew. The further we go, the more we are going to need full-time weapon coverage. I'm particularly interested in this game," she grinned, and I did too.

"Yeah. That sounds kinda cool. I might have to give that a blast myself."

"Yes. The roster should help greatly. We can change things around until we set off to our destination. If you are happy with the plans that I have laid out." Acclo sad.

"It's more Elyek you'll have to persuade. They and Calegg have been responsible for running most of the ship's functions. We just step in when they're overworking themselves. However, things have changed a lot in a short space of time," I said.

"They really have," Ember added. "And while Elyek would have addressed these issues in time, you have already done so much to help in their absence. We'll discuss it with them when they get back aboard. But I think that they will agree that you are perfect to oversee the logistics of Uprising."

Acclo blushed, replying, "I would love to be involved in anything along those lines. I love prioritizing and organizing things perfectly. It's a fascination of mine."

A thought sprung to my mind when they said that, but I buried it for now. I couldn't see how it would work, and it might be cheating. Acclo interrupted my thought process. "You really need to address the Calegg problem soon. He is presently doing 18-hour shifts to cover the two disciplines. There is no need for him to multitask the work of four people every day."

"Ha! I agree he needs to choose pilot or engineer. Still, we should let him continue the 18-hour shifts. I think he'd be heartbroken to have that taken away from him; he loves it," I said.

"Yeah. I agree he needs to choose. Though it sucks to be you, to be the one to tell him," Ember smirked.

"Well, actually, I felt like it was more your job. I'm terribly busy at the moment and, well, you hired him," I said with a smirk of my own.

"You're a real asshat, Shaun. I'll tell him what you've decided, and that you were too cowardly to tell him to his face."

I was about to retort, but Acclo spoke before I had a chance, and it was possibly just as well.

"I'll be happy to speak to him as I'll be potentially taking more of a role in the organizational structure of the Uprising."

"No," Ember said firmly, "it really should fall to me. I foisted any responsibility for this whole thing onto Shaun, so I suppose I should get my hands dirty with this. Plus you're right, he needs to reduce his workload. I'll speak to him."

"Oh, so you can answer reasonably when Acclo says something, yet act like a total fruit loop when I say anything."

"Yeah, well. I like Acclo."

"What's that supposed to mean?" I said, getting ever-more agitated.

She gave me a long, dangerous look, "I love you, you fuckwit. It makes everything much more… *murky*."

I didn't even know how to respond to that. I was happy that she said she loved me, nevertheless there were serious layers of confusion added to that statement. So I said nothing. Acclo saved me from answering, or from more awkward silence. "Would you like to see the roster, in case you feel any changes should be made?"

"Yeah. I'd like a look at what you've done, Acclo. Show me," Ember said, and they both walked over to the co-pilot monitor.

Feeling slightly relieved, I decided to have a walk around and talk to everyone on the bridge. I needed to build some bonds with these people, or this whole thing wouldn't work.

I approached a Torax who was engrossed in his screen, running through a simulation. He was moving in his chair, trying to personally dodge the incoming imaginary missiles.

"Looks fun," I said, leaning over. "Do you think it will

help?"

"Definitely. It's amazing!" Then he turned his attention to me with a big grin. "And intense!"

I knew I wouldn't get much convo out of him, so with a pat on his back, I wandered off to do the rounds with the rest of the seated crew members.

Once I'd talked to everyone, or at least made some kind of connection, I sat in the captain's chair. I still had a serious case of imposter syndrome, but you know what they say: 'fake it 'til you make it'. I wasn't dwelling in self-doubt: I knew I could fight, I knew I was near immortal, and with Havok I was all but invincible. I had some sweet powers on my own account, too. But even so, I had nagging doubts that I should be leading anyone. Fuck, I could barely lead myself. Yet it seemed to be working so far.

I resolved to just trust in the people around me and do the one thing I knew I could do, and wanted to do with all my heart and soul: to make sure everyone was okay and treated with respect, whether they were smaller, weaker or simply different. That was the reason I stayed as captain. I might not be able to do all the high-tech shit, or any of the other stuff, but I could, and damn well would, look after all these people. I had some serious powers now, and that is what I would use them for. Give a man a fish, and you can feed him for a day. Teach him how to fish, and you can feed him until some fucker takes his fish off him. That's where I come in to smash the shit out of his oppressors and give him half a chance.

I was relieved when Ember came and sat in her seat next to me. She nodded in Acclo's direction, who had already gone back to man the copilot terminal. "One clever fucker, right there. They must be exhausted after yesterday, and they've literally organized every last person on the ship, including strengths and aspirations."

"Seriously?"

"Seriously, Shaun. I don't even think it's to get in our good books. I think they're just obsessive as fuck about ordering things."

"Sounds like a real boon. How do you think Elyek will take it?"

"I think they'll be fine, to be honest. We've put a lot on their shoulders, so hopefully it'll be a welcome relief. I'm sure the bigger we become, the more we'll all have to do."

"Yeah, I hear you on that. Luckily, we're surrounding ourselves with pretty decent folk."

"Plus, I actually feel like I can learn now! That Mental Clarity shit was a real handicap."

"Especially for you," Ember nudged me. "We should probably do some inventory, Shaun. Every little counts."

"I was thinking earlier, I wish I could put Acclo in my head to do my inventory. They'd have it done in a day, I reckon."

"Nice theory, but they wouldn't have a Scooby Doo where to put anything, would they? They're your memories, dumbass."

"Ah, yeah! You make a good point. Shall we go somewhere more private then?"

"How about, fuck inventory, and practice levitating instead? Not really had a chance to try it out since we updated our vision," she replied.

"You know what, that actually sounds fun."

We both stood up. For some reason I found myself telling Acclo where we were going, then we popped out to train while we waited for the other ships.

Once in the gymnasium, Ember sprinted off as soon as we went through the doors. She leapt into the air and kept on rising and rising, moving upwards and forwards at an impressive rate. I followed her and did the same. It was exhilarating to say the least. She came to a halt and turned around, grinning like a Cheshire cat. "This is fucking sweet, Shaun," she said, breathlessly.

"Yes, it is," I said, gliding up alongside her. As soon as I spoke, I dropped altitude quickly, before I righted myself.

She dropped down towards me. "Nice loss of control, Shaun."

"Yeah. It takes a lot to move forward and upward at the same time. Talking as well isn't a good combo."

"I know what you're saying. I don't know if it's a Clarity thing or a practice thing. Either way, give it another month and we'll have it sorted out. We've promised a lot of people a lot of things. We're going to have to be on our A game."

"Oh wow, Ember. Way to fill someone with self-doubt."

"Get over yourself, Shaun. You signed up for this with me. Don't go start being a drama queen. We're doing this. Now, come on motherfucker. Let's fly." She zoomed off, downwards and ahead, before levelling out and going in a slight arc to fly around in circles. I followed her and managed the same maneuver, just executed in a more ungainly fashion. We spent a few hours flying around. No other training at all, just whizzing around laughing and having fun. It distracted me from the knot in my stomach about Elyek and the two ships.

When the call came in saying that the ships had appeared, my relief was palpable.

C14

Shake it Up

The Thoth and Seshat had appeared close to where we were, and it felt good to be together again. There was a certain amount of comfort brought by the extra protection.

We wasted no time in setting up a video link once they were in range. Ember and I sat in anticipation in our quarters, waiting for the other two captains to pop up on the screen.

To my immense relief, Elyek was with Astrid, which kinda fucked my flow up a little, because my first question was going to be, 'Did you get Elyek?'.

"Elyek! Thank god you're okay!" Ember all but shouted, then said to Astrid, "Well done for getting them out. Was there much trouble?"

"No, none at all. I know you love your ship and all, but you might want to consider changing it. It seems to be becoming quite recognizable," Astrid replied.

"Yeah. It's looking like it might be necessary," Ember said.

Elyek cut in. "Perhaps it is not. I am sure we can rename her and change the registration number a little to throw our pursuers off."

"You can do that?" I asked.

"Well, hacking systems just so happens to be a specialty of mine, in case you forgot."

"No, I didn't. And I'd much prefer to do what you're suggesting, rather than change the ship. I'm quite attached to the Uprising."

"I'll get straight onto it when I come over," Elyek assured me.

"I look forward to having you back," I replied. "While we're on the subject of transferring Elyek back, I wanted to talk to you all about mixing our crews up: spreading the Torax and Veiletians across the three ships and bringing some humans onto the Uprising. Only those who wish to come and go of course, we won't be forcing anyone."

Both Astrid and Rufus looked uncertain at what I was saying, which annoyed me a little. Especially since one of Acclo's concerns was how they'd be treated on the other ships. Before either of them could respond, I continued talking. "I'm aware not everyone is as well-mannered as we all are on our ships," I said pointedly, looking at each of them in turn. "So I'm asking you to keep an extra close eye on any xenophobia that floats to the surface."

"Why do we need to spread people around?" Rufus asked, confusion clouding his face.

"Do you have a problem already, Rufus?" I asked, a little bit of anger touching my voice.

"No!" he replied quickly, "I just wanted to understand the thinking. We've built a pretty tight-knit team over here. Seems counter-productive to disrupt that."

"We're trying to expand our army, Rufus, and we're heading into a war zone. As strong as you may think your crew is, do you have any members who are naturally resistant to laser-fire? Or shoot fireballs? Or even fucking explode, doing massive area of effect damage? Do you have any members who understand all of this Galactic Empire technology in depth and can hack their systems? Oh and let's not forget, turn invisible? Now before you answer, don't; those were rhetorical questions. You don't have any of those skills, and though you can survive without them, you can thrive with them."

Ember clapped, and Astrid and Elyek joined in. Seems my impromptu little speech was well received by them at least.

Rufus looked suitably chagrined. "Okay. You make a very good point."

"Thank you. Now, I really want you to ask who's willing to come over to the Uprising. I don't expect masses to flock over because *apparently* I'm not well liked, but hopefully a few will want to."

"Not well liked, Shaun? You're damn-near worshiped. We'll be fighting them to stay," Rufus said.

"Oh? Genuinely, that's surprising. If that's the case, I'll let you both be the judge of who's the best to send over. We should try to balance all our numbers out in terms of supplies and fighting capabilities. If anyone has any ideas on the best way to transport people between the ships, I'm all ears. For now, keep in touch, and good luck organizing people's preferred placements."

"While it's certainly going to be odd having new crew members, it will definitely shake things up a little," Astrid said. "I'll put the word out for people who might wish to come over to you. I've a feeling I'm going to lose Mick and Gus in this, and that will leave us without our best technology expert."

"Some of my people will be more than up to the task of filling in for Gus," Elyek interjected.

"I'd second that. The four who helped us with the folding drive were amazing."

"I look forward to having their expertise on board," Astrid smiled.

"I'll see if the Veiletians here with me would be happy to either stay or move over to the Seshat," Elyek said.

"That's great. We've four Veiletians here who'll definitely be staying, but I'll make the offer of transfer to the other seven. We want, what? Eight Veiletians on each ship? I'll speak to the Torax, too. But I won't be a dick about it."

"This I have got to see," Ember added.

"What?"

"You not being a dick," she grinned.

"Thanks, Ember. Anyway, moving on. Tell me what and where this new contract is."

Rufus got excited now. "Yes! I've managed to negotiate an excellent deal. Although the job is far away, we will be paid handsomely. We are traveling to the Perseus system. There is a space station, Beler 3103, that is under attack from some sort of rebels. They were unclear on the exact details, but the long and short of it is that they're assembling a fleet to retake the station and then defend it."

"Rebels? Sounds interesting. I wonder who's rebelling?" I said.

"It's more than likely just a territorial dispute between two different races. The Empire must be taking a side in the conflict. It is not uncommon," explained Elyek.

"It's a job at least. How much are we being paid?" Ember asked.

"Ten thousand per fully-manned ship, per week," Rufus replied proudly.

"Ten thousand?" Ember said. "That's not great."

"Not great! It took a lot of negotiating to bring them up to that number," Rufus said, outraged.

"If I may speak," Elyek interrupted, then continued on anyway. "Considering the distance to the Perseus system and the high potential for damage to our ships, ten thousand is on the low side."

Rufus began to bluster. I could see his face going red with embarrassment.

"However," Elyek added, "as a new, unheard of mercenary group, we would never be offered a decent rate. Not until we had proven our worth and have recommendations. Luckily, we have enough senlars to cover any damages, so we can afford to do this. Nonetheless, we should be careful to protect our assets."

"Fair enough," Ember said, "I suppose the main point in doing this is to build the Uprising's profile and attract more members, so well done, Rufus."

"Um, thanks," he answered with uncertainty.

"Yeah, good job," I added, "We have a clear plan, so all's good."

"If that's everything, we should get on with sorting out our crew numbers and getting moving. We've sat here long enough," Ember said, pushing things along.

"Ah, just one more thing," Astrid said, sheepishly.

"Yes, Astrid?" My curiosity piqued.

"We're in a really dangerous position out here; outnumbered and outgunned. I could do with your help."

"What the fuck are you talking about, Astrid?" Ember answered. "We're helping you!"

I noticed Rufus had perked up and was looking extremely interested in what Astrid was asking for.

Astrid's face clouded in anger. "I want to fucking transcend!" she shouted, taking us all by surprise. I don't think I'd ever heard her swear.

"I don't know how you both did it, but I'm *begging* you to show me. I worked under Ogun for so long and never felt like I was getting any closer, like he was almost hiding the secret from me... us. But he's gone now, and our people need to become stronger. Can you teach me?"

She was so desperate, and I could tell Rufus was begging to ask the same question too, only the intensity of the situation held him back.

I looked at Ember, who looked at me. We both had stern expressions on our faces. She winked at me on the side that couldn't be seen by the video screen, then turned back. "I'm really sorry," she said to the desperate Astrid, "we think it's just too much power for you."

"What?" Astrid said in deflated disbelief, "But..."

"I mean, what if your head explodes?" I jumped in before she could say any more, a serious expression on my face. "It can happen you know."

Rufus had a downcast expression now, "Really? How?"

"Ha, ha! Your fucking faces," Ember laughed, "Of course we'll help you to transcend!"

"Ideally, we want all the humans with us to transcend, if they can," I added, laughing along.

"You pair of shitheads," Astrid huffed, but she had a wry smile, too, "I'll be coming over when we ferry crew around between the ships, *so prepare yourselves.*"

"Yes, sir," I said, saluting Astrid, who just beamed.

"I'll come as well?" Rufus said, but phrased it as a question.

"Of course, mate. Hopefully, what I did with Ember will work for you guys. If it does, you can try to transcend the rest of the crew on your ships, if you think they're ready."

"Start with those who achieved the highest level in Anatoli though, and work your way down through the ranks," Ember added. "From what Ogun indicated to us in the past, we don't even know if someone who made it to level 21 would be able to transcend. We don't want to lose anyone by being over eager."

"That makes sense," Astrid replied, regaining her usual composed demeanor.

"Okay then guys. It'll be nice to meet face-to-face again when you come over. See you all soon," I said with a wave. Unfortunately, I didn't know how to turn the damn thing off. We sat there awkwardly for a few seconds longer, waiting while Elyek broke the link.

After the meeting we went to find Acclo and Koparr. It wasn't hard. They were both on the bridge as usual, Acclo scrolling through a data pad, Koparr on the shooting simulation.

"Acclo, Koparr, a word please!" I shouted over. There was a lot of chatter on the bridge, it reminded me almost of a diner's atmosphere, and more than a few people had a coffee with them. The Uprising even provided coffee holders at the various workstations. Now there's something you don't see in the sci-fi movies.

"Yes, Captain!" they replied loudly, coming straight over.

"I need you to speak to the other Torax and Veiletians onboard and offer them the opportunity to work on the other ships. We're spreading everyone around a bit, so we've got more multi-skilled crews on board all ships."

"Yes, of course. Leave it to me. I will speak to the Veiletians and I will coordinate with Elyek to arrange the transfers."

"Acclo, you're a star," I patted them on the shoulder

with a small bow. They left to continue their tasks. I looked to the still silent Koparr. "Everything okay, dude?"

"This may be difficult. We should find Calparr first. He's training the men. He'll be better equipped to deliver the news, or at the very least, keep them all in line should they start complaining."

"What? You don't think I can keep them in line?"

"Nah, Captain. You're too nice," he replied, then added, "Except when you're not."

"I don't even know what that means, Koparr."

A smile was all I received in answer. We found Calparr training in the gym with four other Torax. "Hey, Cal," Koparr shouted.

He stopped what he was doing and walked over to us. "What can I do for you two?"

I sighed inside a little, having to go through it again. "I want to spread out the Torax and Veiletians across the three ships, and I also want to bring more humans on to the Uprising. We all have vastly different skill-sets and abilities. I think we'll work better together if we mix ourselves up a bit. Can you help out by asking anyone if they're interested?"

"No. I can't help with that, but I can help with the problem."

Koparr laughed. "Yeah, Calparr. Whatever you think best."

"I don't get it?" I said, baffled. "What are we talking about here?"

Calparr explained: "Our people will not choose to leave here, they've no reason to go. They're happy, comfortable and fought in two space battles and survived. However, what you're proposing is to spread our abilities and expertise among the ships of the Uprising. There-fore, it's not a matter of if they want it, it is a matter of telling them they will go!"

"Hey Calparr, I don't wanna force people to do things they don't want to do."

"You are not forcing anyone, Captain Shaun. You're giving the soldiers of the Uprising an order to go and serve on another vessel for the betterment of us all. If you intend to conquer the galaxy, you must learn to make these decisions."

I groaned. "I don't actually want to conquer the galaxy. I just want to right the balance a little. Even so, I suppose you're right."

"Yes, I am," Calparr said.

"Yes, he is," agreed Koparr.

"Okay. Fuck it then! Calparr, Koparr, you pair of wankers. Will you pick balanced teams of Torax for each ship please? And I think I'm just gonna delegate this task outright, because I'm sick of you smart-arsed fuckers."

They both started to laugh at me. "Of course, Captain," they said almost in unison.

"One more thing, Captain," Calparr added. "I'll lead a group on one of the other ships. Koparr is more than capable of taking my place here. We'll need training and knowledge of the command structure on both the Thoth and the Seshat."

"Really? But I was just getting to like you, Calparr," I said, jokingly.

"You can still get to like me, Captain. Give me a call if you ever need advice on leading men again."

"I'm sure you weren't this much of a prick when we were on that fucking moon!"

"I'm growing into my role, Captain," he said with a

smug expression.

"I'll be sorry to see you go, Calparr. But I won't lie, I'll be glad to know you're looking out for our crew on whichever ship you go to."

"Everything will be fine, just as long as we receive the same treatment and respect we have here."

"Of course. You will. I'll tell you the same thing I told Acclo: if there's any discrimination, let me know directly as soon as you can. I'll make sure I've a direct link with you, so any problems that come up can be dealt with quickly."

"That is enough for me. I have trust in you at least, Captain, and Ember of course. I believe with all my heart that you would protect our best interests. It is an honor to serve under you." Then he bowed.

I didn't have a clue what the fuck to do, so I patted him on the back. "It's an honor to have you with us, Calparr. I feel really blessed. Now, I'm gonna fuck off before this gets weird. I'll see you before you go, Calparr."

I extracted myself from the gym and went to have a shower. I didn't need one, but I could really do with the stress release before we started shipping people around.

C15
Sharing is Caring

After my shower, I found Ember chilling on the bed. She was talking to Acclo and Calparr.

I was not expecting company after my beautiful, hour-long shower. My suit was on the bed. Ember was half lying on it. By the smirk she gave me, she knew it, too. I poked my head out the bathroom door, said hello to the two guests, then said to Ember, "Hi, dear. Would you pass me my clothes, please?"

With a wry grin, she threw my suit at me and continued talking. I quickly got dressed and went out to join them. "Ah! The hide and seek champion 2025 has finally joined us," Ember declared. "While you've been hiding in there, all transport between the ships has been arranged. That crew that'll be transferring has been finalized."

"Cool, cool. So, when's everyone moving?"

"We can do it straight away. We only need to anchor the ships together. If we do this, we can fire our outward-facing weapons, but otherwise we'll be sitting ducks for an hour or so. For some weird fucking reason we decided to wait to run it by you."

"Oh, right. What do you guys all think? Anchor, or wait until we can land?"

"Anchor. We'll be more vulnerable on a planet," Calparr said.

"Agreed," Acclo added.

Ember looked up at me from the bed, "I'll bow down to the man who had 5 out of 1000 Wisdom not so long ago for his answer. Because I know he's got a hidden jammy-bastard stat somewhere that's at 1000."

"Very funny, Ember. I'll bow down to the knowledge of my trusted advisors. Let's shake this shit up."

Acclo spoke into a comm on their wrist. "Commence anchors!"

And that was it. Everything went like a well-oiled machine, and I had to do sweet fuck all, other than say, 'Yes, we'll do anchors'. I could get used to this kind of life. I then cursed myself for even thinking that thought: Sod's law states everything is due to go horribly wrong any second now.

Calparr left to get his men ready, while we made our way to the bridge – more for appearances than anything else. We waited for the people to start flowing between ships before moving to the room next to the loading bay. It was going to be a bit of a fart on, in all honesty. The landing craft shuttles could only handle eight people at a time. It must have looked flippin' mental to any ships driving by.

I didn't actually know which humans were coming. But two things surprised me as they arrived. The first was that they were all wearing fancy green suits with black and gold detail. I had to admit that I liked them a lot, and they set us apart from the Fystr.

The second thing that surprised me was the arrival of Roger, formerly known as Thor, on the Uprising. My interest was insatiable, so I walked up to the big man. "I've just gotta know why?" I asked.

He shrugged. "Hey man. You may not realize this, but

there are only so many times someone can kick your arse and prove you wrong before you have a choice to make. I could easily hate you for embarrassing me, repeatedly. Especially when you suddenly reappear from the fucking grave in an amazing ship full of OP aliens. Oh, and a ton of money. Or I could give in to the fact that you're actually an impressive guy. I could learn a lot from you." He went red when he said it; nonetheless, he seemed sincere.

"Well, I'm glad to have you here *if* you want to be here. It's gonna be an intense undertaking building Uprising up."

"We'll do it. With you leading us, I'm sure we will. Ogun did a lot for us, but he really let us all down when he left, you know? Lucky for us, you came along when you did, 'cause we were dying on our asses out there."

"Thanks, dude. I hope that's what I've done. Get settled into your room and get yourself some food from the FSU. It's much better than the Thoth's: everything tastes awesome," I nodded.

"Really?" He beamed and wandered off.

Gus and Mick's arrival was a real moment: we'd bonded a lot with these two in our short time together. A massive group hug ensued with Ember, me and the two men. No one else was invited to the hug; we had been through some shit together.

"Sorry we left you. We didn't feel like we'd any choice at the time. Looking back on it, we were wrong. We should've stayed."

"Hey, guys. You did what you could. If I blame anyone, it's Ogun."

"Don't be too hard on him, Shaun. He took losing you both really hard. I genuinely think he may have left to go find you both, or at least confirm if you were dead," Mick replied.

"Let's not get into it again. I'll take your word for it, and I do feel kinda bad for talking shit about him. Plus, you did lead the Fystr away, so we were able to escape. I suppose I'll have to lessen my annoyance at being left behind."

"Well, you were certainly doing better than us when we met. So I think it may have been for the best that we split up for a bit, in a really fucked up kinda way," Mick said.

"Yeah, we did okay, I suppose," I replied, strangely accepting his logic.

"Shit and roses, Mick. Shit and roses! Cling on to this big, daft fucker and you'll never go far wrong," Ember chuckled.

"Yeah, I can see that." He raised an eyebrow, looking around at our spanking new ship.

"Did I hear the FSU here tastes like real food? 'Cos that's the only reason we came," Gus said. They were essentially the first words he'd spoken.

The three of us started laughing our asses off at him. He may have had Asperger's once, but that should've been healed. I was beginning to think that perhaps Asperger's wasn't a disability at all, just a different way of being. "It's awesome, Gus," I replied. "Only first go and see Acclo for your rooms. There's bigger ones for couples, so let them know." I pointed towards the industrious Acclo.

"Will do, Captain. Pleasure to be aboard." Gus saluted, and Mick gave his usual chilled grin. They toddled off, then I went through a procession of greeting the 50 or so new inhabitants of Uprising.

It was odd to be among humans again, and I thought I should make an effort with everyone this time around.

I wanted a close-knit crew, with no fuckheads fucking things up, like Roger. Despite the flowery words, I'd be watching that motherfucker like a hawk. By the time the meet and greet was done, I found myself oddly exhausted. In the last ship from the Thoth came Elyek and Astrid.

It had only been a few days, but boy was I glad to have Elyek back. I was more excited to see them than I was Astrid. After Ember, Elyek was the solid rock in the Uprising that held me up. Although to be fair, Acclo was quickly ingratiating themselves into an important position. I didn't mind; in fact, I was very impressed with them. I would have to speak to Elyek about their role, I didn't want them to step on Elyek's toes.

Group hug, round two ensued. "Elyek! It's so good to get you back," I cheered. "Once you're settled, I'll need to cover some things with you. First, we just have a few things to go over with Astrid and Rufus first."

"Sure, I'll be around. Just give me a shout on my comm when you're finished. Astrid's great by the way, I really like her. I thought all humans would be like you two, but none of them are. In fact, I would say you two are real anomalies in your race."

"Yeah. Well, Shaun is a serious fucking anomaly, to be honest," Ember laughed.

"Ha! And Ember's a sharp-tongued shithead."

Elyek grinned. "I love how you're different. Who would have thought it was possible to make insults the language of love?"

"It's a strange skill Ember has; I'll give you that."

Ember punched me on the arm.

Next, we made our way over to Astrid and Rufus, who were waiting expectantly. I thought about a hug, but then decided against it; we weren't on that friendly of terms. Astrid and Ember hugged, and that was enough. "Right, you two," I greeted them, "welcome to the Uprising."

"Thanks for having us over," Astrid replied, smiling. I definitely sensed nerves from her: she must have been worried about the whole transcendence carry-on. She continued, "We've brought uniforms for everyone on the Uprising. The Torax uniforms, so I've been told, have exponentially more fireproof fibers woven into them. Gerome believes their suits will be able to withstand the heat they create. Any damage should self-heal, too."

"That's some great work. Will you thank Gerome for us?" Ember said.

"Yeah. He's done good," I added.

"Of course I will. He'll enjoy the praise, I've no doubt."

I noticed Rufus looking a bit forlorn. "You okay, dude?" I asked.

"Yeah. It's a beautiful ship. How did you come buy it?"

"We bought it," I answered flatly. We had already covered this story during our first meeting. Rufus could be a doofus at times. "Come on. Let's get settled in the office and we can go through this whole transcending business."

"I can't actually believe you're going to help us transcend," Astrid said, excitedly.

"It's a piece of cake, really, I don't know why Ogun held you all back so much," Ember answered.

"He seemed to view the whole process with great reverence. Maybe it was a cultural thing he couldn't let go of," Astrid replied.

"I think he was full of shit to be honest. But never mind, we're going to fix that now," I added.

We entered the captain's office from the main corridor. It was great not having to go through the bridge, and I imagine crew members wanting to visit the captain would prefer not having to trudge through a load of people at their workstations.

"Alright guys, take a seat," Ember began. "Shaun will talk you through everything."

"I will?"

"Sure Shaun. You pulled me through, didn't you?"

"Well, yeah. Except, you've got like 63% wisdom, compared to my poxy 34%, and you always tell me I can't do everything by myself. We're a team, right?"

"Fair enough," Ember said with a smile, then turned to the two seated captains.

"Okay. So both me and Shaun felt like there was a curtain of darkness over us when we entered our minds. Do you know what I mean by this?" Ember asked.

"I do, indeed," Astrid said.

Rufus nodded in agreement.

"Well, let's lift that veil. I'm gonna enter your head, Astrid. Your mental representation will be sitting in a chair in your Control Room with its eyes closed. I'm gonna go in and take your hand, then I'll ask you to open your eyes. You need to concentrate on my hand; that's your link to the Mindscape. Don't let go. Don't even think about letting go. If you do, I can't promise you we'll ever recover your mind." She stared at Astrid intensely, who returned the look with a worried but determined expression.

"I can do that, although I've a natural fear. Can you both come in and take a hand each? I don't know why, but I'd feel better about the whole thing."

"Sure we can," I replied.

"Okay then," Astrid said, exhaling deeply, "do it."

Ember and I both entered Astrid's Control Room, and there she was, sitting calmly.

"Hey, Astrid. We're both here. We're going to take a hand each now. It'll feel weird, but just focus on it being our hands," Ember said as we both took a hand.

"I can feel it," Astrid gasped, "but it feels nothing like hands."

"Yeah, that's where your imagination comes in, Astrid," Ember said a little abruptly, I thought.

"I don't really know what you mean, but I'll try."

"Well, that's it. That's all I've got for you. You can either imagine the sensation being our hands, or not. If you can't, then I don't know how to help you," Ember replied.

Astrid fell silent. After a while she spoke again, almost pleadingly. "I just can't do it, guys. Is there another way?"

"No. This is the only way we know," Ember said, but I had a different idea.

"Raaaar!" I shouted at the absolute top of my voice and squeezed Astrid's hand as I did it. The result was dramatic; Ember jumped out of her skin and immediately started shouting and screaming at me for being an absolute prick. Astrid opened her eyes, blinking rapidly in panic. I stayed calm and held her hand firm. Ember quickly grabbed her other hand again, still cursing at me, while Astrid began flickering. Just like Ember had before.

"Okay, Astrid. Stay calm. You're in your Mindscape and everything is fine," I said, soothingly.

"Yeah, Astrid. We're here to help you. Come on," Ember added.

The flickering intensified, and we both held her tighter in our group hug, until finally she began to settle down. " Wow! That was insane!" she said, exhausted.

"You did it, though. You transcended, thanks to this absolute ass," she turned to me. "You could've warned me. I nearly jumped out of my bloody skin."

"That's kinda the point, Ember. Anyway, it worked, and we've another thing we can try going forward."

"Oh, guys! This is amazing. It's all I've wanted since I came out of Anatoli. I've finally leveled up."

"Do you know already?" I asked puzzled.

"Know what?"

"About the stats," I stated.

"What stats? What do you mean?"

"Never mind. Come on, back out of your Mindscape and we'll go and transcend Rufus."

"I want to explore," she said almost petulantly.

"No," I said, firmly. "We need to get moving. I don't want to explain everything twice. Rufus first, then we'll show you everything you need to know – that *we* know, at least. Obviously there's lots we don't know yet, but Ogun drip fed us information when it could have all been so much easier. Now let's go."

We all entered our normal state and looked to Rufus like a pack of wolves staring at a deer. "Okay, Rufus." I eyeballed him with mock seriousness. "You're up! Astrid is done."

"Excellent. Hit me with it."

"You okay if Astrid comes in? We need to walk you both through a few things, and it'll be better to only do it once."

"Why not? The more the merrier. My mind is gonna be like party central."

"Yeah, man. It's going to be great!" I said, before turning to the others. "Now, the same script as before. Yeah?"

"Sure," both women said, grins stretching across their

faces. With a nod from me, we all entered Rufus's Mindscape, meeting Astrid in the corridor. "Wow! What is with the corridor?" she asked.

"It holds all the rooms in your mind. Once you're a bit more experienced, you can appear directly in the room you want to be in," Ember answered.

"That's amazing, and interesting. I can't wait to study this place."

"Yup, it is. But shall we go and wake Rufus up?" Ember said.

"Of course we should. Lead the way." Astrid said, still looking around in wonder.

Rufus broke through the barrier to transcend pretty quickly: probably because I brought my shock tactic into play a lot earlier in the proceedings. He also stabilized quicker, and the general consensus was that it was down to having three people involved. Worth thinking about for people in the future.

"Okay, Rufus. Any dark secrets I need to know about?"

"Uh, not since therapy, no," he chuckled, and looked uncomfortable.

"So, are you okay if we use your mind as a walk-through?"

"Yeah, sure, why not?"

"Ember, would you like to do the honors?" I asked her.

"Might as well. Okay, guys. This is your Cognition Room. This is where you operate from, when you're outside your body. That screen next to the chair displays all the thought images you process. You can use it as a lie detector. It's cool."

"How?" Astrid asked.

"Simple. If a person says one thing and thinks another, lie. Boom! Simple. You'll work it out. Just as long as you know the basics, which we never did, for far too long. Come on. Next room," she said, abruptly.

As we walked out into the corridor, Astrid and Rufus looked around, awe-struck. It was hard to remember just how awesome these places were when you had spent so much time in them. "Okay. While we're in the corridor, you should know there's a bad juju room; it's essentially death to enter. It's filled with all your despair and self-doubt. Don't go in," I said with finality.

"Really? You're taking the piss, right?" Rufus scoffed.

"No, not at all. You'll know what I mean when you come to it, but I'm just letting you know. It isn't hiding the land of milk and honey. It's genuinely bad, according to Ogun. Right, here we are, the Interface Room. Come on in, guys. This is where things get very interesting."

We all piled into Rufus's room. "Okay, guys," said Ember, taking the lead again. "That big screen allows you to navigate and use your telepathy. We were led to believe by Ogun that you had to reach a certain level of ability and Mental Clarity to be able to compartmentalize your mind. This would, in turn, allow you to work from without and within.

"However, Shaun and I very recently discovered you can apparently attain a visual upgrade. We don't exactly know if our increased Mental Clarity allowed for it to happen, but it's something we'll show you how to do once you get your bearings. The most interesting thing about this upgrade is that Ogun evidently didn't know about it. In fact, a large percentage of Fystr didn't know about it."

"You're saying you two just happened to stumble upon this amazing secret that hardly any of the Fystr knew about? How would you even know that? It seems more likely Ogun just hadn't told you yet," Astrid said.

"Ogun only told us how he navigated the Mindscape, which was by his ability to devote part of his mind to the Mindscape while still functioning in normal state. It was Havok who told us that Jotun did it differently and that he'd got the information from one of the Fystr ruling class. Evidently they like to control access to power and knowledge, even for their own people," Ember said, smugly.

"Wait, wait, wait," Rufus jumped in. "That was a lot of information. My main questions are, who is Havok? And who is Jotun?"

Astrid spoke next. "I know of no Havok, but I've heard Jotun's name mentioned before. Was he one of the Fystr? A famous one at that, and you killed him on the supply station?"

"That he was," Ember replied.

"So, who is Havok?" she asked.

"Havok is my axe," I smiled.

"Ah! That was Jotun's axe. Am I correct? Is it alive then?"

"He identifies as male, and he is very much alive, with a very distinct personality of his own. That actually reminds me. Do you have any music from Earth? We really need some."

They both looked at me like I had gone insane. "Yeah," Rufus finally answered, "we've a load of entertainment, so does the Thoth. Music, movies, eBooks, audio books. You name it, we've got it. There's even a few of them that are similar to what we're going through now, believe it or not. I'm reading a fantastic series at the minute called *Cond...*"

"Rufus! Stop prattling on. We need to get on with your

Mindscape tour," Ember snapped.

"Okay," Rufus said, holding his hands out in a conciliatory gesture. "I can send copies of everything over to you."

"Sounds good. I look forward to it," I said, taking some of the heat off Rufus, before continuing about Havok. "So, yeah. Havok doesn't necessarily know a lot, because he freely admits the Fystr are boring and he didn't listen to them too much. But he did know enough to point us in the right direction to get our visual upgrade. It's my thinking that there must be more forcible upgrades like that. We need to keep our minds open to opportunities. There's so much to learn."

"Thank you, Shaun," Ember said, curtly. "Are you ok if I move on with the tour *you* asked me to do?"

"Yeah, of course. Crack on with it," I smiled.

"There are other things you can do here, but what we've discussed covers the main things. Even if you can't do the visual upgrade yet, it'll be good for you both to practice here. Now, if you have a look over at that screen, I think you're gonna be a little surprised."

As one, they turned and looked toward Rufus's stat screen. They moved quickly to moon over it. "Is this for real?" Rufus asked. "This is amazing!"

"It's for real," I replied. "Let's have a look at whatcha got, then."

Name: Rufus Camacho
Age: 35 GY
Transcendence Level: 58
Strength: 80/1000
Agility: 71/1000
Speed: 70/1000

Intelligence: 35/1000
Constitution: 70/1000
Wisdom: 45/1000
Mental Resilience: 40/1000
Mental Clarity: 16%
Potential: 80%

I couldn't deny I was impressed with Rufus's stats. They weren't as good as Ember's or mine, which was possibly a little unfair considering how long he'd been training. I wasn't complaining that I was at a much higher level. I secretly hoped that Astrid would be a lower level, too. I know that it was a petty thought, but... well... nope. I've got nothing. I wanted to be stronger than them.

"Right, you guys. You can moon over your stats later. We must move onward. We've the most important room to go to, and it's the absolute fucking pits. Let's go!" Ember shouted.

We all piled out of the Interface Room, and I had a realization that I was so used to this now that I genuinely felt like I was in some random building, rather than in some random mind.

We arrived at the shit-tip room. I knew it wouldn't be great, because Rufus only had a Clarity of 16%. And to be honest, upon entering, the room looked similar to how it appeared in my mind at first.

"Okay, guys. I'm not gonna beat around the bush. This room is key to your ability to progress and develop in so many areas," Ember said.

"Basically, you've got to clear all this shit up. That's what Ogun told us," I said.

"With the experience of hindsight though, we've found a relatively efficient way to clear it."

"But you won't have Havok's sweet tunes," I chuckled.

"Ignore him and listen closely. Make a path through the junk to those shelves over there. Once there, you need to just start putting things on the shelves as quickly as possible. Once you fill a shelf, it disappears. Keep going until the room is empty."

They looked at us like we were mad. I was about to explain in more detail, but Ember stopped me.

"Look everyone, we need to keep moving. Astrid, Rufus, follow our instructions and you'll do better than we did for the first few months, or do whatever you want and waste your time," she said.

She wasn't wrong. We had given them far more advice than Ogun had given us, and would continue to support them, "Ember's right, guys. Get stuck in. Learn the ropes and we'll talk about it again soon. If you find new and better ways to do things, then pass that information along. We need to work together on this. The Uprising needs to rise up *quickly*."

They both nodded at me, respectfully.

"Thank you so much for showing us this. We've a few people who did very well in Anatoli, so we'll try to bring them through to the Mindscape soon. Hopefully, we can become a true force to be reckoned with," Astrid said.

"Sounds good to us. Just one more thing before, well, before we go our separate ways. Astrid, I wanna see your stats, or you can just tell me them. We need to know where you're at."

"Oh, right. Sure, just come over and see. I wanted to see them myself, like, an hour ago."

"You know what to do, Rufus?" I asked.

"I think? Is it just the same as entering a mind in our normal training?"

"Pretty much, yeah," Ember said.

We all jumped over to Astrid's Mindscape again and went to her Cognition Room.

Name: Astrid Vaughan
Age: 31 GY
Transcendence Level: 60
Strength: 79/1000
Agility: 79/1000
Speed: 75/1000
Intelligence: 49/1000
Constitution: 50/1000
Wisdom: 52/1000
Mental Resilience: 40/1000
Mental Clarity: 22%
Potential: 80%

"What the fuck, Astrid? How is your Mental Clarity so high?" Ember said.

"I don't know." She said, looking puzzled but proud. "I mean, I've always been an extremely careful person, I suppose. Before Anatoli I avoided as many situations as I could where anything unexpected could happen."

"What, like going to watch a horror movie?" I asked.

"I never went to the cinema. I never really left the house."

"What about shopping?" Ember asked.

"I had it delivered to the door, and my mother would deal with the delivery driver."

"Oh, wow. I'm sorry. So, how did you end up in Anatoli? Sorry! You don't have to answer that," Ember said, looking a little embarrassed that she'd pressed Astrid.

"No, it's fine. I'm quite over it now. When I look back

over my life before Ogun and his therapy, it's like I'm watching a TV show.

"Basically, my mother died. I spent two weeks alone in the house with her body. I couldn't bring myself to ring an ambulance, or anything. I just covered her up and tried to carry on as normal. The food ran out after a little while, but I remember not minding too much. I didn't eat a lot anyway, back then. When they found me, I believed I'd gone quite mad.

"I was taken to a hospital and was about to be committed to a mental institute when Ogun appeared and offered me a lifeline. Not that I chose it; I was incapable of choosing anything at that point. He actually worked with me for a month before he put me into Anatoli. I don't think I'd have lasted an hour in there otherwise."

"I guess you feel extra hurt by Ogun disappearing, then," Ember said.

"I really do, though I've a developed the ability to cope with unexpected situations now," she laughed, which I was bloody grateful for, because it had turned morose as fuck for a minute there.

We all came back to our normal states and walked back with Rufus and Astrid to their waiting shuttles. This time we had a group hug. The whole Mindscape tour and the transcending stuff coupled with Astrid's story had pulled us all together. Closer than I would have expected. I realized that Rufus was probably just as fucked-up in the past too, and that I didn't need to compete with the pair of them. We all just needed to grow stronger together to face whatever came our way.

We waved them off, then went to find Elyek.

C16
Six P's

We entered Elyek's quarters and took a seat, and I began what I hoped would be a positive conversation. "Hey, Elyek. One of the Veiletians, Acclo, has made some changes to how things are run around this place. I've warned them that they would only stand until you came back to approve them."

"Okay," Elyek said, raising one eyebrow.

"They've, um, set up a roster for permanent bridge crew, except for a few blank positions to allow a place for newcomers. One of the things they've suggested is that pilot might not be the best role for Calegg, but I've straight away stomped that down. Still, I did agree with Acclo that Calegg shouldn't be covering both posts. Especially since we have a lot of skilled people now."

"Oh, that is fantastic news. I had hoped one of the newcomers would be skilled with logistics. That will take a huge amount of pressure off me, and yes, we need to reduce Calegg's workload. He will not like it, but he does need support. Let him choose of course between engineering or piloting the ship."

"So, you're okay with Acclo taking charge with this?" I asked, surprised.

"Yes, Captain. Only, what will I do? Be Calegg's co-pilot?" Elyek said with a laugh.

"Whatever you want. You'll always be one of the most valuable leaders in the Uprising. You could just hang about the place, causing trouble like me and Ember."

"Sounds like fun! Let's go speak to Calegg. This needs to be addressed immediately in order that we can plan for the rest of the crew."

We all agreed and went off to find Calegg.

He was on the bridge, as always. "Calegg! Old buddy, king of open space, can we have a word in my office?"

He looked over to Elyek, Ember and me and nodded grimly. Saying a few quick words to the Veiletian next to him, he followed us to the captain's office.

Before we could even get a word out, he spoke. "I know, I know. There's much better pilots here than me. At least let me serve as a copilot?"

"What! Calegg, no. You're chief pilot here, and where everyone else has nine-hour shifts, you're the only lucky bastard that gets to pull double."

"Seriously? I thought for sure I was getting a demotion."

"You are dude. Sorry."

Calegg looked confused.

"We need to be the best we can be. You're a founding member. There's four of us, and will only ever be four of us who made this happen. But you do double shifts day in and day out when you don't need to.

"And yes, here comes the boom. You can't be both pilot and engineer. You'll have to choose. We've too many good people who are deserving of jobs. You decide which. We'll give you space, of course, and you'll be in charge of whatever uh… department you settle in."

"Oh, right. I mean, yeah. You're totally right of course. It'd be stupid for me to continue to work 18-hour shifts covering two important posts when there are so many people now. Um, I'll think about it as I work. I'll let you know in a few hours, at most."

"Okay, thanks Calegg. You're still the man!"

He smiled, then headed for the door. When he stopped, he turned around slowly. "Engineering," he said as he finally faced us.

"Really?" I asked, surprised.

"Absolutely. I'll take other responsibilities as you need, but I've to face the truth. Even if Elyek or Hwista trained me, I'll never be as good a pilot as them, and I accept that. Though I do love being in control of the Uprising, and I will miss it."

"Well man, I'm sorry it's a decision that has to be made, I know you love flying this baby," I said, patting the wall I was standing next to.

"Well, my main skills are in engineering. Not to mention the fact that I've nearly exploded about five times when we've had to escape life-and-death situations. I still like to think I'm getting better. One of these days, who knows?" he paused, looking thoughtful. "No. I came on as a ship's mechanic who can fly a bit, and it's what I'm best at. Elyek, I'll happily hand the pilot position over to you."

"Oh, Calegg. I'm honored, but I hope you know you're highly skilled and would have easily been as capable as me or Hwista with a little time. We are technophiles as a race, so it stands to reason we have a natural affinity. Plus, we all have a lot more practice than you. But if you ever want to join in as co-pilot just let me know, yes?" Elyek said, coming across as both sympathetic and informative. I would have just sounded like a patronizing asshole.

"Well, that was pretty intense," Ember said loudly. "But for what it's worth, Calegg, we all would have been happy with whatever you chose."

"Thanks, Ember. I think I've made the right decision. I'll finish my shift, so it's not awkward or embarrassing."

"Whatever you want, pal. But if you are going to switch full-time to engineering, I want this ship running like a damned dream. No excuses."

"You'd better believe it, Captain."

"Good. Now, get us to the Perseus system so we can go and fight in this war, for an Empire that hates us and hunts us like criminals!"

As one they all looked at me and gave me a what-the-fuck expression.

"What?" I said petulantly. "It's the truth!"

"Just don't say that in front of anyone else, Shaun. We need to build morale! Now, we should probably let Acclo know about Calegg."

"Yeah. Give them a call to get up here."

"What? You give them a call, you lazy bastard. I think this captaincy has gone to your head."

I laughed, "Yeah, you're probably right. I mean you literally have never listened to anything I've ever said. I don't even know what got into me."

"Acclo is on their way," Elyek interrupted, pulling the comm away from their mouth.

"Elyek!" Ember grumbled, unhappily. "We should have made Shaun do it!"

"Not really. Although you say we four are the founding members of the Uprising, and we are, Shaun is the one who freed me. And we did all agree that he was the captain. Not to forget the fact that he is Onnekus, which we also previously discussed."

"We should still wind him up, though. It's fun!"

"It is difficult for me, nonetheless I will continue to try," Elyek said, looking genuinely conflicted.

"Good! Keep trying. He already has a big enough head. We need to keep him grounded."

"I'm not that bloody bad," I protested.

Ember laughed. "Nah, you're not at all. But it's fun, remember?"

Acclo came in at that moment, and I was glad for the reprieve. "Hey Acclo," I said, while everyone else greeted the diminutive Veiletian in their own way.

"Hello, everyone. Is everything okay?"

"Yeah, it's all good. Just need to catch you up on a few things."

They raised an eyebrow, then looked at Elyek, who smiled warmly in return and said, "Acclo, it appears you are going to be our new logistics officer."

"Oh, thank you Elyek, that is fantastic news!" they said, seeming to almost shudder with happiness. "I love coordinating everything to where it should be. It consumes me."

I looked around to see if anyone else thought Acclo's' intensity for organizing was hilarious. It seemed I was alone in this. Never mind. I spoke to them instead: "Acclo, we've spoken to Calegg. He's assuming the engineer's role, full time."

"Excellent. That is perfect for him. I am most happy he chose that role. He was unsuited to flying the Uprising."

"Yeah," I grimaced, "but please never tell him that. Despite seeming like he's chilled out, I think it'd affect him to hear it said out of someone else's mouth."

Everyone nodded in agreement; I don't think any of us wanted to hurt Calegg's feelings. He's a pretty cool dude.

"Okay. With that all sorted out I'm gonna have a lie down. Acclo, organize your heart out."

"I will, Captain. I assure you we will have this whole operation organized to the second."

"Brilliant stuff, Acclo. You are now our official Six Ps Officer."

"Six Ps?" Acclo asked, inquisitively.

"Yup, it's short for Proper Planning Prevents Piss Poor Performance Officer. It's a new role, but an important one, and I know you'll crush it. So long as I don't have to hear about every second. I want to know when big decisions need to be made, but otherwise just crack on."

Elyek looked concerned by my statement and spoke to that effect. "Acclo, you can speak to me about all aspects of what you're doing. The captain has an incredibly special kind of intelligence. We must work around it, but I am always here for you."

"Thank you, Elyek, I am very grateful for that, and will speak to you often."

Ember looked a little unsure about where she wanted to fit in. The next words out of her mouth made me chuckle internally a little. "Acclo, think of me somewhere between Shaun and Elyek." And that was it; all she had to add. Fucking hilarious.

"Right! I really am going this time. Catch you guys later." I said

"Me too!" Ember said behind me. "I could do with a shower, seeing as I couldn't get in it earlier," she grumbled, looking pointedly at me.

C17
Alpha Team

I stretched out on our room's chaise longue, enjoying a few blissful moments of peace and quiet.

"Hey, Shaun. Don't think you're just gonna be sitting around on your ass for the next two weeks. We've some serious inventory work to do," Ember said as she walked out of the shower, a towel wrapped around her.

"Ha, ha! Yeah. We've plenty to do on that score, I'm thinking we also need to build some togetherness with our crew mates. I was just mulling over the danger of people feeling alienated… Shit, can I even say that now? Is it racist or something?"

Ember stood silent for a moment, thinking. "You know what, you might be right. Shaun, I think I'm sensing an improvement in your Wisdom already!"

"Ha fucking ha! Ember, do you think when you up your Intelligence stat some more, you'll be less bloody obnoxious?"

"Hope not. It's part of who I am. I mean, yeah. I want to be max level on all available skills, but not to the point of no longer being me. Would you even like me anymore?"

"What? Would I like you if you weren't constantly giving me shit? Yeah, I think I'd be okay with that," I laughed.

"Well, don't get your hopes up, Shaun. It's my favorite bit of entertainment. So, you were talking about togetherness?"

"Yeah, maybe we should make sure to form mixed groups to train in. People are people, and will always be a little competitive. Let's have them compete group to group, rather than race to race."

"I've no doubt some dickheads will have made their way over from the Thoth and Seshat," Ember replied, "but I think once they get a feel for what our alien friends can do, they'll soon change their tune."

"One-hundred percent," I agreed. "And if they don't, I'll shoot them out into space."

"You know you can't do that, don't you?" she chuckled. "Even if we really want to."

"Why? Racist fuck nuggets deserve to get ejected into space."

"Yeah, but everyone on the Uprising will then be fearful that if they make a mistake, they'll get the same treatment."

"Mmm, so what should I do? Maybe just give them a good beating? Show that I'll deal personally with bullies."

"What if it's a woman? Or a Torax? Or Veiletian?"

"Easy! You beat the women up, Elyek can beat Veiletians up and Koparr can beat Torax up."

"Just when I thought you were showing signs of improvement, you come out with that shit," she laughed. "You really are a fucking idiot, Shaun. You're a leader now, and you've gotta start thinking like one. Your days of beating people up because they were assholes needs to become a thing of the past, with the crew anyway. We need a solid, fair and consistent set of rules for discipline... for everything, really."

"Shit, you're right Ember," I sighed. "I suppose we've been flying by the seat of our pants."

"Well, to be fair, we haven't really led a big crew before. It's just we need a fair set of rules on the Uprising that people can rely on."

"We should have a meeting with Elyek, Acclo, Koparr, Mick and Gus to look at the best way forward for training the crew and setting rules."

"What about Calegg?"

"Yeah," Ember agreed, "might as well. I wouldn't want him feeling left out."

"Okay, then. It's a plan. Get Acclo to get everyone together in the captain's office."

"I'll do it, only there's one more thing; we need to start transcending humans."

"Yup. But," I paused, "I say only transcend Mick and Gus for now. They're the only ones we trust enough. Then we'll ask them to find the next candidates."

"Agreed. They'll know the other people here better than us, anyway."

I walked over to the desk and pressed the comm for Acclo. A few seconds later their voice came back at me. "Hello, Captain. What can I help you with?"

"Acclo, I want to hold a meeting in 20 minutes with Elyek, Koparr, Mick, Gus and Calegg. Oh, and yourself. We'll meet in the captain's room. Can you arrange that for me?"

"Of course, Captain. I will get right on it. Is there anything else?"

"No thanks, Acclo. See you there."

The connection died, and I turned to Ember. "Sorted," I announced, grabbing my suit from over the chair. "I'd better get ready then."

"You could've given me a bit longer. Twenty minutes, you ass. Let's hope no one else is in the shower, or you've put them in a right stressful situation, haven't you?"

"Do you think I should change it?"

"Nah, you'll just look stupid. We need to avoid that as much as possible."

"Well, there's a lot you could do to help with that perception, Ember."

"Yeah, I know. I *am* going to try harder."

"That would be nice," I grinned, then turned to pick up Havok, who stood in the corner. "Hey, pal," I said, "Do you want to come with us to the meeting?"

"Oh no, Shaun. I want to stand alone in the corner of this room."

"Do I sense sarcasm?" I laughed at Havok. "Come on, then. On you get." I grabbed him and swung him over my shoulder, where he settled into position.

Within ten minutes, Ember was ready, and we made our way to the office. We passed humans on the way who looked like they wanted nothing to do with me. I realized that maybe they weren't being assholes, they just probably didn't know how to act around me. So I made the effort to be friendly with them, whether I wanted to or not. "Hey," I smiled, offering a wave to those I passed.

Most smiled sheepishly back but said nothing. Only one, a small, brown-haired woman, made the leap to talk back. "Hello Captain Shaun, Ember. Thank you for allowing us to come over to join you on your ship, I'm truly grateful to you for rescuing us. It's marvelous what you have both achieved."

"That's okay. We're pleased we found you all again. Sorry I don't know your name," I said, feeling unexpectedly happy for the interaction after all.

"Oh, of course, sorry I should have introduced myself, I'm Janet. I came from the Seshat."

"Well it's nice to meet you, Janet. Things should be much better now for all of us."

"I do hope so. We were devoid of hope once Ogun left. I couldn't believe we were taking bounties as work! Always going further and further away from Earth. I know we're going further away now, but at least we have a solid plan. Right?" she finished hopefully.

"We've a plan, Janet, don't you worry about that," I laughed like I meant it. "We're gonna build and train the toughest little army you could dream of. Then we're gonna start righting some wrongs."

"And some healthy dismembering, Shaun, don't forget the dismembering," Havok said, interrupting my thoughts.

I tried to ignore him and focus on Janet. "I don't know how long it'll take, but I do know that we are going to live for a long time now, and I don't intend to stop until we've leveled a few things out with the Fystr, and the Galactic Empire for that matter. The overall plan is to one day get back to Earth and see what we can do there."

"That is good to hear, Captain. I have no expectations, but I'm just thrilled to be part of something that matters."

"It's a pleasure to have you with Uprising," Ember said before me, "but we must go to our meeting now. We'll catch up later if you've any questions. We'll be happy to help."

"Of course, thanks for taking this time. It was an honor to finally speak with you both," she said with a genuine smile. We parted ways, continuing along to the bridge.

"Well, I hope they're all as friendly and as happy to be here as her," I said.

"They will be, Shaun, they will be. Now, come on.

Chop, chop!" she said, shooing me down the corridor. I took the next few seconds to speak to Havok.

"Seriously dude, dismembering?"

"We all have our hobbies, Shaun, what else am I supposed to think about? I am an axe. I love heavy metal music and killing things."

"You know what, Havok? You're absolutely right, you just do *you*, man, I have no criticisms," I replied as we entered my office.

Acclo was there already, and was setting out glasses of water and terminals at eight of the seats. "Acclo, thank you for being so organized. You're an absolute boon to have around," Ember said.

"Oh, you're welcome. I like things to run smoothly, and I find they always do when I am in charge. I would blame myself if I let an incompetent planner arrange things and they didn't get it right."

"You do a great job, Acclo," I said, as I took my seat at the head of the table, Ember beside me.

Elyek, Koparr and Calegg entered the room from the bridge side, chatting amiably. I assumed they'd been at their stations.

Gus and Mick arrived only a few seconds later, looking almost nervous. Mick was trying to hide it behind his chilled demeanor. Gus was silent, his face expressionless.

"Mick, Gus, dudes!" I greeted. "Come and take a seat." They relaxed a little, and I continued as they made themselves comfortable. "Right you two, I'll start with you first. Are there crew members who you'd consider to be higher ranking than yourselves who came over from the other ships? I don't want to upset anyone, so they can be involved if they're okay. Still, I'd rather just have you two helping us with our human contingent."

"Nah, I'd say there are others of similar stations, but no one who would be above us."

"Okay. Going forward, you two are my main guys for dealing with humans here. Cool?"

"Just Mick, I don't want to be in charge. I've too much on," Gus said.

"How can he have too much on, he's just bloody well got here!" Havok said into my mind.

"It's Gus, he's probably brought a ton of *projects* from the Thoth."

"Yeah, he's kinda weird, but he's solid. I like Gus," Havok said back with finality. With a chuckle, I pushed him from my thoughts.

"That's fine Gus. Mick's the man for the job."

"Shall I leave, then?" he replied.

"No, you daft ass. We still have things to discuss, but you don't have to come to future meetings, if you don't want to."

"No, I don't want to. I'm happy to stay today, though."

"Well, we're all here to discuss a few rules and everyone's training. I think Acclo will have most of that planned out, anyway," I said, smiling and turning to Acclo.

They beamed back at me. "Of course I have, sir. It is good to meet you, Mick. Now, I will discuss my plans for the humans with you. Koparr and I have spoken at length about the Torax, and Wulek will lead the training of the Veiletians."

"Great to have someone overseeing each race, just to stay aware that we must have people in mixed groups. We need to build elite teams that can train and learn together through each other's unique strengths. By combining everyone's skill sets, we can have truly formidable groups.

"Also, I have my own awesome team, which has everyone here in it! I might add one or two more humans in time, but I consider this team pretty elite as it is."

There were smiles all around the table, and I had to join them. There was no way I was breaking this team up. Acclo was new, as was Koparr, but they had proven themselves beyond doubt so far, and I liked them too.

"It makes sense, Captain," replied Acclo. "I will liaise with everyone and put that into place."

"Sounds fun," Koparr grunted. "Means we can have little tournaments of evenly matched groups. Competitions to bring everyone together and make them work that little bit harder."

"Though I'd agree," Gus said, "there should also be some kinda signaling system if we're in a large battle that involves everyone. There may be instances where it makes sense for each race to group up again."

"What do you mean, Gus?" I asked. I knew better than to doubt the odd man. I knew he had a lot of knowledge around military tactics and history.

"I mean that the Torax are laser-resistant and can go supernova, from what I gather, yet they can also act as ranged troops: different functions for different instances. We could use them alongside humans shooting, or as shock troops. The Veiletians can go invisible. We can use their element of surprise. It would be foolish to have them in either of the two previously mentioned categories. If everyone is in individual autonomous units, they need to also be able to merge seamlessly back into groups that match their strengths."

"I get what you're saying," I said thoughtfully, and he was right. We didn't want to lose our strengths, like a group attack of exploding Torax. "With that in mind Gus, whether you like it or not, you're now in charge of overseeing our training and military tactics."

"That's okay boss, but I'll only be comfortable passing information onto team captains."

I laughed at him. "Awesome. Now, one more thing for you two; when you left Anatoli, what levels were you guys again?"

"Thirty-four for me, and Gus here was 38," Mick replied on Gus's behalf.

"Good stuff. Well in that case we'd like to try to transcend you both. We'll start with Gus first. He's the highest level, and it's also a good test on sub level 40."

"Yeah!" Mick slapped the table. "I sooo wanna transcend. Did Astrid and Rufus manage it?"

"Yeah. Easily, in the end."

"Fantastic!" Mick said with a laugh, throwing himself back in his seat. "We're gonna be seriously OP man, this is awesome."

"It still takes a long time, Mick," Ember added.

"That's cool. We're in it for the long haul! We're Damn near immortal, remember!" Mick replied.

"We will go through it after the meeting with you. But first, we need some clear plans. Acclo, please tell us everything we need to know." I said.

"The first item is to make you all aware that it will take 15 days to get to the Perseus system, based on the various engine capabilities in our fleet. Despite the Uprising's ability to make the distance in eight days, we must work with the Thoth's and Seshat's smaller jump distances and longer recharge rates.

"I advise we also make a stop off before we arrive at our destination to ensure we have everything we need prior to the battle. In my opinion, it would be unwise to turn up under-prepared, therefore Elyek and I have plotted a detour. As we approach the Perseus system, there are several supply planets we can make use of. It is a far more desolate section of the galaxy, meaning we can pick up what we need without risk of attack. Then we'll travel to Beler 3103 using only propulsion engines for that stage of the journey. That way, if we need to jump out of danger, our engines will be recharged and we can move quickly."

"Seems to be a very well-thought-out plan with no glaring flaws I can see. Questions, anyone?" I asked, looking around at those present. No one spoke, so I took that as acceptance and continued.

"Last thing on the agenda, *rules.* I want you all to come up with a series of important rules and suitable responses to rule breakers from your own experiences. Have a good think after the meeting, then we'll look through it together to share practice and form our own code."

"May I suggest we arrange a meeting every couple of days to catch up and discuss how everything is going?" Acclo suggested.

"That's a great idea, Acclo. Book it whenever suits."

"Of course, Captain."

"Right, guys. Anything else?"

"Don't forget we need to change the name and registration on the Uprising," Elyek added.

"Damn Elyek! You're bang on. Are you okay sorting that out?"

"Of course, Captain. I was going to, anyway. I just thought I'd bring it up, so no one had concerns at a later date. It will be done. Is there any name you'd like to use in particular?"

"Anything you think fitting, Elyek," Ember interrupted. "I trust you more than Shaun when it comes to naming us. He has his strengths, and names are not one of them."

"Hey! Havok's a good name, so is the Uprising."

"Havok is a fantastic name, which perfectly fits my outlook in life," Havok laughed into my mind. I chuckled back while Ember was speaking.

"You didn't come up with the Uprising, and it took you over two weeks to give Havok a name."

"I don't mind, anyway." I said. "I trust Elyek, and this ship will always be..." I pumped my fist in the air and shouted, "*Uprising!*" As usual, the response was not what I would have hoped for, but probably what I expected. The miserable fuckers. At least Mick shouted '*Uprising*' back, and pumped his fist, so I wasn't totally hung out to dry. "Okay people, time to wrap it up unless there's anything else? Nope?" No one was forthcoming with anything new. "In that case, you can all fuck off, apart from Mick and Gus. We've got some work to do," I said, grinning at the pair of them. Everyone said their goodbyes, leaving us alone.

"Here we go then, let's see what happens," I said as Ember and I approached Gus. He seemed surprisingly relaxed considering, sitting with his eyes closed. We entered his mind, following the same procedure we had before on Astrid and Rufus, only this time we didn't need to give him the shock treatment.

Gus opened his eyes within seconds; the fastest I had seen it happen, so far. He flickered just the same, and if anything, he seemed to be panicking more. He was difficult to contain. We managed it though, bringing him safely through.

We went straight to Mick's mind next, and the absolute opposite was true. It took ages to get him to open his eyes; even the first shock treatment didn't work. In the end, it took all three of us to deliver a shock as one before his eyes opened. Once they did, he got a group hug from us all. His flickering settled almost instantly.

We showed them everything we knew. The two guys were amazed, as you'd expect, and Gus's eyes blazed when he saw the stats screen.

Name: Mick Greenall
Age: 32 GY
Transcendence Level: 54
Strength: 80/1000
Agility: 74/1000
Speed: 78/1000
Intelligence: 40/1000
Constitution: 86/1000
Wisdom: 25/1000
Mental Resilience: 39/1000
Mental Clarity: 14%
Potential: 72%

"Not bad, mate, not bad at all. Now, come on. Let's go and look at Gus's," I said.

Name: Gus Vallance
Age: 30 GY
Transcendence Level: 56
Strength: 81/1000
Agility: 65/1000
Speed: 60/1000
Intelligence: 70/1000

Constitution: 35/1000
Wisdom: 52/1000
Mental Resilience: 31/1000
Mental Clarity: 30%
Potential: 86%

Like Astrid, Gus's Mental Clarity was already remarkably high, all things considered. But it made sense when you took into account his personality: he processed things carefully. It probably helped that his Intelligence and Wisdom were fucking sky-high, relatively speaking. I could imagine Ember quietly seething that his Potential was higher than hers. Mick probably wasn't too happy either. His Potential was the lowest I'd seen so far.

We walked through Gus's Mindscape. His Cognition Room didn't look too bad at all. Plenty of work to do, but that wasn't a surprise. We explained the best process for tidying them, pointing out that Ember and I often worked in tandem to lessen the boredom, which was something they could do between them if they were comfortable being in each other's Mindscapes.

Unsurprisingly, they were more than happy to be in each other's heads. Although whereas Gus's eyes showed an almost rapturous hunger for ordering his room, I sensed nothing but dread from Mick.

Once we had told them everything we could, I said, "Right, guys. It's been emotional, but now me and Ember have a shit-load of inventory to do. We'll all start training together from tomorrow. If you discover anything useful in the Mindscapes, let us know. We need every edge we can get."

"Sure will, Captain. This is amazing, what you've done for us. Really amazing," Mick said. Gus was lost in Gus's world.

"Bah! Behave yourself, Mick. We're a team. And, I've been meaning to say thanks again for levitating me on Xonico when I asked. Beautifully done."

"Xonico was my favorite time," Havok mused.

"You're welcome, you mad bastard. Although you didn't give me much choice," he laughed.

"I don't need help levitating any more, but I'm sure there'll be plenty more mad endeavors in the future."

He nodded, a serious expression on his face. "We'll be there, Captain. I promise."

"I know you will, Mick."

We all left the captain's office and went our separate ways.

Back at our own quarters, Ember stopped me before I could enter my Mindscape.

"Shaun, should we mess with the climate controls a bit?"

"Oh shit, yeah! For the constitution boosts? I can't deny, that's a good idea."

Ember nodded smugly while she messed with the controls for our room. The drop in temperature was instant. She shivered wrapping her arms around her. "Oh fuck that," she said teeth already chattering. "Let's try low oxygen this time, huh?"

Within a few seconds the temperature was back up to ambient, followed by a noticeable shortness of breath for me.

"Right, that should be low enough to make a difference without killing us," she gasped. "Now let's go Mindscape side."

"Yes, let's," I said pulling at the neck of my suit, feeling like I was slowly suffocating. We would be doing the inventory work separately now to make the best use of our time, which I was sad about. "Best hold on to Havok, Ember. Just in case you messed up with the levels."

"I didn't mess up, but I will all the same, thanks," she smiled, but it looked more like a grimace. We both sat on the bed with Havok between us.

"I'll keep you guys safe. You've got nothing to worry about," Havok said in our heads. Then, we entered our Mindscapes.

I appeared in front of the terminal, relieved to not feel like I was dying. I stared blankly for a few moments at the glowing screen. "Boring!" I shouted. "Come on Havok, hit me with something good!"

"I have just the thing. It's called metal."

"Sounds good, pal," I said, as heavy thrashing guitars screeched through my mind. It helped me to get past feeling overwhelmed from the sheer amount of work that I had to do at the terminal. I soon got into a flow.

There were plenty of things I had no clue about, things that could have happened at any time in a five-year-period, but the newer representations of memory were easy to file. I imagined my 75% Mental Clarity was being put to good use in the work. I toiled for most of the day, a whole seven hours. It wasn't until I was coming away from the inventory terminal that I checked the notification at the bottom.

Rebuild mind-database: 3% complete.

Depressing, but at least I had a frame of reference to go with my Mental Clarity stats. I figured I would get an extra point in Clarity every time my Rebuild went up by 4%. So if it took seven fucking hours for a lousy 3%, then this was going to be a long, slow process. If I kept to this pace, it would take around 230 hours to reach full Clarity. We'd be nowhere near done by the time we landed in the Perseus system.

The following days saw the training commence. Acclo made sure that all the ships were following the same, or similar, training methods. We made sure to keep in touch and abreast of any problems arising. I named our group the Alpha Team – Ember wouldn't let me call it the A-team, and apart from Mick, who supported my call, nobody else cared enough.

We practiced levitating and fighting together. It was massive fun! Calegg and Koparr shot fire at the new fire-resistant targets, while Elyek and Acclo turned invisible and flanked our imaginary enemy, moving in after four volleys of fireballs. Mick, Gus and Ember floated along behind me, levitating metal balls at the training bags ahead of us, and deflecting the odd training-laser that came their way with their Fystr swords. I levitated just in front of them as I always did, ricocheting the harmless training-lasers.

I told Havok not to help me with the lasers, I wanted to develop the skills myself. If anything ever happened to Havok and I didn't have his abilities for some reason, I'd have to be able to defend myself. With an increased Mental Clarity, I did well. Although it was astronomically more tiring wielding the heavy axe with my own power, and I had no doubt my strength went up in those first few days. Obviously, with Havok's muscle repair skills, those changes happened quickly.

We made sure all the other teams followed a similar drill to ours. After the first full week, when we felt like we were all working well together, we concentrated more on mass battle tactics. Gus was intrinsic here, as the main dilemma we had was to figure out how to use the Veiletians' abilities without killing them. His solution was to devise a number of signals for set events that he would deliver.

By the time we arrived at the supply station, I was feeling rather proud of the work we had been doing. Watching the pure carnage each team could create was mind-blowing, and I hoped it would be enough to stand up to most situations. On land, anyway. In a space battle, maybe not so much. We could get by I supposed, but generally speaking, space warfare wasn't one of the Uprising's strong points.

C18
Supply and Demand

We arrived safely at the supply station, a day out from the planet we needed to reach in the Perseus system.

We were not in any danger: no one had threatened us or approached us in the past two weeks. We had come a hell of a long way across the galaxy, and I hoped that would be enough to throw off any pursuit. Elyek had changed the Uprising's name and registration to some random selection of numbers and letters, and I was actually glad they hadn't chosen a proper name – this way we weren't really losing the Uprising's identity, but the change meant we wouldn't alert the Empire's tracking systems. It would be interesting to see whether we attracted any unwanted attention before turning up at this big battle we'd been hired to fight in.

The biggest decision, as always, was whether to take all three ships down to the surface. Taking them all down would make loading much easier, but it was potentially risky. After much deliberation, we decided to keep a ship in orbit to provide cover and keep a lookout for incoming hostiles. Rufus volunteered to keep the Seshat in orbit, and he would swap places with the Uprising once we had loaded up. We hadn't had any trouble since Arus, but I'd rather be safe than sorry.

Obviously, in hindsight, I made a huge shit-stain of a

mistake. You see, it's overlooking the finer details of any plan that will fuck you over. In this instance, it all began unraveling when I received a call from the Seshat.

"Shaun! There are two Fystr Hunter ships on our scanners!" Rufus told me.

"What?" I replied calmly, while my mind processed the information.

"Two Fystr Hunter ships, they're around ten minutes out!" he continued to yell at his comm.

"Ten fucking minutes Rufus? How did they get that close before you identified them?" I practically screamed down the comm.

I was in the captain's office, with the entire alpha team looking at me in horror. "Tell Astrid," I mouthed to Ember, and she raised her comm, nodding.

"They jumped in close, and they're moving fast," Rufus replied at the same time.

"There's no way we'll make it into orbit in time, Rufus. Give me a sec," I said, then turned to talk to the others. I know we can't get up in time, so what do we do?"

"They won't be able to attack from orbit, the supply station's defenses will be too strong, and it would be an act of war on the Galactic Empire," Elyek offered.

"That's good to know Elyek, so they'd have to land and face us, which suits our strengths really. What about the Seshat?" I asked.

"Two Hunter ships will tear them apart," Gus offered in his grumpy deadpan way. "They need to run, or get their asses down here."

"Thanks, Gus. And they're not fucking running, were going to need them down here," I said, then jumped back on the comm. "Rufus, you're going to need to get yourselves down here now."

"A… are you sure that's wise, Shaun?"

"Am I sure I don't want to get the Seshat blown up? Or am I sure I want our full army in one place to deal with the threat, Rufus? Get your ass down here quick."

"Okay Shaun, we're coming down. I was just wondering if we had better options."

"If we had more than eight fucking minutes, you could wonder all you like. See you soon Rufus," I snapped, then closed the call. "Ok, where are we at?"

It was Gus who responded. "Astrid is rallying her crew, as are we. I've told everyone to line up into race at the front of the ships, and I've ordered the Veiletians to keep out of sight until after the first volley. Then they're to stay low and take out people when it's safe to do so."

We made our way out to the docking bays, just in time to see the Seshat landing. "Gus, can you relay everything to Rufus?"

"Sure thing, Captain, I'll get right on it," he said, bringing the comm to his mouth.

Everyone was scrabbling from around the docking bay, leaving whatever supplies they were carrying. The station security guards started to look a bit on edge. Poor fuckers had no clue that hell was about to descend on them. Everything was a little chaotic, with the Seshat's crew pouring down the loading ramp to join us.

The tension was vibrating in the air of that cold metal supply hanger, and it only got worse as the two Fystr ships came into view, casually descending like they had all the time in the world. I felt sick, and I'm sure everyone shared the sensation. But I fought to stay calm: we had this, it was going to be okay. I looked around, seeing the sheer terror on the surrounding faces.

"Uprising!" I shouted at the top of my lungs. Thankfully, my voice came out clear and with way more confidence than I felt. "It's been an age since I last killed a Fystr. Three of them, if I recall correctly. I didn't even have Havok then," I said, thrusting Havok in the air. He screamed in my head with the excitement of a kid on a roller coaster.

"They like to think they're invincible, but I promise you they are not. We can do this!" I shouted, and a cheer rose up from the crew as they looked to each other, confidence building.

It settled down as the Fystr began to leave their ship. Huge, imposing bastards that they were.

Their arrival also prompted a full station security force to appear, around 80 of them all told, armed to the teeth, lining the exit of the docking bay. With the Fystr across from us, we had a three-way standoff.

A giant Fystr raised his arms. He was as tall as Jotun at well over seven-feet, but he looked more in proportion, well-muscled and capable. There looked to be around 40 Fystr with him. He spoke in a commanding voice: "People of the galaxy, please put your weapons away. We are the Fystr, and any sign of aggression against us will be considered an act of war by the Galactic Empire against the Fystr Empire. You do not want to let that happen."

There was a lot of talk; hushed whispers passed between the planet's security personnel. The hairball leading them spoke on his comm amid the quiet clamor. Finally, he raised his hand to his men, beckoning them to pull back. Now, it was just us and the Fystr, deadlocked in the open space.

"So, my little monkeys. You have led us quite the merry dance! Almost halfway around the galaxy," the imposing Fystr shouted, a wry grin on his face.

"Sorry, mate. I think you've got the wrong little monkeys. We live here, now run along and bother someone else, will you?" I shouted back.

He laughed, "Oh, very good. You must be Shaun. I've heard quite a bit about you. In fact, Ogun told me everything about you all. So, are you the leader of this collection of misfits?" he said, waving his hand disdainfully at the surrounding members of the Uprising.

He'd shook me at the mention of Ogun giving him information, but I tried not to let it show. "Okay. Sorry, I didn't get your name. Shall we start there?" I said, stalling.

The dick puffed his chest up proudly, looking around to make sure he had everyone's attention. "I am the eighth commander of the Fystr fleet, Heiliun the Great."

"Only eighth? I'm disappointed. So, *Heiliun the Doesn't Matter*, do you and your poxy crew a favor and fuck off back home, will you? You're starting to bore us."

Ember started snickering by my side, and I couldn't help but smile.

"You dare…," he started to speak, but I turned away.

"Sorry about this, guys. But are you all ready?" While I spoke, I winked at Gus, who had been watching me like a hawk. He immediately signaled. The effect was awesome. Within seconds, all the Torax burst into flames. In unison, the humans brought up their guns or levitated metal projectiles. Havok simultaneously flew into my hand. The Veiletians were already invisible and ready to rock.

The expressions on the opposing Fystr, were comical. I couldn't help
the smile on my face. "I don't know what you thought you were gonna face here, but we're not exactly lambs

for the slaughter, Heiliun. Now, last chance. Fuck off, or this place becomes a living nightmare for you," I threatened.

Heiliun struggled a little, but his shock slowly became a sinister smile. "You think you are such a powerful monkey with your fiery friends! You do not truly understand the pure might of the Fystr," he said, sneer still on his face as he began to rise smoothly from the floor. He had regained his composure, and the others around him began to look more confident again. That was until I copied the feat, rising from up the ground myself. For the second time in less than a minute, the Fystr's expressions fell to dismay.

"How is this possible? Ogun had not informed me that you had transcended!" Heiliun tried to scream angrily, but it came out more like a whine.

"I'm surprised! You made it sound like he was happy to tell you everything about us."

This time Heiliun laughed, "Oh, no. He was without question *not* happy about it. We had to use our finest torture techniques, and it appears we still did not get all we needed from him. We will have to revisit our little traitor again. After this display, I am glad I didn't just execute him now," he snapped.

I was thrown a bit by all of this. "You mean you have Ogun with you, now?" I asked.

"He is held captive and in pretty bad shape," Helium chuckled. "You're welcome to return with us and see him for yourself."

"No, thank you. But we'll have him back, if you don't mind!"

"No, no, no. That will not be happening. We must take him back with us to Fystr Prime to stand trial alongside you. The others can go free; we don't need all of you."

"You must know you won't win this fight, right? You're not seriously that delusional?"

"I am not delusional! I am supremely confident. I accept you have developed further than I anticipated. You will always be seen as vermin to the Fystr, you fool. You really do not understand the extent of our abilities," Heiliun said.

I didn't even care enough to respond. It was going to be a fight whether I wanted one or not, but then I knew that from the moment they landed. Heiliun seemed to be talking to someone internally, because he fell quiet for a few moments before speaking again. "Here is the situation. We have traveled a tremendously long way and used a lot of vital resources hunting you. This fight, despite what you may think, would result in our victory. However, it would be unpleasant for everyone concerned. So rather than bicker here, I am prepared to give you an offer. Your planet Earth has not yet been destroyed, and currently we work on reducing their available technology. Be warned, if you do not return with us, I will give the order to have it destroyed."

"Hey, you fucking tool! Why would we agree to that?" Ember shouted over. "If we just kill you now, then you can't order Earth's destruction."

The daft arse actually went red with embarrassment or anger, or maybe both. "You must be Ember. I have also heard about you," he said, distaste dripping from his words. Looking back at me, he continued: "How about a duel of honor, then? You against me? If you win, you walk away. If I win, your people come back with me, peacefully."

"Oh, yeah. Great idea!" I said sarcastically, though the

grin lightening his face told me he hadn't picked up on the sarcasm. I carried on before he could speak. "Couple of things first; how old are you? And what transcendence level are you?"

Havok shouted at me. "Shaun! We can do this cocksucker. I've got this. Trust me."

"Havok, I believe you. We could do it, but we don't need to. If we fight and win, I really don't think they'd honor any deal they've made. They're purebred wankers. Now, tell me honestly. Do you disagree?"

"No, I don't," he said, "and I don't think this is ending without a good fight, anyway. So fuck it, it doesn't matter, though duels *are* fun."

Heiliun stuttered in response to my question. Looking at one of his crew, he then finally spoke, "I am 6000 years old. Transcendence level 800."

"Okay... so that seems like a little bit of a mismatch, if you don't mind me saying. I've only just gone above transcendence level 100. Oh, and I'm like 32 years old, or less in galactic years. Anyway, you get my point: no duels."

He looked outraged. "Fystr do not refuse duels, especially those which could save their people."

"Number one," I raised a finger, "I'm not a fucking Fystr. Number two," I raised another, "My people will be okay. Yours, however, are fucked."

"How disappointing," he said, then launched an attack on my mind. I smiled grimly as I felt his presence. So predictable: I'd left my mind unguarded intentionally. This time I wasn't taking any chances. I went into my Mindscape to face Heiliun.

He was there in my corridor, waiting for me. "You don't get a choice whether to duel or not," he cried. "You're mine, Shaun. You're not getting away from me. I will jump at least two commander ranks for killing you and bringing your people back."

I leaned on Havok. "You're a fool, Heiliun. All those years of experience and skills, and you still waltz in here like you're an untouchable god. You're not."

"Compared to you, I am. Child! I can have you weeping on your knees in seconds."

"Nope. No you couldn't," I grinned.

He was getting angrier and angrier.

This was so much fucking fun. "You're an ignorant prick, Heiliun," I continued, "and unless you get the fuck out of my head quick, you're going to die in here."

He laughed an insane laugh, then lunged with the six-foot sword that he held one-handed. Havok came up on his own accord to deflect, then reversed in a heartbeat to take Heiliun's head cleanly from his shoulders."

It missed, as in a remarkable feat of skill, Heiliun disappeared then reappeared a foot out of Havok's range. Heiliun came back with a series of blistering attacks, wielding his heavy sword like it was a bamboo cane. Not that Havok gave a shit; he blocked tactical missiles for fun, and easily resisted every attack. We were at a standstill for a few seconds, when Havok and I began pushing Heiliun back. He teleported backwards again, which I assumed was a skill that was only possible in Mindscapes, and it was one I had to learn.

"You have uncanny skill with Jotun's blade. I do not understand how you fight so well. I have far more advanced sword skills, yet you seem capable of meeting my match. I have tested you, and now it is time for you to die."

I sighed like a bored teenager. "This is just getting stupid, now. Guys! Come out will you. I'm getting bored."

Mick, Gus, and Ember all stepped out of various doors into my corridor, Fystr weapons in hand.

Heiliun paled. "How?" Then before we could answer, disappeared.

"I assume that was a rhetorical question then?" Ember laughed before disappearing herself. We all did the same.

"Take them down!" Heiliun was screaming as I came back to my normal state. This coincided with a good number of my crewmates falling to the floor, writhing in agony.

I knew it would not take long for them to be killed if I didn't act quickly. "Attack!" I shouted at the top of my lungs while I charged Heiliun, hovering over the top of the ground faster than I could run. I was pretty confident that I could take him in a melee now, so I took the initiative.

Havok screamed in delight and rage while playing my favorite metal song as we hurtled through the air like a bullet. Balls of flame flew past me into the ranks of waiting Fystr. The accuracy of the Torax was remarkable. Yet even though most of the Fystr were busy attacking my crew mentally, they were still able to deflect most of the attacks. What they couldn't cope with, however, were the 20 invisible knives coming from behind them, slicing into arteries. Heiliun levi-hurled objects at me while waiting angrily, sword raised and ready to attack as I came into range. His second in command stood by his side, doing her darndest to protect him from any distractions.

Havok was a blur, deflecting anything and everything in our path, until I landed like a boss right in front of Heiliun. "Impressive monkey...," he began, but I lunged straight at him without pause. He deflected the blow, and our fight began in earnest, this time for everyone to see. I could feel Ember was in my Mindscape, watching out for attacks, so when I felt the pressure of a Fystr enter, I remained unconcerned. I knew it wouldn't be Heiliun.

He came at me enraged, trying desperately to end the fight quickly, but again Havok had no problems in dealing with his attacks. To give Heiliun his due, he hadn't allowed us to get in any attacks either.

I felt a sudden pain in my head, which I instantly recognized as a mental attack. I quickly glanced to Heiliun's second. I could see they were in some pain. I assumed from Ember protecting me.

While Heiliun was still holding his own extraordinarily well, I worried for Ember. "Havok, we're gonna take that bitch out. Are you ready to switch targets for a second?"

"Sure," he said, though I could hear the strain in his voice. I jumped backwards and to the side, out of Heiliun's range. He stopped his attack for a moment, clearly thinking I was trying to back out. He should have kept up his attack, as Havok swung in a wide arc to the right, and split Heiliun's second in half.

Heiliun's eyes went wide with horror. "My wife!" he gasped. The fight fled from him entirely as he dropped to his knees next to the dissected woman to his side.

Havok raised himself up to finish the job on Heiliun. "No! Havok, don't!" I shouted, but Havok was in the zone, and he took Heiliun's head, shoulder and arm off in a wicked cut.

"Dude!" I shouted, "I told you no!"

"He needed to die. They all do, Shaun. Don't worry, I'll keep you on the right path."

I was speechless. This was the first time Havok had

gone solo against my will, and it terrified me. I couldn't do much about it at the moment, though. I needed him to make sure our people survived, and I couldn't start an argument with him just yet. But afterwards, he was in deep shit with me.

I looked around to assess the situation. There were 11 Fystr left alive, desperately defending themselves against fireballs, laser fire and one incredibly angry human with a mass of flame-colored hair. I watched for a moment, impressed as he hacked through a gap in one Fystr's armor with a pulsating hand axe, followed by a brutal punch to their face. They went down hard. He stomped on their head, crushing their skull with the force. It was an utterly brutal display, leaving only ten Fystr left.

"Stop!" I yelled. The barrage ceased instantly. I was almost embarrassed with how quickly my command had been followed. Even the head stomper backed off immediately. I'd have to find out who he was.

The change of noise level was almost deafening. Quietness punctuated occasionally by the whimpers of those badly injured. I made my way over to the remaining bloody and battered Fystr, while taking in the bodies of my own fallen crew. There were more than a few people down and not moving, killed on a distant rock almost a galaxy away from where they should have been. And I was furious about that. Ember fell in beside me as I walked, but stayed silent. Her presence both comforted me and enraged me, as images of her lying dead sprung into my mind. She was fine now, obviously, but what if she wasn't the next time these fuckers showed up? I pulled away from my reverie as my eyes fell back on the Fystr in front of me.

"You," I shouted, pointing a finger at them. "You could've left! Now look at what you've achieved. All of this death, for what?" I shouted at them, my anger on show. "So your race can continue to abuse the galaxy? For your pathetic worthless pride? All because we got one over on you. We're light-years away, and yet you still hunt us like dogs, for no good reason at all."

"You are dogs," one of them spat.

I threw Havok out of my hand and he knew what to do, flying to skewer the one who had spoken. I had no doubt they tried to stop the throw with their mental abilities, but that shit wouldn't work on Havok. He returned to my hand a heartbeat later.

"Listen to me. Nobody else needs to die here. Although I strongly advise that not one of you insults me or my people again. If you do, understand I will kill you instantly. You think you're gods among men. You're not. You rule with fear and lies. Now, which ship is Ogun on?"

As soon as I'd spoken, I gave a mental command to Elyek to make sure the next person to throw an insult died from an invisible knife. That would really freak these fuckers out.

None of the Fystr answered. They stood there like sullen children.

"Lead me to Ogun and you can live. I'll let you take the other ship and crawl back to your people, tail between your legs."

"We will be imprisoned and humiliated for this failure, you stupid fool," one of them snarled, promptly followed by a gurgling sound as a knife from nowhere penetrated his throat. Blood jetted from his arteries across the eight remaining Fystr, whose expressions turned to horror as yet another of their number bled out on the floor.

"We won't insult you again," said another voice, a dark-haired woman with a blood-smeared face. "But I want you to understand a couple of things. Our lives are over if we go back, and no matter what we do, our people will never stop hunting you down."

"So, what will you do if I let you go free?" I asked, genuinely interested in the answer.

"We have no choice but to continue to hunt you and make sure we are more successful when next we meet."

"So, basically, I have to kill you all here then?"

"I do not wish that end, but there is no other way."

"Could you not join us?" Rufus said, coming to stand by my side.

I think I actually fish mouthed. I was more than a little gobsmacked that Rufus had suggested it.

The Fystr began to snicker among themselves. The new leader hushed them. "An interesting offer," she said, eyes flicking from Rufus to me. "Would you have us?"

I turned to Astrid and Rufus. They looked at me for my reaction, but instead of speaking to them, I spoke to Ember in her mind. "I can't believe Rufus just offered them that, can you?"

"He's a bit of a dick at times, so yeah. What are we gonna do about this?" she asked.

"Even if they say they'll work with us, they won't. It's not in their nature. They see us as animals. They'll just kill us later. They've no morals."

"Yeah," Ember sighed, "I'd have to agree with you. Can we imprison them in any way? How do you actually imprison a Fystr?"

"Astrid or Rufus might know a way," I replied.

"Ogun will definitely know a way if we can get him

back alive. He seems to have kept a lot of information from them about us, even under torture."

"Yeah. I picked that up, too. Right!" I asserted. "You need to go in and find Ogun. Take all our team, along with Astrid. I'll keep an eye on these fuckers."

"Okay, Shaun. Will do," she said before returning to her normal state to speak to Astrid. "Come with me, Astrid." She waved to the other members of our team – that she could see, anyway. Astrid nodded uncertainly; Rufus looked confused, but I ignored his stupid face, turning back to the Fystr.

"If you're honest in your intentions to become part of the crew and support us in all of our future endeavors, including against your own people, then yes we'd have you," I offered.

Her eyes almost seemed to glint as I said those words. "I will discuss it with what remains of our troop," she replied.

"One more thing," I said, "you'd have to give me access to your Interface Room."

Her face fell at that, smug grin gone. "Just a moment, then," she said, and turned to converse with the others.

Ember and Astrid had peeled off, and I gave Rufus a frustrated look, but the daft shit was oblivious, seemingly happy with his work.

After a minute of conferring, the lead Fystr turned back to me. "We are against mind invasion of this sort. However, in the promise of goodwill, one of us will submit to this interrogation."

"Why not all of you?" I asked, heat entering my voice again.

"As I've just explained, we consider it an affront."

"Better than death though?"

"Maybe not. However, those are our terms."

"Very well, then. Let's have a look and see when my friends get back."

"Where have they gone?"

I didn't reply. I just waited. It took ten minutes before Ember popped her head from the ship. She spoke into my mind: "Ogun is alive, barely. He seems to be in some kind of stasis capsule. We don't know how to free him. Gus thinks he can get him out, but not quickly. Shit Shaun, they've really done a number on him."

"Damn. I'll see if any of these bastards know how to free him," I replied.

"Yeah, that would be good. I'll go back in and tell Gus and Elyek."

She went back into the ship, and I spun to face the Fystr once more. "I need one of you to get Ogun safely from the stasis capsule before we take this any further."

"No. We won't be doing that just yet," the Fystr woman replied. "We will keep him in there as our insurance that you will not do anything to us."

"Are you kidding me? I could've had you killed at any time. You fuckers are infuriating."

"Yes, but you have considered letting us go. You have also kept us alive. There is obviously value to you that we do not die," she said with an I'm-cleverer-than-you look spreading across her face, like she had somehow backed me into a corner. She really hadn't.

With Elyek and Acclo helping Ember, I found Hwista's mind for my next order. "Kill them all, except the speaker. All at once if you can. I don't want to give them a chance to retaliate, hurt or kill any of you. We've already lost too many. And, sorry for asking you to do this." And I was, I felt like utter shit.

"It's okay, Captain. I agree with this course of action. I sense they are nothing but evil and have already indicated they wish nothing but ill will to us."

I watched the lead woman intently for a few seconds when all those around her dropped to the floor, blood spurting from deep neck wounds. The Veiletians were brutally efficient.

"Okay", I said. Her face must have been exhausted, from the amount of expressions it had been through: it had now settled on horrified. "I hope that clears up how much I value you all. Now are you going to help me get Ogun out of the stasis chamber?"

"I… I will. I need assurances from you that…"

That was the last thing she said as Havok took her head from her shoulders. It was so quick she barely saw it coming.

"My god, Shaun!" Rufus said over my shoulder. "That was brutal!"

I spun round to meet his eyes and spoke into his mind. "Don't ever go over the top of me like that again," I snarled into his head.

He went white and nodded in response.

"You should have killed them straight away," Havok said into my mind, "You just wasted your own time there."

"Havok, me and you are going to have a serious talk too, now shut he fuck up," I said, with a mentally projected growl.

He fell silent after that, leaving me to my thoughts for a moment. I would have to go and explain what had happened out here to Ember and the gang. There were a lot of eyes on me right now, and I would be glad to be able to get away from their stares for a moment.

"Everyone!" I shouted, as unfortunately I couldn't just walk off. "Thank you all for your hard work. I'm sorry we were caught flat-footed like that, but you all did amazingly. I'm gonna go check on the situation with Ogun. I won't be long!" Then in a quieter voice for Rufus, I said: "Try to clear this mess up as best you can. We need to save who can be saved. We also need to deal with the inhabitants."

He nodded in response, still looking pale and shaken.

With that I walked off into the Hunter ship to find where Ogun lay. Ember saw me first. Gus was leaning over the control panel.

"Shaun. Would any of them help?" she asked.

"No. They were uncooperative," I said grimly.

"What are we going to do about them, then?"

"Nothing. They're all dead," I said, struggling to make eye contact.

Everyone but Gus looked up at me. No one looked horrified, which was good. I just got nods of grim acceptance.

I walked over to look through the transparent cover of the capsule, seeing Ogun's battered form lying there. I felt a surge of queasiness; for some reason the bastards had cut his hands and feet off. It was a disturbing sight. If he had tried to protect us through all this torture, I owed the man a massive solid. Although I didn't know the full extent of what had happened, I felt a real sadness at how I'd thought about him in the past. For some time now, I'd begun to feel bad for him as my Clarity and Wisdom increased; I could see more clearly the choices he had to make each time he left us. There were really no choices at all. He had done the right thing each time. I'd even kinda done the same thing with Elyek on Arus. Though I knew Astrid was there to pick up the slack.

"What's the score, Gus? How do we do this?" I asked.

"We can't do anything at the moment. Elyek has looked over it with me, too. It needs the captain's bioscan, I think,"

"Right. Well, let's go get his body then!" I said, a little confused that this hadn't been done already.

"It will not work, Captain," Elyek jumped in. "This is a different type of technology from what we used in the bank. This detects the vital signs of the operator in the scan. It will make sure the operator is not under the influence of any chemicals, or in a state of fear or heightened stress."

"Oh, shit. That's no good then, because that fucker hasn't kept it together at all," I said, for some reason trying to bring levity to the hellish situation we were in.

"Shaun, you fucking idiot! Now is not the time for your shit jokes," Ember said, thankfully just into my head, which was kind of appreciated.

No one else had spoken, so I continued. "Any suggestions, then?"

"We take the ship and the captain's body with us. There will be something we can do. It will just take time," Elyek responded.

"Sounds like a good enough idea to me. Do we have enough crew to take both ships?" I asked.

"Yes. Although we are stretching our resources thin," Acclo piped up immediately.

"It would be madness not to take these ships, Captain," Elyek added. "They seem to be very advanced, even in comparison to the Thoth."

"If we can, we will totally take them. Plus, it'll mean we can put butts in the seats of even more weapon stations. We can get more crew eventually, even if it means going back to Torax and that fucking smugglers' moon. It'll be nice to know we have a stronger fleet for space battles; that's something we've been massively under-powered for. Agreed?"

Everyone nodded, including Mick, but he looked thoughtful. "These really must be some of their best ships, right?" he said. "To catch up with us this far away. I mean, I still can't believe they found us. Does it seem odd to any of you guys?"

Everyone looked confused, excluding me. "Yeah, Mick. I don't know why, and we have a lot going on, but it feels like something was a bit off with them turning up like that. But to be honest, I wouldn't know what to do about it. Everyone just keep their eyes open for anyone behaving suspiciously."

Astrid replied, "Absolutely, Captain. I will have the Thoth covered."

"Cool, let's leave it at that for now. Acclo, Koparr, work with Astrid and Rufus to get well-balanced crews for each Hunter ship. Ten should be enough on each, right?"

"Yes Captain, right away," Acclo answered before they left with Astrid and Koparr.

That left me, Ember, Calegg, Elyek, Mick and Gus. I slumped against Ogun's pod and slid to the ground. I wanted to cry, to hurl, to be in a coma like Ogun.

"Shaun, are you okay?" Numerous voices said at once, worrying around me. Ember crouched down and put an arm around me.

"I really don't think I am. I'm not the right person to be running this shit-show. All those deaths. Plus, how many did I coldly order myself? I'm turning into a fucking monster, just like the Fystr."

"Stop being a daft-ass, Shaun," Ember said from my

side. "You're a pretty awesome guy. We've just survived a stand-up fight with 40 Fystr. That would've been impossible even a month ago. Now, I'm glad you're upset; we've lost a few good people and it's heart wrenching. It's one of the reasons why I love you, too. But the only thing similar about you and the Fystr is how big your heads are. You can't take credit for everything we've done that's a success. We're a team, and we've worked together to get where we are now."

"I know that! I'm not trying to take credit for everything!" I said, offended.

"Really? Because it sounds to me like you're trying to take all the responsibility for everything that's gone wrong or isn't very nice. You can't have one without the other."

"No, it's not that. All those deaths are on my hands, including the ones I just ordered."

"No, they're not, Shaun," Mick said next. "All of those deaths are purely in the Fystr's hands. Every last one. Now, you're a crazy, odd bastard, and I don't know how you achieve one-tenth of what you do, but I'm proud to follow you. I think I can speak for every single person of the Uprising when I say that."

"You do for me," Gus said, while the others nodded agreement.

Then Gus added: "Although it's closer to one-fifth for me," which brought some chuckles.

Calegg bent down. "It's worse for me. I don't want to put a number on it, but I'd still follow you to my death," he said as he patted my shoulder.

Ember leaned in. "Right, Shaun. That's enough of us all blowing smoke up your ass. We know why you're feeling like this, but you need to give your head a wobble.

We've just won an impressive battle, and that's what the people of the Uprising need to see and hear from you. Not this morose, motherfucking self-pity. We only let you off because we're pretty much a family, but those guys out there need a lot more from you."

"Argh! Fuck off, all of you, okay! I just needed a moment to pull myself together, and you all ruined it." I pulled myself to my feet and gave everyone a red-eyed smile. I hadn't cried, but I'd been bloody close. Especially after they all started trying to make me feel better. They were right though; I had a job to do, and I needed to keep going for everyone else. I decided I'd just cry my ass off in my favorite hiding spot tonight: the shower.

We all walked back off the ship, and I pretended I was overjoyed with our victory and filled with confidence. I actually felt bad that I was lying to everyone with my body language, but I pushed it down to the welcoming recesses of my mind.

I saw the main security officer was standing next to Rufus, looking distraught but cowed. We all walked over to see how we could help, because so far, I was not hugely impressed with Rufus's decision-making.

"We'll remove all the bodies," Rufus was saying.

"The place is ruined," the security officer said, outraged. "I'll get into so much trouble. This is a Galactic-Empire-sanctioned docking hanger. I'll have to report everything that has happened, and I'll be punished. No matter," he whined. He was about five feet tall, with a body covered from head to toe in coarse, yellow hair, and he showed large, flat, white teeth when he grimaced.

"What would it take to report none of this?" I asked.

"I must report it. If anyone turns up and it's in this state, there'll be even more trouble."

"We'll fix it then," I said, feeling a little irritation growing in me.

"With what? My maintenance budget won't cover a fraction of this!"

"So, how much do you need not to report it and get it fixed up?" I sighed. "For fuck's sake, man. What I'm saying is, we give you money, you don't report us, you don't get in trouble. You dig?"

"Dig?"

"Arrrggghhh!" I yelled in frustration. I was clearly on edge. "Give me a number and make it reasonable. Or, I can just kill you and deal with the next in command here."

"Urr... I'm not sure. It's all a bit much today," he stuttered. His body quivering in fear. I felt terrible, and really wished I hadn't just threatened to kill him.

"I think 50,000 senlars will suffice for repairs," Elyek said, helpfully.

He stuttered again, "Urr... okay."

"Will that buy his silence and pay for the inconvenience, Elyek?"

"Perhaps not. We can go to 80,000, but I wouldn't give more."

"How does that sound?" I asked the head security guard.

"Y... yes...," he stammered. "That's more than fair. Thank you, thank you. And, if you don't bring great warrior enemies along with you, come back any time. You'll be honored guests!"

"Sounds like a fair deal," I said, turning away from him to talk to my friends. "I suppose now I'd better speak to the whole crew."

"Yes. That would be wise," Elyek said. "I will arrange for everyone to gather."

"Thanks, do we have the names of who we lost yet Elyek?"

"I will find out," Elyek said, reaching for their comm. A few calls later, and I had the sickening list. Twenty-two people had died in total. Somehow only four from Uprising, not that it mattered which ship they were from. I recognized only one name on the list, and my stomach lurched. Janet! Poor, hopeful Janet. I'd only spoken to her the once but she appeared in my mind with crystal clarity. The bastards had killed Janet. I decided I would kill a Fystr in her honor, next time I came up against them.

Ten minutes later, a weary crew stood in front of me, and I had to strengthen my backbone once more. "Well, everyone! That was a very unexpected visit from the Fystr. Being so far away from their territory, I honestly thought it'd be a long time before we saw them again. It appears even this far out they're dogged in their pursuit. Hopefully, we won't be seeing them for a while.

"The ships they've kindly left us look to be their finest advanced Hunter ships, which explains why they had the ability to catch up with us. But now we can use them to defend ourselves and become an even more formidable force!"

The crowd cheered at that, and I was happy to pause for a few moments to get my words in order. Once the noise had died down, I continued. "What I want to say though, is that I'm so fucking proud of how you all handled yourselves. All that training and hard work you put in before today has really paid off. I don't think the Fystr knew what the hell to do with themselves. The combination of Torax, Veiletians and superhumans was truly amazing. I hope you all appreciate what everyone is bringing to the table. Everyone here today played their part in this victory."

Again, cheers and applause went up. Different races patted each other on their backs, some even hugged. It looked as though team bonding was going well. That made me even prouder than the victory. Ember moved closer and took my hand, squeezing tightly. I was feeling a little more buoyed now and forged on. "I also want you all to remember that this was 40 Fystr, and they still made it bloody hard for us. We lost nearly as many people as they did today, and I can't stand losing a single person. So we need to keep training, because one day we'll be faced with thousands of Fystr arrayed against us".

"Millions," Ember whispered behind me. What a knob.

"And I don't want to lose so many in the future. Now, everyone! We're going back on the ships, and I'll make sure we respectfully mourn everyone we've lost. I just needed you all to know how proud I am *of all of you!*"

A final, massive cheer went up again.

I couldn't have been prouder. We took horrible losses, but it was still a glorious victory.

C19
Lovers Tiff

Once I walked away from the crowd my adrenaline must have fled me, because I went from feeling confident to feeling like a car wreck in seconds.

As soon as I arrived on the ship, I headed straight to the shower. It was becoming my go-to hiding place when I didn't want to talk to anyone, including Ember. It was about the only place on the ship where I might not be interrupted. I needed desperately to level myself out and get my thoughts in order. No matter what I did though, I kept replaying the moment that the remaining Fystr – the ones I'd ordered Hwista to kill – dropped to the floor in pools of gushing blood. No matter what anyone said, that blood was on my hands. Don't get me wrong, I didn't think I'd made the wrong decision, but I still felt dirtier than a tramp's underpants from ordering the deed. I seriously hoped I'd never have to do it again – but deep down, I knew the likelihood was that I'd be in a similar position someday. Then I thought that I'd rather do it myself than put that responsibility on anyone else. After about half-an-hour of such thoughts, I realized that I was going round in circles. It wasn't helping me at all.

To escape, I went to my Cognition Room and began madly tackling the inventory. All the while the shower drummed into the back of my neck. Havok was uninvited, but showed up nonetheless. "Hey, Shaun. Would you like some music?"

"No, Havok. I'd like for you to fuck off so I can be alone."

"What's wrong with you?" he asked, inquisitively. Though I reckoned he knew exactly why I was angry.

"You bloody well know, Havok! You killed Heiliun when I told you not to!"

"He needed to die, Shaun. I was happy to make that decision for you. You were too emotional, and I did tell you I'd protect you. Even from yourself."

"You crossed a fucking line, Havok, and I'm not happy about it. The fact that you don't see that is making me question a few things about our relationship."

"Well, tell me then Shaun. Explain what your problem is, because as I see it, all those Fystr are dead and would have been whether I was there or not. Only I made it easier and probably saved lives," he said, almost smugly, and I wished he was a person so I could punch him.

"No Havok, you shithead! I make those calls. When I told the crew not to fire on those last few Fystr, they did it. I showed mercy, and they threw it in my face. But if I have no compassion, then I am no better than a Fystr. I lead people, and they don't want to see me losing my shit, killing everyone without remorse. A lot of these people have lived under the oppressive rule of compassionless assholes. They expect something better from me.

"When you take control away from me like that, you make it look like I've no compassion. You affect how the people I'm leading see me and my choices. I can't have you do that! You're either with me doing as I ask, or you're a fucking liability."

"After everything I've done for you!" Havok said, indignantly.

"Yes, Havok. After everything you've done – and you've done a lot, no doubt about it. I wouldn't be here if it wasn't for you. That doesn't mean I can have you making those calls for me. You were in my hands, and I said stop. You didn't stop."

"You're not getting it, Shaun, what I did…"

"Get out, Havok. Now! I needed time to myself and you've interrupted that, again when I asked you not to. Just get out of my head. We'll deal with this later when I'm not so emotionally charged."

He left and I sighed. Now, I couldn't even concentrate on cleaning. I punched the shelves with all my force, and they crumpled. Then I moved back into my normal state, under the drumming pressure of the shower. A piercing headache in my temple made me curse the stupid act of aggression inside my own mind. That might not have been the cause, but it probably was.

When I came out of the shower, Ember was lying on the bed with her eyes closed. When I lay down next to her, they flew open in a flash. "Wow! You really upset Havok," she stated. "He said you didn't want to use him anymore."

"No. I didn't. I just said he can't do things I tell him not to do when he's in my hands." I sighed and rolled to face her. "I told him to stop when Heiliun was mourning his wife. I knew he would have had to die eventually, but that's not how I would've killed him. Havok didn't listen and carried on anyway. Fuck it, Ember. I can't trust him if he's gonna do shit like that."

"He really, genuinely loves you, Shaun. You need to talk to him. He's beside himself."

"I will. Goddamn it. I don't need this shit."

"That's what being a leader is about. You can't just enjoy the sweet captain's privileges without all the hassle that comes with it."

"Why not? You do."

She laughed. "Yeah, I do. But we're not talking about me, are we Captain?"

I growled, "Right. I'm gonna talk to him again." I closed my eyes. I could feel her nestle into me and couldn't help but smile. That one little act of affection relaxed me more than an hour in the shower did.

I let myself drift into Havok's Mindscape. "Alright, you damned axe. Where are you hiding?"

His form appeared before me; he looked sad. I don't know how, perhaps duller, smaller. It was hard to put my finger on, nonetheless I definitely got that impression.

"Okay, dude. I love you, okay. You're like a brother, or something. But you have to think about how this shit looks, or just fucking listen to me. I know it doesn't matter to you because you're a different kind of alive, or lifeforce... fuck, I don't know. That guy gave up his life to mourn his wife. Yes, he was a dick. Yes, he would've had to die anyway, but I have to think about the way people die sometimes. What you did made me look like a vicious, uncaring shit, and that's not who I am. As much as I do want you by my side, you have to promise to stop if I ask you to in future."

He let out a long, sad sigh. "Okay Shaun, I'm sorry. Though I still don't really understand, and I just want to freely slaughter all of our enemies. I accept that you have responsibilities, and I don't want to hurt your ability to lead. So I promise it won't happen again. I'm going to do everything else I do on my own though to make sure we're safe. Just don't ever abandon me."

"I won't, dude. I definitely won't. Just try to remember, I'm not a 4000-year-old, bloodthirsty axe, and I can't afford to think like one."

"Ha, ha, ha!" Havok laughed. "That position is already taken!"

"Okay dude. And seriously, aside from that, thank you so much for everything you do for us all. You're amazing." With that I left his Mindscape.

Ember was still snuggled right in. Barely awake, she asked, "How'd it go?"

"We're good now, thanks. How are you doing by the way? We both survived this encounter unscathed, but damn, that was crazy back there."

"I'm good, and proud of you. It was a tough situation. You handled it well."

"We were lucky again, Ember. Our people fought bravely. We're still surprising them with our strengths and abilities. That's not gonna last forever. And as you kindly reminded me during my speech, there's millions of fuckers after us."

"It's a big old universe. We can just keep hitting the bastards and running."

"Until they finally corner us."

"That's why we're trying to build an army, dipshit."

"I know, I know. I suppose we're training as hard as we can."

"Yeah. We're doing everything we can, and we still have a fuck-ton of things to learn. Don't feel demoralized. We're gonna be good. Promise."

"Don't listen to me. Let's just keep doing what we're doing."

"Exactly. Now, rest that crazy head of yours. It's been a

shit-house of a day, and it'll feel better tomorrow."

"Should I be sleeping? We've just left what was essentially a war zone. Will our crew not need me there?"

"They need you fresh and sane. Not whatever you are now. You did a hell of a lot of the heavy lifting back there, too. So shut your eyes and get your ass to sleep."

I did as Ember commanded. Thoughts ran sprints in my mind, and I could see no way of getting to sleep; then it was morning.

I took my time getting dressed. I was much calmer than the day before. I still had contrasting feelings on everything, but I was able to deal with it now. Ember got ready alongside me, and we chatted about the smaller things. It was a nice release.

By the time we made it to the bridge, I was actually feeling pretty good. I took Havok with me. I thought he could probably do with the bonding time after our tiff.

"Good morning, Captain, Ember," Miraek said as we took our seats. "We're around eight hours out from the relay station."

"That's quick. Have we picked anything up to be concerned about?" I said, somewhat relieved that it was Miraek flying and not Hwista; I didn't know how I could look them in the eyes after the order I had given.

"No, Captain," Miraek answered, "everything looks as we would expect, although we are being extremely cautious. The Hunter ships have much faster propulsion engines than any of our bigger ships, so they are out scouting in front and at the rear. I hope we will have plenty of warning should anything untoward approach."

"That's a great use. Good to know we have that extra layer of security now. Any news on Ogun's condition?"

"No. I don't believe anyone is actively trying to revive

him at the moment."

"No, of course not. Now is probably not the time," I replied.

Miraek nodded and concentrated on the terminal at the pilot's station.

"Sounds like everything's okay. What are we gonna do about all the bodies? They deserve some kind of funeral, and I have no clue how to even begin organizing all of this."

"There's a Veiletian for that," Ember smiled.

"They might be asleep. I'll wait until they show."

"Yeah, it was a tough day for everyone yesterday," Ember replied.

We sat on the bridge chatting to each other and the crew around us. Koparr was manning the weapons, and it was nice to catch up a bit with him. Just over an hour later, Acclo appeared on the bridge. They smiled when they saw Ember and me and came straight over.

"Is there anything I can do for you, Captain, Ember?"

"Hey, Acclo. Nice to see you. And, well, yeah, although I'm sorry for putting on you all of the time."

"Why? This is my place, and I feel completed by the position. Life in the enclave was like a prison for my mind. This opportunity has been a dream come true! So please, give me your problems, and if I can't solve them, I have an excellent network of crew members who can," Acclo said, beaming.

"Alrighty then. It's about some kind of cross-ship memorial for those we've lost in the battle. We also need a way to *dispose* of the bodies respectfully and honor their bravery." Janet popped into my head unbidden, and the image hit me hard; she now represented everyone we lost, everyone who I barely knew, but who had a full and intricate life all the same. I struggled to return to what Acclo was saying, even though they were answering my question.

"... and we have the cross-ship memorial service arranged for later today, in four hours and 20 minutes. The main question is, how would we do it? There are options on all the ships for recycling of the bodies. They could feed the FSU, water supplies and even atmospheric units. However, Captain Astrid seemed aghast at this notion. I checked with a few other humans, and it seems this is a standard human response."

"Yup, definitely not doing that," Ember said from my side.

"Too close to cannibalism. Very taboo with humans, generally."

"That is fine. I am happy to abide by people's customs. Nonetheless, in the interests of free beliefs, we as Veiletians would be honored to be recycled in this way. It would be fitting for us to know that we had helped sustain and even become part of that which we gave our lives for."

"You're damn right too, Acclo! And I 100% agree with you. But we humans can be rigid with our views. What other options do you have for us?"

"The Torax bury their dead, as they don't burn very well, but we don't have burial procedures. Also, on this occasion no Torax died, so that's a null point."

"Can we direct the recycling to other things? Just not the FSU or water?" Ember asked.

"I am unsure, but I will check," Acclo said, pulling out their comm. "Gus? It's Acclo."

Gus's voice replied: he sounded a little sleepy. "Hey Acclo, what can I do for you?"

"Can we reroute the recycling units so our deceased don't pass freely into the FSU or water supply?"

"Sure. I don't know if there's that option, but there will be in an hour. You can count on it."

"Thank you, Gus. Helpful as always."

"No problem," Gus replied, and his comm disconnected.

"So Captain, everything is arranged. Is there anything else I can help with?"

"No thanks, Acclo. You've done everything I could've hoped for."

"Very well. I shall return when everything is in order." With an unexpected bow, Acclo left.

I sat deep in thought about our losses. I didn't know any of those who had died personally other than Janet who I'd met briefly.

Hwista walked in seeming almost nonchalant; any lingering traces of the slaughter I had asked them to carry out were nowhere to be seen.

"Good day, Captain," They said as they entered.

They were about to engage with Miraek when I called over. "Hwista! Can I talk with you in my office, please?" I said, getting up from my seat. Thankfully, Ember stayed where she was.

"Of course, Captain. Right away."

They closed the door behind them as they entered after me. I took a seat, then gestured for them to do the same.

"Is everything okay, Captain?" Hwista said, a concerned look on their face.

"I honestly don't know. I am genuinely sorry to have given you those orders yesterday, but I thank you for carrying them out in the swift and efficient manner you did."

"You really don't need to thank me. Serving the Uprising is not just a job, it is like a new family. One I hope will help to balance out the power distortions in the galaxy. I have researched the Fystr: what they did, and what they continue to do. They are a supremely powerful race without remorse or compassion. You absolutely made the right decision, and I remain honored to have carried out your orders." They stopped, and I was about to give out various platitudes, but then they started talking again. "In fact Captain, if you did not remove them, I admit I would have been disappointed in you. In our circumstances one should never leave an enemy at their backs. We have too few people and too many enemies to be so forgiving or naive. That said, you gave them an opportunity to repent and toe the line with the Uprising. If I feel any emotion over the whole affair, it is sadness for those lost and concern that you are hurt by the deaths of our enemies."

"Don't get me wrong, I'm not hurt by their deaths. There were no other options. Although just because a job is necessary, it doesn't mean it's a good job. And it doesn't mean it won't leave psychological scars."

"I think I understand what you are saying, although a lot of it is lost in translation between our species. You are an emotional race, which seems to lend you great strength and resolve. The Veiletians are naturally a very fact-based race; we tend to follow a rational course, rather than be governed by emotions."

"Yeah, I get that about you guys. Thanks for your understanding about where I'm coming from, and I'll try my best to acknowledge your culture as much as I can within the Uprising. Only, if we recycle Veiletian bodies in the future, I'll have to find a way to divert you from the FSU. I've a bad history with that kinda shit, and I'm not going back to it."

Hwista laughed. "I have no idea what you're talking about, Captain Shaun, but I do trust you. If there's anything that needs doing that your human emotions make difficult, please let me know. If it is the right course of action, I will carry out whichever task you see fit."

"Wow. This isn't how I saw this conversation going, but thanks Hwista. Now go on and take over from Miraek. I get the feeling they could do with a break."

"I will, but I doubt it. They would have taken rest as they needed it. Veiletians do not have sleep cycles. We can rest for seconds and minutes at a time. As long as we hit a certain time scale, over 40 or so hours, we are fine."

"Really? That's fucking brilliant. Wish I could do that. Once my head hits the pillow I'm basically dead for eight hours, and if I don't get those hours I'm unbearable."

"You have my sympathy, yet you seem to navigate your shortcomings very well."

"I try. Oh, and thanks again Hwista."

With that, they turned and left. I had to admit the conversation both eased my conscience and made me nervous as hell about the Veiletians. Those fuckers were cold as ice. Still, they balanced the crew out nicely, along with the Torax, who had none of that coldness. They were fiery and emotional, but when you're laser-proof and can shoot fire, you can do as you damn well please.

I sat in my extremely comfy chair mulling over our people, what we were trying to do and how well it was working. As well as the fact that last year I was a fat-ass on a couch who'd almost given up on life. Ogun had royally screwed me at the same time as he had elevated me into an existence that was like living an amazing book or movie. I knew how bad life could be, and that I'd been given an unbelievable second chance. Those Fystr could go fuck themselves. Gus was right; only one person had brought this on and it sure as shit wasn't me. But I was going to end it, someday, somehow.

When the time for the memorial ceremony came, we all moved to the Uprising's loading bay, which was the only place that could hold the whole crew comfortably. There was a big screen showing each other ship's loading bay, too, so when I spoke, everyone would hear me. Astrid and Rufus would also be speaking.

I said a fuck-ton of words, but honestly, I don't want to bore you with them. It was morose, and I didn't really know any of the fallen that well, which means you didn't know them either because I've never spoken about any of them before. Let's just say it was really sad and the dead got a dignified send off. Although the thought that I was now breathing in our recycled warriors was strange.

C20
It was a Stupid
Idea Anyway!

Beler 3103 lay near the outer limit of the Perseus system. I think we all took a collective gasp when we saw it. I could barely get my head around the fact that an artificial structure could be so vast; it was essentially a planet, with arm-like projections reaching into space both horizontally and vertically, giving it a feeling of further enormity. And to top it all off, there must have been a thousand ships in orbit.

We had the Seshat lead us in, as it was Rufus who had negotiated the deal for the contract and who knew most about the situation we were entering. I was really fucking nervous about it now. I hadn't spoken to Rufus about what had happened at the supply station, but I wasn't exactly pleased about it. As horrible as it was, I just didn't trust him anymore. He was either an incompetent idiot, or he wasn't working with the Uprising's best intentions at heart. I hadn't brought it up with anyone yet, I just wanted to keep watching him for now.

Thankfully, nothing went awry; we weren't attacked out of hand, which was a relief. We called up a joint meeting between the ships to hear what Rufus had found out from his contact with the fleet.

"I've spoken with Fleet Admiral Mollissan. Beler 3103 has been retaken from enemy aliens. They attacked from what is known as the Dark Sector, whatever that is, sir," he said, overly respectfully, probably because of our altercation over Fystr amnesty. He needed to do a seamless job here, or I would be putting someone else in charge of the Seshat.

I pushed that from my mind for the moment to ask: "What exactly is the Dark Sector, then?"

"I didn't ask because it was spoken as if I should know. I didn't want to appear ignorant. I intend to ask some of our alien crew members. Perhaps you could do the same?"

"Yeah, I will. I thought the Galactic Empire covered everything that wasn't controlled by the Fystr?"

"As did I. It seems we don't know everything this galaxy has to offer. What I have learnt is that we are on the border of the Dark Sector. Beler 3103 has always laid in Galactic Empire territory, until a recent attack by the Dark Sector aliens. The Empire retaliated quickly and reclaimed it."

"So do they even need us now?" I was confused. This was a seriously odd scenario.

"Yes, they're expecting a fleet from the Dark Sector to retake the station. So they're building their current fleet up, making it large enough to prevent any surprises. We'll be part of that fight. Our current orders are to wait and be ready. I've been led to believe they've got a lot more ships coming. We just need to hang around, waiting and hoping that the Dark Sector fleet doesn't arrive first."

"Sounds like they're concerned by whatever's coming, doesn't it?" But I didn't wait for a response. "Everyone, stay in touch, and any info on what Dark Sector is would be greatly appreciated. We'll try to find out more ourselves. For now, I'm gonna move us away from the main fleet. I trust these fuckers about as far as I would trust myself with a packet of cookies a couple of years ago!"

Silence greeted my statement. Miserable bastards! I continued, "We could also do with carrying out training drills. We haven't fought in a battle like this before, so if we can devise anything that will bolster our chances, that'd be excellent."

"That's a good idea," Astrid said, quickly. "I'll see what the Thoth has in its data banks for that."

"I will too!" Rufus said, more hopefully.

"Okay. Time to go. Speak later," I said, and our connection ended. I immediately sent an order to Hwista to move us slowly away from the cluster of ships around the station.

"Shaun," Ember said, quietly. "I thought we were trying to big you up a bit?"

"We are. What's your problem?" I replied, baffled.

"Well, I'm no expert on confidence building, but discussing your weakness for cookies with the two people you need to respect you the most, doesn't seem like a winning strategy," she grinned as she spoke.

"Maybe, but it was funny to me at least. And I'll take those wins where I can get them."

She spoke into my mind next. "Stop being a fucking idiot! We all know you're better than that, and I think it's gonna be more important than ever in the coming days."

"Thanks for the advice, and thanks for not undermining me at every turn anymore. I know it's hard for you, and it's appreciated. However, we're doing okay at the moment, and though I don't buy into all this Onnekus, jammy-bastard shit, I don't want to try and change who

I am, unless it happens naturally over time. You never know, it could be my general attitude to life that's helping us."

"In a fucked-up, typical Shaun kinda way, that possibly makes sense. But try to keep the self-degradation to a minimum, whether you think it's funny or not. Otherwise, what's the point in all this effort I'm putting in?"

"Fair enough. I'll remember not to put myself down. The big question now though is, what in the actual fuck is the Dark Sector?"

"That does seem like it would be important information." Ember smiled. "Elyek and Calegg should be on the bridge. Let's go and see them," she said, offering her hand to me to get off the couch. It was comical because of the size difference, and actually made it harder to get up from my seated position. But it was the gesture that counted.

"Elyek, we need to pick your brains. Do you have a minute?" I said as we entered the bridge.

"Certainly, Captain," they replied. "Hwista, are you okay to hold the fort?"

"Yes. Take all the time you need."

"Oh, it won't take long," Ember said.

"Calegg! You too, man. The enemy we're about to face is from the Dark Sector."

Elyek's face dropped.

"That bad huh?" I asked.

"I'm really not sure, Captain. What I do know is that the Empire would love to possess that part of the galaxy but have never been able to get a foothold there. Whoever lives there must be very capable at defending themselves. In fact...," Elyek turned to the terminal and began checking something intently. A second later they spun back around, "As I suspected. This station is actually in Dark Sector territory. We have most certainly been lied to."

"I don't know anything about it," Calegg said with a shrug. "Although I'd love to know what we're flying into."

"I believe this is actually a land grab by the Empire," Elyek answered, "and now they are waiting for the inevitable retaliation to come."

"Oh, shit. That's not good. I mean, we don't really want to be part of a conquering force. It's kind of the opposite of what we're supposed to stand for," I said.

"I don't think they'll get any further into the Dark Sector if past engagements are anything to go by," Elyek replied, concern etched on their face.

"So, these Dark Sector aliens, whoever the fuck they are, are very capable of smoking Empire attacks. What are we gonna do?" Ember asked.

"Get the hell out of here?" Calegg offered.

"That will hurt our mercenary credentials a great deal," Elyek replied.

"How about, just stay near the back, as far from the action as possible?" Ember said with a smirk.

"So we're staying, but we're not risking ourselves in this shit-show?" I said.

"I don't know if we have a lot of choice at the minute. We need to increase our reputation if we want to grow and be taken seriously," Elyek answered.

"We're all agreed on this?" I asked.

Three heads nodded.

"Let's keep training in those maneuvers then. Looks like we're gonna need them."

I took my seat on the bridge, watching the training exercises unfold with Ember by my side. I'd pretty much phased out, staring into the darkness outside, when Ember broke me out of it. "Wonder if there's been any progress with getting Ogun out of the chamber?"

"Oh, man. I'd almost forgotten about Ogun. We should really check in with the Hunter ship he's on."

"We should, and we should also give both of those ships names," she said.

"Ha! Yeah, though that can wait."

"I thought it was unlucky to not name a ship."

"I don't even know who's on the damn ships. I never asked Acclo."

"You did tell Acclo not to tell you every little thing, if you remember. Fortunately for you I know, so you don't have to. Wulek is captaining the ship that holds Ogun's body, and a human called William is flying the other. Apparently, he and his team are very capable. He was highly effective in the battle against the Fystr."

"Is he from the Thoth? Can't say I recall the name."

"Nope, the Seshat, although he begged Acclo to have one of the ships. As far as I can gather, he doesn't get on with Rufus at all."

"Hmm, I like him already. So, we need to talk to Wulek then?"

"Yup," she agreed, and brought Wulek up on the small screen between our chairs.

"Hello, Captain and Ember. What can I do for you both?"

"Hey, Wulek. Is everything okay over there?" Ember asked.

"Yes. Certainly quieter. It will be good to get more crew members on board."

"Hopefully we can fill your ranks soon. Have you named your ship yet?" I asked.

"Informally, as it's bad luck to have an unnamed ship. We are calling it the Photia. Two of our Torax members wished to name the ship Fire, predictably. One of our human crew members, Felicity, offered the name Photia, which is fire in an ancient Earth language, apparently. We've gone with that. Obviously the choice is yours, Captain."

"Hell no! I don't want that responsibility. Photia is fine by me."

"Then, the Photia we are," Wulek smiled, and I think they were happier with that result than they let on.

"Next question, Wulek. Has there been any progress with releasing Ogun?" I asked.

"I think we are making progress. There is a plan to release him, but the general consensus is not to bring him out until we are somewhere safe and can transport him to one of the medical bays on the larger ships. None of his wounds have healed. The stasis pod is holding his body in the exact condition it was when they placed him inside."

"Shit, that's an evil thing to do. The bastards! I see why you've left him. Hopefully we can get this stupid battle over with and get somewhere to free him in safety with the care he needs."

"Yes, Captain. A sound plan."

"Okay Wulek, thanks for taking on the Photia. Keep in touch," I said, before ending the communication.

Looking to Ember, I said, "I can't believe how much I'm looking forward to getting him outta there. I hope he's okay, you know, up there," I tapped my head.

"There's a good chance he won't be, Shaun. We don't know what the hell they've done to him, but you know it will be bad."

Thinking about that depressed the shit out of me; even

if we managed to free him, he could be totally fucked. "Let's just wait and see, shall we? Guessing the worst won't help anyone," I sighed.

"Yeah," replied Ember, "you're right. Come on. Let's give this William a call. Introduce ourselves and see if he has a name for his ship." With a few jabs on the terminal, Ember brought up William's face. His wild, bright-red hair and beard made him instantly recognizable as the extra-energetic fighter against the Fystr we battled on the last supply station. I had intended to seek him out at some point. Now I didn't have to.

"Ach, helloo there Cap'n," he said in a strong Scottish accent, big grin stretching across his face, "A thought I'd never get te speak te the gaffer!"

"Hey, William. It's nice to meet you, too. I was impressed with your work in our last battle. How are you finding the Hunter ship?"

"Och well, a do like killing Fystr. As for this," he said, gesturing around him, "aye, it's a canny wee ship. Got some good folks wi' me, so it's no so bad. The food synths are shite! There's nae even an option for lager or whisky!"

"I mean, should you be drinking when you're in control of a spacecraft?" I questioned.

"Christ alive! A man has te 'ave a minute te hisel', no? It's no like I'm hammered at the wheel," he brayed out a raucous laugh. I couldn't help but grin back. It was hard not to be endeared by him.

"Fucking hell, William. Have you been drinking already?" Ember asked.

"No! Ye daft bugger. I've just bloody told ye there's no drink over here. Anyways, a get all maudlin when 'ave had a slurp, so ye'd know."

Ember started laughing her ass off. "Who the hell put

you in charge of a ship?"

"Well I'm fucked if ah know! But you're nae gettin' it back. This is ma baby now. Named it and everythin'!"

"We're not taking it off you, William, but I'm very happy to hear you've named your baby. What have you called it?" I asked.

"The Flying Scotsman!" He broke into hysterics again.

"Hilarious, William. But seriously, what have you called it?" Ember asked.

"No, really. Any vehicle ah 'ave, gets called the Flying Scotsman. Every bike, every car, at least 'til ah got banned for life drink drivin' again. A cannae very well break with tradition now!"

Ember looked at me, as if to say, 'Are you going to do something about this nutter?' I just shrugged, "It's different, I'll give you that. But you know, if you get a bigger ship in the future, you can't just rename it right?"

"I'm quite happy with ma baby here," he said, slapping the unit next to him with a big thud.

"Great. It's been good to meet you, William. Hopefully, we'll meet face-to-face soon, after this battle's over."

"A look forward tae it, Captain. Thanks for callin'."

I ended the communication.

"We need to speak to Acclo," Ember said. "Why the hell have they put him in charge?"

"He's alright. Might be good to have a different outlook," I replied.

Ember shook her head, but I could see she was holding back a smile.

"Captain!" Elyek said loudly. "There are more ships arriving. Lots more."

"Good," I said. "Hopefully, we can get on with this, so we can get the hell outta here. I'm liking it less and less by the minute."

"Yes. I hope so too," Elyek replied.

We watched the ships arrive over the next two days. And still we heard nothing from the Fleet Admiral. Not until the fourth day, when we received a call from Rufus, with Astrid, William and Wulek all linked in. He began speaking quickly: "There have been reports of a large fleet moving through the Dark Sector. Fortunately, we have been heavily reinforced by the arrival of ships from a mercenary group, a powerful one called the Rotushna. This has prompted a call to arms."

"What's the plan?" I asked.

"We're now apparently moving forward to meet whatever is coming. The Uprising ships need to go to these coordinates to be positioned in front of the fleet, along with the other smaller mercenary groups. We'll be the first into the fight. A position of great honor, so I was told."

The expressions on the faces of everyone involved in the conversation told its own story. "That sounds more like a death sentence than a position of honor," I said dryly. "You all heard that shit. What do you think?" I addressed everyone present.

"We are being sent in as cannon fodder, Captain. To draw fire and hopefully soften up the enemy for the Empire fleet and Rotushna to claim the real glory. We will not even be a sidenote if this battle goes well. Although if we lose, we will probably be blamed for that," Wulek said. Astrid nodded in agreement.

Surprisingly, William just sat calmly, listening.

"Are they fucking serious, Rufus?" Ember ranted. "I bet they're looking to save money on our fee too! Don't have to pay us if we're space dust."

I had to say, my anger was bubbling a little at the insult, too. "Rufus, get the Fleet Admiral up and patch him through to me. You've done a great job so far, but now I need to speak to this son-of-a-bitch myself," I fumed.

"Are you sure you want to change who communicates at this stage, Shaun? It will look odd. I'm perfectly capable of getting us moved to another position."

"Rufus! I'm at the head of the Uprising. This situation could cost *all* our lives. This Admiral's obviously a complete stuck-up prick. If we must deal with him, then I'll do it."

Rufus seemed to sulk. "Very well, Shaun. I will do as you ask." His screen went black.

"I'll keep you all up-to-date with what's happening," I said before everyone's links closed.

A few minutes later, Fleet Admiral Mollissan appeared on the screen of the Uprising in all his glory. He was a pudgy, pink-colored alien that looked for all the world like a cross between a pig, a cat and a man. He even had big whiskers sprouting from his flat nose. "Captain Rufus," he said, not even looking at the screen, "I haven't got time for idle chat with you. We're planning the engagement here. Why have you not begun moving into..." He stopped, finally noticing he wasn't talking to Rufus. "Who are you? This is an outrage. Who put this communication through?" he yelled, looking around his own bridge for a culprit.

"Hey, Admiral. I'm the leader of our mercenary group. Rufus is one of my captains," I seethed with barely concealed anger. "Having discussed your request with my crew, we can't understand why you'd send the smaller mercenary groups, who are unfamiliar with each other, into battle first. Wouldn't it make more sense to send larger, well-connected groups first, with smaller groups providing support?"

He was flustered by the fact I'd called him out; he was obviously used to having his orders followed without question. "You have been sent here for a good sum of money to be under my command!" he yelled, angrily. "And while you are under my command, you will do as I say. Now get up there to the front of the line and do your damned job!" He snapped the last few words as if that were final.

"Admiral, our ships are worth probably four or five million senlars, and there are 200 people on board. I guarantee you that I'm not throwing all that away for a few thousand senlar at the order of some joker who wants to use us as cannon fodder."

"So you are deserting!" he declared.

"Don't think so. I mean, can you desert as a mercenary?" I replied seriously.

"You most certainly can. Mark my words, you will become the enemy of the Galactic Empire. I will make sure of it."

"But don't you need to pay us for being here before we can actually desert?"

"What?" he blustered.

"We haven't been paid anything yet, so I'm saying we can't really desert because we're not officially part of your fleet. Which is probably intentional, as you're intending to use my people to soften up some unknown enemy and make your job easier," I explained.

His response was to bluster speechlessly.

"Look, Admiral. We'll fight this fight with you, but it'll be as equals. Not as pawns. Have a think about it and get back to me." I flipped the comms off, then announced to the bridge: "What a turd burger!"

Elyek was staring intently at me. In fact, most of the crew was. Only the Torax looked amused. The Veiletians and humans looked horrified. "Was that wise, Captain?" Elyek asked.

"Is dying on the whim of an ignorant prick a better alternative?"

"No. Only, perhaps you could have been more diplomatic?"

I looked at Ember, and she just smirked at me.

Calegg shouted suddenly, "Captain, they're charging their weapons!"

"Oh, shit! We need to run quick! Someone let our other ships know. Tell them to follow us."

Luckily, we still had lines open to them. "Follow us where, Captain? We can't go backwards. We are surrounded by Empire and mercenary forces. What should we do?" Elyek actually screamed the last part. That was the first time I'd really seen them lose their shit.

I looked to Ember, who just shrugged. "Sorry, Shaun. I've got nothing other than to go back in time and tell you not to piss off the admiral of a Galactic fleet. This is on you. Suck it up, buttercup, and get us out of this." Then she leaned back in her chair like she was going to have a nice nap!

"Fuck! Alright then. Elyek, head toward the Dark Sector. Match the Thoth and Seshat's top speed," I said.

Astrid and Rufus both appeared on the screen. "Shaun, what the fuck is going on?" Astrid screeched.

Rufus just didn't speak.

Probably praying for a decent answer from me, which I really didn't have. I just had a very vague plan... okay, it was a very vague hope. "Just get your jumps charging, *now*! The Galactic Empire is a bag of dicks. They were gonna outlaw us for not agreeing to die like the utter, fucking morons they must think we are. Although that kinda doesn't matter because we're already outlawed here." I was mildly distracted for a moment while our ship jerked suddenly to avoid a shot.

"I hardly think starting a damn fight with a whole fleet of them was a good solution," Rufus said coldly. "Perhaps you should have let me continue the negotiations."

I could tell both the Seshat and the Thoth were also making evasive maneuvers from the unsteadiness of Astrid and Rufus. I wanted to switch Rufus off from the conversation, but knew it would look petty.

Astrid broke me from my thoughts. "And why are we flying straight toward the Dark Sect… oh, no… there's a fleet of ships ahead of us; the enemy is here!" She let out a low growl.

Rufus abruptly added, "I thought the whole point in you talking to the admiral was to save us, Shaun. Yet it seems you've just pushed us into certain death."

"You're gonna have to trust me here, guys. Whatever happens is probably gonna suck badly, but not half as much as the situation we were in."

"How can you be sure?" Rufus asked.

"I can't, but as long as we give it our best shot, and keep pushing forward no matter what happens, I know we'll get out of this and be stronger for it."

"So we're just going to fly straight at the enemy?" Astrid deadpanned.

"Yes, we are. Think about it. Whoever lives in the Dark Sector has been strong enough to keep the Empire at bay. I'm hoping the enemy of my enemy is my friend. Yeah, I get they could be absolute skin-eating maniacs, but they might not be, too."

"We're seriously going to try to defect in the middle of a massive standoff?" Rufus said, his voice dripping with disdain.

I just wanted to reach through the screen and break his fucking neck; a thought I'd never voice out loud, but it was there.

"Shaun is right, everyone," Ember argued for me. "This shithole of an Empire is our enemy. We were gonna try to affect it from within. Until today we didn't know there was anyone else but the Galactic Empire and the Fystr Empire in the galaxy. I say let's go and see if we can make some new friends."

I was profoundly grateful for her support. One by one, they all started nodding in agreement, their confidence rising. Apart from the pilots and the rear gun station operators, that is: they were a bit busy.

The Empire's fleet had begun moving after us. Once the enemy fleet came into view around the moon base, they stopped cold, content to let the Dark Sector aliens wipe us out. I really hoped that wouldn't be the case. But as we approached the opposing fleet, I won't lie, my stomach was trying to escape from my ass. I really needed a holiday after this. As we moved out of range of the Empire fleet's weapons, I ordered for our pace to be slowed down to a less insane velocity, as we headed toward either doom or salvation.

Looking over to Ember, who was sitting watching the screen intently, I asked: "Hey! After this, do you fancy finding a nice little planet to settle down on? I can maybe find some work fixing alien roofs. I've been checking out their construction techniques, I think I could pick it up easily enough."

She looked at me, her face an emotionless mask. Then she started laughing. "You fucking ass, Shaun."

It was actually a genuine question, and I hadn't intended for that to be her reaction, but her laughing seemed to cut through the tension on the bridge like a hot knife through butter. A few others began laughing. For a moment, everything seemed like it was going to be okay.

That stopped a second later when we were hailed by one of the Dark Sector ships. "Hwista," I said, "bring up the display, please. We're gonna have to be open and honest."

Hwista nodded and up popped an alien on our screen. Whatever they intended to say died on their lips for some reason. They stood there, now open-mouthed.

"Err, hi. Are you okay?" I asked the flustered brown and gold alien.

"What... wh... why are you here?" he stuttered, pure fear written on his face.

"Do you think you know me or something?"

"You are Fystr. What brings you here, to the other side of the Galactic Habitable Zone?" his voice trembled.

"Dude, you need to chill the fuck out. We're definitely not the Fystr. We fucking hate those guys. We come in peace, looking for friends and as you can probably tell we don't get along with the Empire much either."

"I don't understand. You clearly are Fystr. No other species looks as you do."

"Yeah. We're pretty unique looking."

"So, does that mean you are Fystr?" he questioned again. "Although I will admit, the longer we talk, the more I am inclined to believe you, despite your appearance."

"Not sure how to take that, pal. But anyway, we're humans. We are from the Fystr Empire though. The bastards like to keep their foot on our necks, so we don't get out much," I laughed. Don't know why, but I did.

"We know of the atrocities they commit. That still begs the question, how are you here? This is a long way from your home. And as far as I know, if you're one of the hindered, then you should not be capable of spacefaring."

"You seem to know a lot, and you guys must be pretty tough to keep the Empire at bay."

"The Empire is an annoyance at best. They continually encroach in our territory, and we continually kick them back out again. That is of little importance today. Please explain how you are here?"

We didn't have many options available to us, and if these aliens could fuck the Empire off with ease I wanted to be their ally, so with a shrug I told him everything: "The Fystr caretaker in charge of our planet chose not to cripple our society when he should have. Instead, he developed a way to boost a few humans, or 'hindered' did you call us? Anyway, he helped us to surpass our mental barriers. So while we're not Fystr, we're not hindered anymore either."

The yet unnamed alien listened intently to what I was saying, nodding his head. "This is fascinating information and of extreme importance to our leaders. Will you wait where you are while we get in touch with them?"

"Um, that's not impossible. The Empire fleet is coming, and they want us dead. Not to mention you guys."

"We will allow you to pass further into this solar system beyond our defenses. You will be safe from them and us, but you must swear to me that you wish no ill will toward us."

"Sure, buddy. Like I say, as long as you're not a bunch of serious douchebags, we're here to be friends."

The screen went dead. I looked to Ember, who was looking at me. "Well that was weird," I quipped.

"Really weird. I wonder what's going on here. How did he know so much about the Fystr? We're literally on the other side of the galaxy," she replied.

"Never mind that, let's get our asses to the only thing that looks like safety at the minute, the other side of their fleet. You okay with that, Hwista?"

"Sure, Captain. Plotting a course right now."

"Elyek, are you okay letting the other ships know what's going on? Leave Rufus until last."

Elyek grinned a little. "Of course, Captain. I'll get right onto it."

Seconds after we got moving, Hwista spoke again. "Captain, the same ship is hailing us."

"Put them through, please."

The screen came back on. The same alien as before appeared and spoke. "My leaders have requested to connect with you on a direct line. Will you speak with them?"

"Sure. If nothing else, this shit is fascinating," I said, smiling.

He gave me an odd look, then the screen went haywire. When it calmed down, it was my turn to be shocked to bits. The dude on the screen was only a bloody Fystr.

"Okay! What the hell is going on?" I shouted angrily. "We're armed to the teeth and we're ready for you, motherfuckers."

"Calm," he said gently, and not in keeping with the usual Fystr pomposity at all. "We are not your enemy, at least I do not believe we are, if what I have been told is true. Are you really the hindered ones? You have managed to evolve?"

"Yeah. Not to mention escape the Fystr Empire too. Only to find you fuckers in the opposite part of the galaxy."

"We no longer see ourselves as Fystr. Not for a very long time, young man. For example, has a group of hindered ones from your planet ever committed horrible crimes? Would you wish to be judged the same as those people just because you are from the same planet?

"When the great purge occurred, not everyone agreed with the methods employed by our race. Those who did not care for what we had become left rather than be a part of it."

"Why the fuck didn't you stay and fight? Stop them doing what they did to us all?"

"We were far too few in number to counter their cruelty, so we had a choice to make: be executed as traitors or disappear, sequestered as far away as possible."

"That's actually a pretty good answer to be honest. Although I wish you could've stopped the bastards. So what the hell is going on over here? You're at war with the Empire?"

The ageless ex-Fystr laughed. "They are forever nibbling at our borders, like flies on a corpse. But we are not a corpse. We have nothing to fear from the Empire. They are as a child to an adult. Our main aim is to stay hidden from the Fystr Empire. You, however, are just too intriguing. We share both a common ancestry and a common foe."

"It certainly looks that way."

"Will you visit our planet, so we may commune face-to-face?" he asked.

"Seems risky. You could be luring us to our deaths."

"Yet if you are refugees, you have few choices. And I assure you we are not deceiving you."

I couldn't really sense any deception, and this was kind of a big deal. I looked to Ember. She shrugged, but seemed quite positive. Glancing over to Elyek, their expression was as neutral as a gray wall. No help there then. It seemed like I was making this decision on my own. Turning to the not-a-Fystr, I smiled. "We'll come, but no funny business," I said, pointing at him.

He looked confused, then answered anyway. "Excellent! It shall be fascinating to meet our descendants. And perhaps we can be of value to one another?"

"I sure fucking hope so."

The end of *Condition Evolution: Book Three.*

...Incoming from Shaun...

Wow, that was an epic turn of events. Providing these new guys are on the level, things might just be looking up for Uprising. I suppose we will have to wait and see. We still need to build up our strength, and there are a few issues that are popping up. But first we need to see if we can get Ogun back on his feet... or well, whatever we can do for him. Some of the crew have a few ideas, I didn't really understand most of what they were talking about, apart from something about everyone writing down kind thoughts and hopes and sending them into the ether.

"Elyek! What was it we needed?"

...

"Re... what?"

...

"Ah, yeah of course, that's it, reviews! We really need *reviews*."

KEVIN SINCLAIR

Don't miss out on future releases. Visit my website or Facebook page. Also, you can get in touch on twitter, Instagram at kevinsinclairauthor@gmail.com Condition Evolution 4 is Coming Soon....

THE LITRPG GUILD

Who we are: The LitRPG Guild is a community founded by a group of authors dedicated to the LitRPG, Gamelit, and Progression Fantasy genres. We are trying to spread the word of our favorite genres by working together and introducing new people to amazing books. Our goal is to unify and expand these genres that we love, while bringing fans and creators closer together.

Want a free book? Sign up to our Newsletter to receive updates on new work and get the most up-to-date news on all things LitRPG.

Want more information? Get behind the scenes info, LitRPG news, and live interviews. Follow our shared author page on Facebook, visit our Website, and gain exclusive access on our Patreon.

Want to come hang out with us? Find a bunch of other amazing authors, narrators, and fans on our Discord Server and Facebook Group. To get more involved, join our Street Team.

More LitRPG Guildmasters Titles

Altered Realms by B.F. Rockriver
Brightblade by Jez Cajiao
Grim Beginnings by Maxwell Farmer
Primeverse by R.K. Billiau
Shattered Sword by TJ Reynolds
Tower of Gates by Paul Bellow
Cipher's Quest by Tim Kaiver
Watcher's Test by Sean Oswald
Star Divers by Stephen Landry
Fragment of Divinity by Jamey Sultan
Hive Knight by Grayson Sinclair

Condition Evolution by Kevin Sinclair
Berserker by Dimitrios Gkirgkiris
Glitchworld by Damien Hanson

OTHER FANTASTIC GAMELIT AND LITRPG GROUPS AND PAGES

LitRPG Forum
GameLit Society
LitRPG Books
LitRPG Adventures
LitRPG Releases
Fantasy Nation

LITRPG GROUP

To learn more about LitRPG, talk to authors including myself, and just have an awesome time, please join the LitRPG Group